STALKING THE PUZZLE LADY

ALSO BY PARNELL HALL

A Clue for the Puzzle Lady
Last Puzzle & Testament
Puzzled to Death
A Puzzle in a Pear Tree
With This Puzzle, I Thee Kill
And a Puzzle to Die On

BANTAM BOOKS

New York   Toronto

London   Sydney

Auckland

STALKING THE PUZZLE LADY

A PUZZLE LADY MYSTERY

Parnell Hall

STALKING THE PUZZLE LADY
A Bantam Book / November 2005

Published by
Bantam Dell
A Division of Random House, Inc.
New York, New York

Book design by Glen Edelstein

Bantam Books is a registered trademark of Random House, Inc., and the colophon is a trademark of Random House, Inc.

Library of Congress Cataloging-in-Publication Data
Hall, Parnell.
Stalking the puzzle lady / Parnell Hall.
p.   cm.
ISBN-13: 978-0-553-80417-1
ISBN-10: 0-553-80417-0
1. Felton, Cora (Fictitious character)—Fiction.   2. Women television personalities—Fiction.   3. Crossword puzzle makers—Fiction.
4. Stalking victims—Fiction.   5. Women detectives—Fiction.
6. Older women—Fiction.   I. Title.

PS3558.A37327S73 2005
813'.54—dc22   2005045350

Printed in the United States of America
Published simultaneously in Canada

www.bantamdell.com

BVG   10 9 8 7 6 5 4 3 2 1

For Ellen,
a winner in anyone's book

CONTRACT KILLER

I want to thank Murderin' Manny Nosowsky for providing the puzzles that appear in this book. Manny swears he never actually killed anyone, but considering the enthusiasm with which he threw himself into the part, I would say that perhaps the gentleman doth protest a bit too much.

STALKING THE PUZZLE LADY

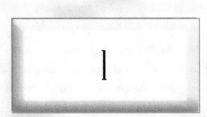

1

*HE COULDN'T BELIEVE IT! She hadn't answered his letter. True, he
hadn't left a return address, but there were so many other ways. And a
clever woman could find them. And she was not just a clever woman,
she was a brilliant woman. When it came to delving, investigating, figuring things out.*

So why hadn't she?

*The thought that tortured him was, What if she had? What if she'd
devised some clever means of communication that he was too slow to
grasp? What if she had already answered him in one way or another?
What if her answer was waiting for him right now?*

*But what kind of answer could it be? An ad in the Personals column?
What Personals column? And what newspaper? How would he know?*

*No, there was only one way she could communicate. Only one way
he expected her to. Only one way that made sense.*

*After all, she had a nationally syndicated crossword-puzzle column.
And how simple it would be to slip a word or phrase into the puzzle.
Meaningless to everyone else, but a wink and a nod to him. And
wouldn't that be delicious. To have a secret. Their secret. In plain view,*

on display, for everyone to see. If only they had perspicacity to glean the hidden meaning. To crack the secret cypher.

Each morning he snatched up the paper, flipped to the Entertainment section, and solved the puzzle, always in under five minutes. For the next half hour he would study what he'd done, searching for a clue.

Which never came.

It infuriated him. Was it possible she hadn't gotten the letter? He had written care of the paper, not having her address. It was only a local paper, but still, they would forward it, wouldn't they? And the breakfast cereal company. He had written her care of that too. She was the spokesman for the company. Surely they would send her mail.

If not, he would have to get her home address. He hated to do it. It would make him seem like an obsessed fan. Like that nutcase who kept showing up at David Letterman's.

And it wasn't that way with him. It wasn't that way at all. He was her confederate, her peer, her equal. Theirs was a true meeting of the minds.

If only he could arrange the introduction.

Should he nudge the breakfast cereal company?

Perhaps.

Or maybe it was time for a special delivery.

2

"I'M TIRED OF LIVING A LIE."

Sherry Carter looked at her aunt in amusement. Cora Felton did not look like a liar. The white-haired, bespectacled lady looked like everyone's favorite grandmother, the type that baked pumpkin pies at Thanksgiving, cookies at Christmastime, and cupcakes for no particular reason on any given occasion. Sherry, of course, knew better. Cora smoked, swore, gambled, had only recently given up drinking, and was somewhat hazy on the subject of how many husbands she'd had. "Mine or other people's?" was her usual deflection.

"Good lord, Cora. Do you have another husband I haven't heard of?"

"It's entirely possible, but that isn't what I meant." Cora pointed at the computer screen, on which Sherry was composing a puzzle in Crossword Compiler. "I'm tired of being the Puzzle Lady. I'm tired of feigning an expertise I have not got."

Sherry nodded approvingly. "See? You even *sound* like the

Puzzle Lady. Do you realize how much more elegant and refined your speech has become since you've been doing it?"

Cora responded with a remark that could hardly be considered elegant or refined by any stretch of the imagination.

"Aunt Cora!" Sherry remonstrated.

"Oh, pooh," Cora retorted. "I'm the Milli Vanilli of the crossword-puzzle community. A hollow subterfuge that has stretched way thin."

"You're mixing metaphors."

A toy poodle scampered into the office and yipped around Cora's feet. She bent down, scooped him up. He nestled against her chest, nuzzled under her chin.

"Look at me," Cora complained. "I used to be tough as nails. Now I'm a dotty old woman with a dog."

"We don't have to keep the dog," Sherry pointed out. "He's here on a trial run."

"Shh! He'll hear you!" Cora hissed. "Buddy, don't listen to her. Cut it out, Sherry. I'm not getting rid of the D-O-G just to make a point."

"And just what point are you making, Cora?"

"I'm not comfortable taking credit for something I don't do. I think it's time you were recognized for your work."

"I don't want to be recognized."

"Why not? It's not like you're hiding from your ex-husband anymore. Dennis knows you're the Puzzle Lady. He also knows where you live. What have you got to lose?"

"My privacy, for one thing."

"Oh? But it's all right for me to lose mine?"

"It's not the same thing, Aunt Cora."

"Why not?"

"You don't *do* anything."

"I beg your pardon?"

Sherry shrugged. "I create the puzzles. Losing your privacy is your *entire* contribution to the project."

"Oh, for Christ's sake!"

Cora jerked a pack of cigarettes out of her floppy, drawstring purse.

"I thought you weren't going to smoke in here," Sherry observed.

"That only works when you agree with me," Cora snapped. "When you argue with me, I gotta smoke." Buddy squirmed and yipped. "Oh, was I squeezing too tight?" She set the poodle down. "All right, I'll go outside. You wanna come, too, or should I finish this conversation myself?"

Sherry followed Cora down the hall through the living room and out the front door of the modest, prefab rental she and her aunt shared together. The house wasn't much, except for the location. On a scenic country road in Bakerhaven, Connecticut, with no near neighbors, the one-acre lot was an idyllic setting.

Cora stopped on the front step, but Buddy pelted by and yipped around the yard. It was mud season, and the tiny poodle's white feet were rapidly turning black.

"You'll wash him off before he comes in the house?" Sherry said.

"Why is it always me?" Cora groused. "Why don't you wash him off?"

"I do when you're not here."

"Yeah, yeah. What's this crap about *I* don't do anything? How does that have anything to do with *you* owning up to what *you* do?"

"It's a partnership. I supply the work, you supply the image."

"I *hate* the image. I gotta be decorous in public, while you run around in jeans and a sweater. Is that fair? You're young and attractive and you happen to look *good* in jeans and a sweater."

Before Cora quit drinking she had often appeared far from decorous in public, but Sherry wasn't about to point that out. "What's really the matter, Cora?"

Cora puffed in smoke, watched the dog cavorting on the lawn.

"I told you what's the matter. I'm tired of the deception. I'm tired of pretending to be something I'm not."

"Cora. You've hated the deception from the word go. Why do you want to quit *now*?"

"Oh."

"Ah! There's an *oh*?"

"It's the damn cereal company."

"The damn cereal company that put you on TV? You'd like to give that up?"

"Sherry . . ."

"What have they done?"

"They've come out with a new cereal."

"And they want you to promote it?"

"Yeah."

"That's wonderful, Cora. That probably pays our rent for a year. We might even think of buying this place, knocking it down, and building something better."

"I don't want to do it."

"Why not?"

"Well, for one thing, it's not a *new* cereal. It's the same *old* cereal, it's just *new and improved*."

"So what?"

"I hate that. It's like saying, 'The stuff I've been selling you for years is crap, but, hang on, I got something better.' "

"All products do that. It's called progress."

"It's humiliating."

"No, it's great. The product launch is a gold mine. So you have to tape some TV ads. What's the big deal?"

Cora exhaled an angry drag. "They want me to tour."

"What?"

"They want me to make *personal appearances*." Her tone was scathing. "They want me to do *supermarkets. Shopping centers. Malls.* They want me to be there hawking their products. They want to let kids meet the Puzzle Lady. Like a Macy's *Santa*."

"What's wrong with that?"

"I'm not good with kids, Sherry. Kids have sticky hands and snotty noses. And a complete and utter lack of tact. They stand there and tell me to my face I look older than their grandmother. It's all I can do to keep from telling them that's 'cause their mother got knocked up when she was fifteen."

"I see your point. Can you do the ads and not the tour?"

"No. 'Cause they're shooting the ads *on* the tour." Cora snorted. "It's all this goddamned reality TV. They want real kids trying the cereal for the first time. Along with the Puzzle Lady. And I *hate* cold cereal. Give me ham and eggs and a buttered muffin."

Sherry Carter looked at her aunt. "You really want to do this? Tell people you're a fake, I mean?"

"I got some money put away. Not just from this, but from my alimony and property settlements. If ever there was a time, it's now."

"If you give it up, what are you going to do?"

Cora shrugged. "Hold a press conference. Do the *Today Show*. We could go on *Oprah* together, tell our story. I could abdicate the throne. Like the way I said *abdicate*?"

"I'm not going on TV, Cora."

"You may think you're not, but TV's gonna find you."

"You'd do that to me?"

"I'm not doing it *to* you. You pushed me out front for years. Was that doing it to *me*? It's just the way it goes. Hey, Buddy!" Cora yelled. The little poodle had ventured too far down the drive for her liking. He halted at the sound of her voice, scampered across the lawn.

"Fine," Sherry said. "That's not what I mean. If you're not the Puzzle Lady, what will you do?"

"Pretty much the same as I do now. I mean, it's not like I spend any time on crossword puzzles. All I do is film a commercial or two a year. At least until this damn tour came up."

"I don't think you've thought this through."

"Why not?"

"Right now people cut you a lot of slack because you're the most famous woman in town. Give it up, you'll be the most *in*famous woman in town. You're gonna spend most of your time apologizing to people for duping them. People don't *like* to be duped. It makes them feel stupid. People *resent* a person who makes them feel stupid. They could make her life a living hell."

"I think you're wrong. I think our friends would come around."

"Maybe." Sherry said it without enthusiasm. "You're doing this just to get out of a tour?"

"Would *you* want to do a supermarket tour?" Cora countered.

"Don't be absurd."

"Well, at least we agree on one thing."

The phone rang. Sherry ducked back inside to answer it.

Cora sat on the front step to play with the dog. The concrete stoop was cold despite her tweed skirt. Cora didn't mind. She put out her arms, lifted the little dog up into her lap.

"You going to snub Mommie if she's not a celebrity? No, you're not. You won't care at all."

From the kitchen Sherry shouted, "Cora!"

"Ooh," Cora said. "I hope that's a poker game. Mommie could use a poker game. Come on, Buddy. Let's go in."

Cora set the poodle down in the living room, and went to answer the phone. "Who is it?" she asked as Sherry handed her the receiver.

"Don't know. He asked for Miss Felton."

"As long as he didn't ask for the darn Puzzle Lady." Cora took the phone, said, "Hello?"

"Miss Felton?"

"Yes."

"This is Charles Coleson, Truestar Investments."

Cora groaned. "Not again."

"Miss Felton—"

"I told you. I don't want to diversify."

"Yes, you did. And we haven't. We've kept all your stock right where you had it. That's why I'm calling."

"What do you mean?"

Cora could hear Charles Coleson take a breath.

"Miss Felton, I'm afraid I have some rather bad news."

3

QUENTIN BURNS COULD NOT HAVE BEEN more annoying. "Is every-thing perfect? I want everything perfect. We are *not* going to shoot before everything's *perfect*."

Quentin Burns wasn't perfect. His chin was too weak, his nose was too short, and his eyebrows were most decidedly irregular.

He also wore a wig. Cora had dated men with weaves, implants, Rogaine IV drips, and hairpieces of all kinds, but there were good wigs and bad wigs. This was an obvious rug perched on a head with no right to have the jet-black hair it sported. The effect was unsettling, at best.

"Who is this geek?" Cora whispered to Florence Evans, a com-fortable woman with a red bandanna around her head, and a black eyeliner in her hand. "Don't squirm," the makeup lady cautioned, but her eyes were twinkling. Flo had made Cora up before, and got quite a kick out of the Puzzle Lady. "That's Quentin Burns. He's the producer."

"For the ad execs, or the breakfast boys?"

"From the agency. He's running this campaign."

"Did he think it up?"

"I'm not sure he thinks."

Cora was boundlessly delighted by that remark, which almost reconciled her to doing the commercial.

Cora and the dorky ad man were filming in a soundstage in Queens, where the art department had designed a perfectly work-manlike replica of a kitchen. Why they couldn't simply film *in* a kitchen was more than Cora wanted to fathom. She sat getting made up, while chaos reigned around her.

"You've never met Quentin?" Flo asked.

"I try to meet as few of these people as possible. Oh, my God, he's coming over!"

He was. Quentin Burns swept down on the makeup chair like the wolf on the fold. Up close his hair looked like a black putting green. "Ah, there you are, Miss Felton. It's so good to meet you. I'm Quentin Burns, and I'm in charge of the shoot. If there's anything you want, anything at all, don't hesitate to ask."

Cora was sorely tempted to order a Tanqueray martini with a twist, in spite of being unofficially on the wagon. "That's very nice of you, but I'm fine."

"Fine? You're more than fine. My God, you're perfect. Isn't she perfect, Flo?"

"Actually, she could use a little powder on her cheek."

Quentin clearly had no sense of humor. He smiled dutifully.

"Tell me something," Cora said. "If we're doing this whole public-appearance tour to film a reality TV commercial, why are we shooting this?"

Quentin looked shocked. "Are you serious? This is the promo that promotes the promo. Didn't they tell you anything?"

"They told me not to curse on camera."

Quentin hoped she was joking. "Ah, yes. Well, this is the spot that gets them in the stores. It runs nationally to introduce the product, then it runs locally with the voice-over tag line, 'See the Puzzle Lady in person Saturday at Wal-Mart.'"

"I'm doing Wal-Mart?"

"That was just a for-instance. We'll be shooting footage at all these local stops for the reality ads, but that, of course, is hit or miss. You never know with real kids."

"We're not using real kids for this?" Cora sounded appalled.

"We're not using amateurs. We're using actors. The kids we hired are real pros."

"Aren't they a little old?"

"Not for TV. Trust me, they're *perfect.*"

"Then you won't use a shot of them smoking?" Cora sniped mischievously.

Quentin followed Cora's gaze across the set. There, the two professional urchins were sharing a cigarette as if it were a joint. "Oh, my God! Lance! Ginger! What are you doing?"

Quentin went charging off, his face a picture of consternation.

"Is he going on the tour?" Cora asked Flo.

"I'm afraid so," the makeup lady said. "But don't worry. It'll be *perfect.*"

"WHAT IS THIS CRAP?!"

Cora turned at the sound of the booming voice, to find a person far too small to possess it standing in the doorway. The newcomer was a compact live wire, and hard as nails. She was also a woman, though one wouldn't have known it from the deep voice.

Or from what it said.

After her initial exclamation deploring the set, the newcomer went on to wonder aloud with whom it would be necessary for one to indulge in a romantic interlude in order to achieve any degree of progress in the immediate vicinity.

Cora's ears pricked up. "Say, who's that?"

"That's Daphne Decker. They brought her in to direct the segments."

"I like her already," Cora declared.

Daphne Decker wore a dungaree jacket and a crimson beret. She flung them both onto a folding chair and strode across the set, seemingly with longer strides than she had legs. She marched up to

Cora, said, "You're the star. No, don't get up. The last thing I need is actors bounding up from the makeup chair. I had a boy once sprang up to see me, poked himself with the eyebrow pencil, damaged his cornea, and missed the shoot. I don't want that happening here. At least, not to you. I can't replace you. You're the goddamned Puzzle Lady. We can't run in a ringer here. Thank God you've done this before, I don't have to teach you."

The director peered at Cora critically. "Makeup's all right, but lose the suit. Jesus Christ, I don't know what Wardrobe is thinking. You're the cheerful grandmother, not the dowdy spinster aunt."

Cora would have let the remark go, but Quentin, materializing behind the director, said maliciously, "Don't be silly. Those are her own clothes."

"Of course they are, dear," Daphne purred, patting him on the cheek. "You think I'd direct without looking at the storyboard? Trust me, I know what my cast is wearing. Good God, are those the kids? They look positively pubescent."

"The kids are perfect. They've done TV before."

"Where? On *America's Most Wanted*? They look like they're planning to knock off a convenience store."

"I assure you—"

Daphne ignored him, zeroed in on the kitchen counter, snatched up the box of cereal. *"New? Improved?"* she read. "Hmmph! What does that mean? The old stuff tasted like motor oil?"

"Miss Decker—"

"Call me Daphne, we'll get along. Call me Dee Dee, I'll punch your lights out."

Quentin could not have looked more nonplussed had Daphne Decker whipped out a scissors and cut his tie off.

"Ah, yes, of course. Daphne. What I mean to say is, we're so glad you're doing this commercial, and we're all here to help."

"You can help by staying out of my way. I got one day to shoot this sucker, and I'm not going into overtime. Not on a thirty-second spot. Larry!" Daphne bounded off to confront the cameraman, who was lecturing the electricians on how to light the set. "It's a promo, Larry, not *Gone With the Wind*. Stop trying to win an Oscar, just aim your lights and shoot."

Larry, a large man with a trim goatee, had clearly worked with Daphne before. He grinned. "You wanna see your actors or not? It's all the same to me, of course. I'm not sellin' the damn cereal."

"Hey! A little respect for our product," Daphne said. "It's the *new and improved* damn cereal."

The electrician, a lanky man with a complacent attitude, leaned on the tripod he had been positioning. "You want me to go on lighting?" he drawled at the cameraman.

"Yeah, Wayne. And if you could try to aim somewhere in the vicinity of the set so I don't have to keep this ad off my résumé, I'd be grateful."

"What's the problem?" Quentin demanded. All eyes turned to him as if he'd just butted in on the conversation, which, indeed, he had.

"Our DP's upset because our gaffer's incompetent," Daphne explained.

"What?"

"Your gaffer's your head light man. Your DP's your cameraman. That's director of photography, if you're studying up for a quiz."

"That's not funny. Who called who incompetent?"

An assistant director, young, eager, with puppy dog eyes, hurried up with a smartly dressed young woman carrying a soft leather briefcase. "We're going on in thirty minutes, gang, thirty minutes," he announced, though where he got that information was anybody's guess. "Daphne, this is Jennifer Blaylock. She's the new publicist for Granville Grains."

Jennifer flashed Daphne a dazzling smile. "I am so pleased to meet you. I can't begin to tell you what this spot will mean for our product—"

"It'll probably mean more kids eating the crap," Daphne cut in. At the publicist's expression, she added, "Hey, it's a closed set, John Q. Public ain't here, nobody gives a good goddamn. Well, let's meet the brats."

Daphne and the assistant director swept off in the direction of the professional children. Quentin tagged along behind, leaving perky Jennifer Blaylock alone with Cora.

The beaming publicist looked barely old enough to be out of college. Her sculpted hair, stud earrings, and slightly overstated makeup reminded Cora of a kid playing dress-up. "Oh, Miss Felton, I'm so pleased to meet you. I didn't know what to expect."

"Oh?"

Jennifer flushed, and hastened to add, "I've heard of you, of course." She wasn't happy with how that sounded, either. "Not that I've heard anything bad. You being famous and all."

Cora smiled and let her off the hook. "You new to this?"

"Yes, I am. Not advertising. The company. I want to do a good job. And it's very hard coming in in the middle of a campaign."

"It's a new campaign."

"But you're an old hand." Her flush deepened. "I don't mean *old*. I mean you've done it before. Oh, before I forget! I have your mail."

"My what?"

Jennifer snapped open her briefcase. "Your fan mail. I have your latest batch."

"Really?"

"Didn't your last publicist give you your fan mail?"

"I didn't know I had a publicist."

Jennifer's eyes were wide. "Oh, my goodness. I was told things were a shambles, but who knew? So how did you get fan mail? Did they send it to you?"

"I get e-mail."

Jennifer pulled out a sheaf of letters. "No, I mean your regular mail. Who handled that?"

Cora vaguely remembered a phone call about what to do with Puzzle Lady letters sometime back in the days when she was still drinking. If anything, she had most likely suggested torching them. "I don't recall."

Jennifer thrust the letters into her hands. "Here you are. I *know* you'll want to answer these."

That rang a bell. "Of course." Cora handed them back. "If you'll just write replies for me, I'll be happy to sign them and send them out."

As before, that did the trick. Cora could practically see the publicist backpedaling in her head.

"Well, now, there's no official letter-writing campaign scheduled. . . . If you want to correspond with a fan, that's entirely up to you. It's completely voluntary. You're under no obligation. Of course, if a particular letter strikes a chord . . ."

Cora, who had no intention of reading any of the letters, agreed heartily. "Absolutely. If a letter moves me, how can I resist?"

"I'm glad to hear it." Jennifer pulled an envelope from the bunch. "I do think you'll get a kick out of this one."

Cora's heart sank. Good lord. On the other side of the studio the director was having some fun with the two kids, who were in stitches, probably over something smutty. And here she was, caught in a shaggy-dog story with a well-meaning publicist from hell. Even now the woman was smiling and nodding, urging her to read the letter.

Cora reached in the envelope and pulled out a crossword puzzle.

"See?" the publicist gushed. "Isn't it fun? You just have to do it."

Cora shrugged. "No big deal. People often send me puzzles. Hoping I'll get 'em published, or introduce 'em to Will Shortz."

Cora felt smug. Sherry would be proud of her for remembering the *New York Times* crossword-puzzle editor's name.

Jennifer beamed. "I just knew you'd be pleased. There's no

letter with it, so there's nothing to answer. Just a nice crossword puzzle to solve in your spare time. Won't that be *fun*?"

"I can't tell you how much," Cora said truthfully.

Cora smiled at the young publicist, thrust the puzzle deep down in her floppy drawstring purse, and didn't give it another thought.

4

THE SMILING FACE OF CORA FELTON filled the screen. "Here's a puzzle for you: What's better than Granville Grains Corn Toasties?"

Cut to the two brats, Lance and Ginger, made up to look young, sitting behind the counter in Cora's soundstage kitchen. Their innocent faces are stunned. They gawk at each other in utter amazement. They haven't a clue. Clearly, neither one of them could fathom such a thing.

Shot of Cora, smiling slyly. "Well, it's *new, improved* Granville Grains Corn Toasties."

Lance and Ginger could not have been more astonished had Pat Boone taken Best Rap Video at the MTV Awards. They gave each other a how-could-I-be-so-dumb look, then dug greedily into the bowls of cereal that had somehow materialized in front of them.

Cora watched approvingly. No parent at a Harvard graduation ever looked so proud. "Yes, folks, how do you improve upon perfection? There's a puzzle worthy of the Puzzle Lady. I'm proud to be bringing it to you, not just on TV, but in person, at your neighborhood supermarket. Consult your local listings for the time and place in your area."

A still of Cora Felton, holding the box of cereal, filled the screen. A voice-over said, *Meet the Puzzle Lady this Saturday, nine to four, at the Danbury Stop and Shop, and try a free bowl of new and improved Granville Grains Corn Toasties. This offer void where prohibited by law. Some restrictions may apply.*

Sherry Carter clicked the TV on MUTE.

"Well, that's not so bad," Aaron Grant said. The young reporter was dining with Sherry and Cora in their living room during the evening news.

"That's me holding a box of cereal with my picture on it," Cora pointed out.

"And doing a dandy job of it," Aaron told her.

"Bite me," Cora said. "No, not you, Buddy." The toy poodle, begging food, couldn't have found three softer touches. He had not only wheedled bites, but had managed to lick the plates clean.

"Hey, I wasn't being sarcastic. You happen to project well on TV."

"It's humiliating."

"Come on," Sherry said. "It's not like you haven't seen the ad before. It's been playing for weeks."

"This time it's playing with the voice-over. 'Come meet the Puzzle Lady. Watch her hold the box of cereal with her mug shot on it. Get your mug shot taken with the Puzzle Lady.' "

"They're doing that?"

"Over my dead body."

"Then what are they doing?" Aaron asked, intrigued.

"You want to go, Aaron?" Sherry interposed.

"I'll kill you," Cora said. "I'll beat you to death with breakfast cereal. So help me God, if a picture of this winds up in the *Gazette*—"

"I have no control over where my editor assigns his cameramen."

"You have any control over your body parts? You wanna keep them, I better not see a camera."

Aaron prudently changed the subject. "How you getting there? They sending a limo?"

"Yeah, right," Cora scoffed. "I'm driving down myself."

Aaron nodded. "No wonder you're miffed."

Cora opened her mouth to protest.

There came a thud from the front door. It was a single sound, and different than a knock.

Buddy darted to the door, yipping frantically.

"What was that?" Cora said.

"You expecting somebody?" Aaron asked.

"That wasn't a knock," Sherry said.

"Then what was it?" Aaron said.

"Well, we could debate it all day, or we could go see," Cora pointed out.

"I'd hate to miss your ad again."

Cora narrowed her eyes at Sherry. "Your boyfriend is aiming for a fat lip."

"Now he's *my* fault?" Sherry protested.

Cora shrugged. "Men are always someone's fault. You know how many I've been blamed for?"

"I thought you'd lost count."

"Well, they do tend to blur into one. Anybody gonna check the door?"

"If it was a knock, they'll knock again," Sherry said.

"My niece is incredibly lazy. Good thing she's a good cook."

"Among other things," Aaron said.

"I'm going to pretend I didn't hear that rather racy comment." Cora heaved herself to her feet.

Buddy was still yipping at the door. "You probably want to go out after that feast, don't you, boy?"

Cora opened the front door. Buddy darted out onto the stoop. There was no one there. But Buddy was barking hysterically.

"Is someone there, Buddy?"

Cora looked down. But the little poodle wasn't looking off into the darkness. He was facing back toward the house and the open front door.

"Buddy, what's the matter?"

Cora's eyes widened.

Sticking out of the bottom of the door was a huge carving knife.

5

DALE HARPER WAS LESS THAN PLEASED. The Bakerhaven police chief stood in the open doorway, and frowned at the embedded knife. "You didn't see anyone?"

"No," Cora said.

"You didn't hear anything?"

"No."

"None of you?"

"We were watching TV," Cora said.

"You couldn't tear yourself away?"

"The commercials were so riveting," Aaron said.

Cora shot him a dirty look.

"How long from the time you heard the knife hit the door until you actually opened it?" Harper asked.

"We didn't know it was a knife," Sherry said.

"Of course you didn't. What did you think it was?"

"Someone knocking."

"So you decided to leave them out there?"

"I don't think there was any conscious decision."

"Give us a break," Cora said. "We heard it hit, we didn't know what it was, we talked about it a little, I went to open the door. Plenty of time for whoever threw the knife to get away."

"You think someone threw the knife?"

"I doubt if they walked up to the door and stuck it in."

"Why would anyone throw a knife at your door?"

"Maybe they didn't like the ad," Aaron suggested facetiously.

"Who doesn't like what ad?"

"I don't," Cora said. "But I didn't do it."

"You didn't hear a car drive away?"

"No."

"So what happened?"

"There was a thud. The dog started barking."

"The dog wasn't barking before the thud?"

"Only to get things to eat."

"You're spoiling your dog?"

"The dog was spoiled when I got him, Chief. He's a prespoiled dog."

"Okay. But the dog didn't bark at the knife thrower until the knife was thrown?"

"I don't even know if he barked at the knife thrower *then*. I know he barked at the *knife*."

"He doesn't bark when people come to the door? He doesn't bark until they knock?"

"If I'd wanted a guard dog, I doubt if I'd have gone for this breed."

"Aha," Harper said. If he was convinced, one wouldn't have known it.

"You want to make a move, Chief." Cora indicated the open door. "It's getting cold."

"Okay. I'm going to pull this out of the door, bag it, see if I can get any prints. In the meantime, if you can think of anything helpful, don't hesitate to chime in."

Chief Harper put on plastic gloves. Even so, he touched the knife gingerly by the edge of the hilt, and wiggled it free. "Okay.

We got your basic Bowie knife, eight-inch blade, probably every hunter in the county's got one, except perhaps the guy who threw this."

"You gonna start calling on hunters, ask them to show you their knives?" Aaron said.

"Yeah, there's a plan," Harper agreed dryly. He bagged the knife and stepped out on the stoop. "Your front-door light doesn't do much. A hundred-watt bulb, tops, in that frosted thing there. Not throwing much light beyond ten feet. Guy with the knife could be pretty much in the shadows when he makes the toss." He paced it off. "See, I'm still in the light here, I'd have to back up. Actually, farther than I thought. From here your knife's gonna turn three or four times, probably wouldn't stick. Be a couple of paces in, then I'm in the full light. The minute I throw I'm gonna turn and run. You sure you didn't hear a car?"

"No. But that doesn't mean there wasn't one. We weren't listening."

"Great." Harper got in his cruiser, started it up.

"Where's Buddy?" Cora said.

"He was right here," Sherry said.

Harper backed the cruiser around.

"Where is he?"

"Relax, Cora. He knows better than to run under a car."

Chief Harper sped down the driveway.

"Too fast!" Cora yelled.

"Buddy's not out there," Sherry said. "Aaron, did he go back inside?"

"I think he ran off."

"Wrong answer!" Sherry hissed.

Cora stumbled into the darkness. "Buddy!"

There was no answering yip. Cora felt a moment of dread.

The little toy poodle came bounding across the lawn. He had something in his mouth, which was why he hadn't barked.

Cora dropped to her knees. "Buddy! Here, boy!"

Buddy ran up, leaped into her arms.

"What have you got there, fella?"

It was a torn piece of paper. Cora tried to take it from the poodle's mouth. Buddy growled.

"What's that?" Aaron asked.

"I need a treat."

"Huh?"

"Buddy's not going to give the darn thing up without a bribe."

Cora carried Buddy into the kitchen, set him on the floor. She took a box of small Milk-Bone biscuits down from the shelf, held one out to the dog. "Here, Buddy. Sit."

The sight of a biscuit did the trick. Buddy's jaws loosened their death grip on the paper. The poodle sat expectantly, licked his chops.

"Untrained, my fanny," Cora muttered. She handed him the treat, picked up the paper.

The sheet of paper had been folded in thirds, like a letter. Dead center, there was an even cut, about an inch and a half, perpendicular to the long folded side of the letter. From one end of this cut was a jagged tear through the side. The letter was also perforated by tiny teeth marks of a rather suspiciously poodle-looking variety.

Cora unfolded the paper and groaned.

It was a puzzle.

Crossword Grid

A crossword puzzle grid with numbered cells. Numbers visible: 1, 2, 3, 4, 5, 6, 7, 8, 9, 10, 11, 12, 13, 14, 15, 16, 17, 18, 19, 20, 21, 22, 23, 24, 25, 26, 27, 28, 29, 30, 31, 32, 33, 34, 35, 36, 37, 38, 39, 40, 41, 42, 43, 44, 45, 46, 47, 48, 49, 50, 51, 52, 53, 54, 55, 56, 57, 58, 59, 60, 61, 62, 63, 64, 65, 66, 67, 68, 69.

ACROSS

1 Like a tack?
6 Tale of Troy
11 Hi-___ monitor
14 "M*A*S*H" setting
15 Upright or grand
16 Likely
17 Start of a message
19 Tarzan's kid
20 "Charlie Hustle"
21 Big name in discount clothing
23 Chinese 33-Down
24 ___-toity
25 CPR expert
28 "Shane" actor Alan
31 Wrap up
32 Magician's disappearing word
34 Part 2 of message
39 ___ Chem. 101 (sci. course listing)
41 Toothpaste type
42 Margaret Mead's venue
43 Part 3 of message
46 Thanksgiving veggies
47 Ink or oink place
48 Nil, in Seville
50 Ran into
51 Necklace fastener
53 Hotel amenity
55 Lip-stretching African
56 Ooze through the cracks

61 Stimpy's cartoon pal
62 End of message
64 College test, for short
65 Offer to a hitchhiker
66 Kate's TV partner
67 Letter before tee
68 Ad ___ per aspera (Kansas's motto)
69 Snorkeling places

DOWN

1 Word with hop and jump
2 Hockey great Gordie
3 "I smell ___!"
4 Extend one's "Life"
5 Walk a beat
6 NYSE debuts
7 Take a shine to
8 Writer Fleming
9 One more
10 Average on Wall Street
11 Morocco's capital
12 Strong glue
13 Charon's river
18 Hungarian sweet wine
22 Around 5/15
25 Grist for DeMille?
26 "___ Lisa"
27 Porky or Daffy
29 Rapper Snoop ___
30 Expected to arrive
33 Skillet
35 A, as in Edison?
36 Mosque prayer leader
37 Seward Peninsula city
38 Toward sunrise
40 Snaps
44 Gets off a tackled player
45 Car bomb?
49 Show up
51 Talking truckers, for short
52 Pool paths
54 Bridal path
55 Impulse
56 Use a coffee spoon, say
57 Sicilian smoker
58 Khartoum's river
59 Weekly "Yay!"
60 Change for a five
63 *The Addams Family* cousin

6

"Why aren't we calling Chief Harper back?" Aaron Grant wanted to know.

"To tell him what?" Cora said. "The dog found a paper in the yard?"

"The dog found a *crossword puzzle* in the yard."

"The chief doesn't do crosswords."

"Come on, Cora," Aaron said. "I don't see how you can take it so lightly. Someone stuck a knife in your door."

"I called the chief. I gave him the knife. What more do you want?"

"The puzzle was on the knife."

"We don't know that."

"You know it as well as I do. The cut in the middle of the paper is exactly the same size as the knife blade. Someone stuck that puzzle on the knife, threw it at your door, and ran. The puzzle ripped off, flew around the yard, and Buddy brought it back."

"Will you two shut up? I'm trying to concentrate."

Sherry Carter was solving the puzzle. She had scanned the original, and printed a copy to work on. Her pencil was flying across the paper, writing in answers.

"Yeah, we really seem to be slowing you down," Cora said, ironically.

"Come on, Cora," Aaron said. "Give the chief a call."

"You're not worried. You just want the chief to come back to pump up your story. See, Sherry? Didn't I warn you about dating a reporter?"

"You've dated reporters?" Aaron asked.

"Oh, I must have. Though none stand out."

"Then how could you have warned Sherry about them?"

"Kids. Could you take it outside?"

"Oh, dear," Cora said, ironically. "We're annoying Ellen Ripstein."

"Who?"

"The crossword-puzzle champion. She won the National Tournament."

"Was anyone throwing knives at her at the time?"

"Not that I recall."

"Hey, I got one long answer," Sherry said.

"What is it?" Cora demanded.

" 'I want to know.' "

"Me too. What is it?"

" 'I want to know.' "

"I'm going to hurt you."

"Don't be dumb. The answer is 'I want to know.' "

"Oh. What's the clue?"

" 'Start of a message.' "

"Aha. And the message starts 'I want to know'? Aw, gee, Aaron," Cora said theatrically. "That does it. Call the chief at once!"

"You're going to feel stupid when the rest of the message calls some Incan curse down on your head."

"Incan curse?"

"Or Egyptian curse. Whichever you prefer."

"Remind me never to take you two to a golf tournament," Sherry muttered.

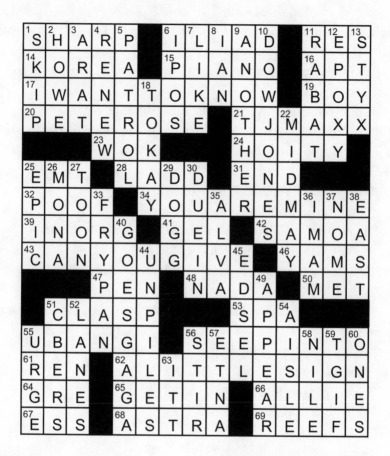

¹S	²H	³A	⁴R	⁵P		⁶I	⁷L	⁸I	⁹A	¹⁰D		¹¹R	¹²E	¹³S
¹⁴K	O	R	E	A		¹⁵P	I	A	N	O		¹⁶A	P	T
¹⁷I	W	A	N	¹⁸T	T	O	K	N	O	W		¹⁹B	O	Y
²⁰P	E	T	E	R	O	S	E		²¹T	²²J	M	A	X	X
		²³W	O	K			²⁴H	O	I	T	Y			
²⁵E	²⁶M	²⁷T		²⁸L	²⁹A	³⁰D	D		³¹E	N	D			
³²P	O	O	³³F		³⁴Y	O	U	³⁵A	R	E	M	³⁶I	³⁷N	³⁸E
³⁹I	N	O	R	⁴⁰G		⁴¹G	E	L		⁴²S	A	M	O	A
⁴³C	A	N	Y	O	⁴⁴U	G	I	⁴⁵V	E		⁴⁶Y	A	M	S
		⁴⁷P	E	N		⁴⁸N	A	D	⁴⁹A		⁵⁰M	E	T	
	⁵¹C	⁵²L	A	S	P		⁵³S	P	⁵⁴A					
⁵⁵U	B	A	N	G	I		⁵⁶S	⁵⁷E	E	P	I	⁵⁸N	⁵⁹T	⁶⁰O
⁶¹R	E	N		⁶²A	⁶³L	I	T	T	L	E	S	I	G	N
⁶⁴G	R	E		⁶⁵G	E	T	I	N		⁶⁶A	L	L	I	E
⁶⁷E	S	S		⁶⁸A	S	T	R	A		⁶⁹R	E	E	F	S

ACROSS

1 Like a tack?
6 Tale of Troy
11 Hi-___ monitor
14 "M*A*S*H" setting
15 Upright or grand
16 Likely
17 Start of a message
19 Tarzan's kid
20 "Charlie Hustle"
21 Big name in discount clothing
23 Chinese 33-Down
24 ___-toity
25 CPR expert
28 "Shane" actor Alan

31 Wrap up
32 Magician's disappearing word
34 Part 2 of message
39 ___ Chem. 101 (sci. course listing)
41 Toothpaste type
42 Margaret Mead's venue
43 Part 3 of message
46 Thanksgiving veggies
47 Ink or oink place
48 Nil, in Seville
50 Ran into
51 Necklace fastener
53 Hotel amenity
55 Lip-stretching African
56 Ooze through the cracks

61 Stimpy's cartoon pal
62 End of message
64 College test, for short
65 Offer to a hitchhiker
66 Kate's TV partner
67 Letter before tee
68 Ad ___ per aspera (Kansas's motto)
69 Snorkeling places

DOWN

1 Word with hop and jump
2 Hockey great Gordie
3 "I smell ___!"
4 Extend one's "Life"
5 Walk a beat
6 NYSE debuts
7 Take a shine to
8 Writer Fleming
9 One more
10 Average on Wall Street
11 Morocco's capital
12 Strong glue
13 Charon's river
18 Hungarian sweet wine

22 Around 5/15
25 Grist for DeMille?
26 "___ Lisa"
27 Porky or Daffy
29 Rapper Snoop ___
30 Expected to arrive
33 Skillet
35 A, as in Edison?
36 Mosque prayer leader
37 Seward Peninsula city
38 Toward sunrise
40 Snaps
44 Gets off a tackled player
45 Car bomb?
49 Show up
51 Talking truckers, for short
52 Pool paths
54 Bridal path
55 Impulse
56 Use a coffee spoon, say
57 Sicilian smoker
58 Khartoum's river
59 Weekly "Yay!"
60 Change for a five
63 *The Addams Family* cousin

"You got any more?"

"Yeah. The second line is 'You are mine.' "

"That's innocuous enough."

"Yeah. It sounds like a valentine. So far, the only thing out of the ordinary is the method of delivery."

Sherry's pencil flew over the puzzle. "Okay, I got it."

"Got what?"

"The puzzle." Sherry turned it around.

"Don't make me read the damn thing," Cora said. "What's the message?"

" 'I want to know
You are mine

Can you give
A little sign?' "

"That's it?" Cora said.

"Yes, it is."

"You gotta be kidding!"

"You don't believe me? Solve it yourself."

"Let's not get carried away," Cora said. "The thing is, that's not what I wanted to hear."

"What did you want to hear?"

"I dunno. Just not that. It's the pits. It's the worst. It sheds absolutely no light on the situation. It's not intimidating. It's not even threatening. It's just a stupid jingle. The type of crap you'd find on a greeting card."

"Isn't that good?" Sherry said. "I mean, you don't *want* a death threat, do you?"

"At least I'd know where I stood. But this . . ."

"What about this?"

Cora grimaced. "It's either totally innocuous . . ."

"Yeah?"

"Or scary as hell."

7

HIS HEART WAS STILL RACING *as he drove out of town. God, what a rush! Who would have thought he could have done it? Skulking through the woods. Sneaking up on the house. Throwing the knife into the door!*

Even after a week of practice, his best was four out of five. And he'd only done that once. Usually three out of five. Or two out of five. Somewhere around fifty percent. And he'd stuck it in the door on the first try.

Not that there'd have been a second. He couldn't have risked that. If he missed it would have lain there, a testament to his inexperience, to his lack of athleticism, to his inability to score. But, no, the knife had gone right in.

A dangerous phrase!

A dangerous game. Oh, what a daring chance he'd taken.

But he had to make sure she had it. After all, she was coming to his neighborhood. It said so on TV. "A shopping center near you." How right it was. She was coming to a shopping center near him. What a colossal joke. That was ironic, eh? That was a good one.

Not that he wouldn't have gone out of his way to see her. He just didn't have to. Not the way things had worked out.

Not the way he'd made them work out.

He couldn't wait to meet her.

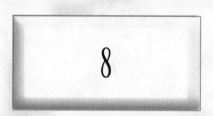

8

THE DANBURY MALL CONSISTED OF a Wal-Mart, a Rite Aid, a Block-buster Video, a sprawling Stop & Shop, and a multiplex cinema. The movie house was closed in the morning, but the parking lot was surprisingly full. In the evening, Cora imagined, it must be an ungodly mess.

The film crew had staked out locations around the doors to the Stop & Shop. There was a camera truck, a lighting truck, a truck the purpose for which Cora could only guess, a makeup and wardrobe camper, and a dozen production cars.

The camper, in Cora's humble opinion, summed up her position in this project. Cora Felton was a nobody who could drive herself to the set. Once there, however, she was the much-vaunted Puzzle Lady, and the public mustn't forget it.

"Did you have to put my name on the door?" she complained to the director.

Daphne Decker raised her eyebrows. "*Moi*? Were you addressing *moi*? Sweetheart, I could care less if Snoopy and the bloody Red

Baron were painted on this camper. I think you'll find that was some cereal person's idea."

"Hold still," the makeup lady advised Cora. "You're about to meet the public. We want them to see you as you really aren't."

"What public? It's nine in the morning."

"So?"

"No one shops at nine in the morning. If they have jobs, they're at work. If they don't have jobs, there's no reason to get up."

"It's Saturday."

"What's your point?"

Quentin Burns stuck his head in the doorway. "Ah, good. Are you about ready? The crowd's getting restless."

"The crowd?" Cora asked.

"Yes, thank goodness. Lance and Ginger can probably go."

"Lance and Ginger?"

Daphne shrugged. "Joe Public isn't always photogenic. Sometimes you get stuck with a bunch of losers. Sometimes no one shows up." She turned on Quentin. "The answer is, no, you don't send the kids home. You're payin' 'em for a day, whether they go home now or at five o'clock. So save 'em for backup."

"How can they be backup?" Cora protested. "You used 'em in the promo."

"So? They gotta live somewhere. Anyway, we're not going to use 'em, but there's no reason not to bust their chops. So, you know what you're gonna do?"

"We've been over it."

"I know we've been over it. I want to go over it again. Because, when this fails to move the product, when this footage isn't sufficient to make the ad, you won't be fired, because you are the Puzzle Lady, and they need you for this god-awful campaign. I, on the other hand, am totally expendable. I'll be the first one out on her fanny when it comes to whom to blame."

Jennifer Blaylock popped in the door. The young publicist was all hyped up. "Are you about ready? It's a riot out there."

"What do you mean?"

"Mothers are killing each other to be the first in line. Everyone wants to be on TV."

"All set," the makeup lady said.

"Okay." Daphne grabbed Cora by the hands, practically yanked her out of her chair. "Here's the deal. Cameras will be rolling, but that doesn't matter. Because there's no set script. Doesn't mean they're MOS. We'll be shooting sound. We may use 'em MOS, we may use 'em sound-synch. Your only concern is to interact with the kids. Get 'em to eat the cereal. If they happen to smile while they're doin' it, that would be real nice. If that happens, you smile, too, like a proud mother hen."

"Hen?"

"No offense, sweetheart. It's called acting. If the kids don't smile, it's a little harder, you may have to tell 'em a funny story while they're eating. If it's a smutty story, turn your head away, or some deaf viewer will read your lips and there'll be hell to pay."

"You want me to trick the kids into laughing?"

"Hey, when was the last time you smiled at your breakfast food?"

The director opened the door and skipped down the steps from the camper.

Cora emerged into the early-morning sunlight, and realized how rock stars must feel.

Two hundred people were camped out in front of the Stop & Shop. All had somehow materialized in the half hour Cora had been in wardrobe and makeup. When Cora had entered the camper, there had been no one around but the crew. Who had clearly been busy. Arc lights had been set up on tripods and aimed at the 4x8 folding table with the bright red bowl, spoon, carton of milk, and upright box of new and improved Corn Toasties.

Larry, the cameraman, sat behind a camera on a dolly, the latter of which, Cora gathered, had been the subject of some spirited disagreement. Quentin Burns had felt handheld cameras would give the shots a reality-show air. Daphne's opinion was, who gave a damn, keep the camera steady.

Next to the camera was a table where two soundmen sat with a tape recorder and boom mike. That was because they weren't shooting MOS. MOS meant picture only, and no sound. Cora was pleased she knew that, more pleased that she knew it stood for "mit-out-sound." Though no linguist, Cora liked that. It also amused her that there was no expression for shooting *with* sound. If you were shooting with sound, you were simply, as the director had put it, *not* shooting MOS.

"There's the Puzzle Lady!" someone in the crowd cried. It was a child's voice.

"God, I hope tape was rolling!" Daphne muttered.

Cora glanced in the direction of the sound table just in time to see Sherry and Aaron walk into view. Her face hardened. Well, of all the nerve. She'd made it perfectly clear to Aaron she didn't want him covering this debacle. And if he wasn't covering it, did he and Sherry have to come to gloat?

Cora turned away, stomped off after the director, producer, and publicist through the crowd. Faces seemed familiar.

Damn familiar!

Cora did a double take and stopped short with a groan. Nerdy cruciverbalist Harvey Beerbaum was in the crowd. The pudgy, bald constructor, hopelessly smitten, was constantly doing utterly inappropriate things to embarrass her. Now he just smiled and waved.

The look Cora gave him might have been more appropriate had she been on her way to the gallows.

And Harvey wasn't alone. Chief Harper was there with his wife, and his daughter, Clara. The kid seemed a little old for the cereal ads; but then, you never knew.

And there was First Selectman Iris Cooper, with whom Cora played bridge. And Dr. Barney Nathan, dapper as usual in a red bow tie. And prosecutor Henry Firth, who always reminded Cora of a rat. And Mary Cushman, of Cushman's Bake Shop. And Judy Douglas Knauer, of Knauer Realty.

And, good lord, there was Becky Baldwin! Bakerhaven's fashion plate cum lawyer had turned up, looking like a million bucks. In fact, Larry seemed to be focusing on her now!

Cora couldn't believe it. This was her *Danbury* personal appearance, and half of *Bakerhaven* was here.

The publicist stepped in front of Cora, and, raising her voice to a decibel level that belied her slender frame, proclaimed, "Let her through! Let her *through*! Nobody gets on TV until the Puzzle Lady gets through."

Marching ahead of Cora, young Jennifer managed to clear the way. She reached the front of the crowd, ducked under the ropes holding the throng back. Ropes, Cora noted, which were manned by teamsters. Who, she knew, were not required to do anything but drive. Evidently, they were getting a kick out of keeping people off the set.

Quentin Burns held up his hands. "Ladies and gentlemen, ladies and gentlemen! This is what you've been waiting for. The Puzzle Lady is here to introduce this exciting new product. Please keep in line, don't push. Everybody is going to get a chance."

Cora's head came up with that one. *Everybody's gonna get a chance?* Every one of them was going to eat the damn stuff?

Cora took her place behind the table.

"There, now," Quentin said. "All set to go, and—Good lord, where's the prop! Where the hell's the damn prop?"

Pepe, who'd been lounging in a director's chair, heaved himself to his feet and lumbered up to the set. The propman had greasy sideburns and a pugnacious attitude. "The props are all here." He pointed to the table. "There's your cereal, your bowl, your spoon, and your milk. The next set's all ready to go. What are you griping about?"

"My floor sign. We're kicking off the shoot without our floor sign?"

"That's not a prop. It's set dressing."

"Nonsense. We're shooting on location. We're not constructing sets."

The property master shook his head. "Hey, I'm the union rep. If it's a set piece, I can't touch it. It's the set dresser's job."

"We *have* no set dresser."

Pepe shook his head. "Not my problem."

"Oh, for goodness' sakes!" The producer stormed to a blue station wagon parked off to the side of the store. He jerked open the back and took out the bone of contention.

It was a life-sized cardboard cutout of Cora Felton, holding a box of new and improved Granville Grains Corn Toasties.

Cora groaned again when she saw it. She'd never posed for any such picture. The darned ad company must have grabbed a still from the footage they shot for the promo.

The producer marched on with the cardboard cutout, stuck it up at the end of the table.

"You can't dress the set," Pepe warned him. "You're not union."

"Oh, come on." Quentin adjusted the floor sign.

Pepe shook his head. "I'm filing a grievance."

The teamster captain, who probably held that position on the strength of being the size of a Mack Truck, fixed Quentin with a gaze usually reserved for virus-infested vermin. "Who drove that to the set?"

Daphne Decker made little pretense of suppressing her amusement over the producer's discomfit. "All right, gang. We'll be taking a fifteen-minute break before we start shooting. Stick around, be ready when you're called." Turning her back on the crowd, she rolled her eyes at Cora Felton. "Care for a smoke?"

"Thought you'd never ask."

Daphne and Cora slipped around the corner of the store.

For the shoot, Daphne was wearing blue jeans, a man's pin-striped dress shirt, and a leather fanny pack. She unzipped the pack, took out a cigarette case and lighter. She offered one to Cora, and the two women lit up.

Cora sucked in smoke. "You care what happens with the shoot?"

"Of course I do. That's my job. But this union fiasco is not of my making. It's the ad agency trying to cut corners. If we can't shoot today, we'll shoot next week."

"Will you have enough footage to cut?"

"Are you kidding me? I could grab enough at any of these spots."

A voice called, "Cora!"

Cora looked at the man peeping around the corner. He had a furtive look, that of someone doing something he shouldn't. Which, in a way, he was. The shooting set was out-of-bounds. By extension, the space behind it was too. The store, of course, was open, but there were roped-off lanes leading in and out. The side of the store, where the film crew were set up, was a definite no-no.

Daphne was quick to point this out, suggesting in a very brusque manner that the gentleman remove his posterior from the premises.

The man didn't take the hint. "But I need to see Cora. Cora, it's me. Freddy. Freddy Fosterfield. Remember?"

Cora's mouth fell open. She remembered all too well. Freddy Fosterfield was one of the few men in the Northern Hemisphere she had not managed to marry, and not for his lack of trying. Cora shuddered at how long ago that must have been. And here he was, the same roly-poly little munchkin who'd made such a pest of himself back in high school. He'd aged well, aside from being bald as a billiard ball.

Cora couldn't have cared less if Freddy looked like the new James Bond. As far as she was concerned, the man was a dork.

Freddy was wearing a three-piece suit. It occurred to Cora that Freddy had worn three-piece suits as a teenager. Only one of the many things she had found odd about the boy.

"You two know each other?" Daphne ventured.

Cora flashed her a look of pure venom. *You two know each other?* was not the phrase she had wished to hear her director utter. Daphne's initial instruction on the placement of his fanny was more like it.

"Oh, we go way back," Freddy answered. "Would you believe

it, we were actually in school together. PS 84. Back in— Well, I shouldn't give the year, now, should I? I just couldn't believe it when I saw on the television Cora was going to be here. I live here, see? It's quite a coincidence."

"It's no coincidence, Freddy. I went to school with a couple of thousand kids. I'm bound to bump into 'em from time to time."

"It's remarkable, even so. What are you doing after the filming? You must let me buy you lunch."

"I'm afraid we're working through. In fact, we have to get back to the set. Come on, Daphne, let's shoot this thing."

The director, startled at being ordered about, nevertheless picked up on Cora's vibes instantly. "That's right, we do. You really shouldn't be here. Go back with the rest of the crowd."

Without waiting for Freddy to respond, Cora pushed past him, stomped around the building, and strode onto the set. The union must have reached some sort of agreement, because the cardboard cutout of the Puzzle Lady was now stationed beside the table. Cora pushed by, grabbed the box of Corn Toasties, plastered on her widest trademark smile, and announced, "All right, who wants some cereal?"

The screams from the kids were deafening.

Daphne, passing the camera dolly, whispered, "Tell me you got that!"

"I'm also getting this," the cameraman muttered.

The sea of prospective commercial kids was besieging the publicist, who was holding her clipboard like a shield as she attempted to write each name down.

"Okay, who's first?" Daphne called to her. "Let's get 'em in, get 'em out."

"First up are Kevin and Molly Wallace."

"Okay, Kevin and Molly. You're on!"

The two siblings were spotlessly dressed in color-coordinated T-shirts and slacks. Molly wore pigtails. Kevin wore bangs. Their hairstyles and dress seemed a vain attempt to make them look younger than they were. Molly's baggy shirt could not quite mask the fact that she was pushing puberty. She was beaming. Kevin seemed downright sullen.

"All right," Cora said, once Molly and Kevin had been positioned on either side of her. "Are you ready to try Granville Grains' new and improved Corn Toasties?"

"You bet!" Molly cheered. One would have thought the kid was being offered a trip to Disney World.

Kevin, however, gave it his best James Dean. "Yeah, sure," he snarled.

Daphne leaped into the fray. "Kids, kids. You wanna do this, that's fine. You don't, there're a lot of kids waiting. You got a problem, young man?"

"They made me cut baseball practice," Kevin griped.

"Your parents did? Are they here?"

"Yeah."

"Then I think we should make *them* come up here and eat the cereal."

The crowd laughed and cheered. Even Kevin broke into a grin.

Daphne called to the publicist, "Have the parents sign a consent form, and get 'em up here."

A sheepish-looking fortyish couple, she in a tan topcoat, he in a blue Thinsulate jacket, were hustled through the ropes and up to the table.

"Great," Daphne said. "We'll do the parents, then the kids, then maybe the parents and the kids together. How will that be?"

That was great with the kids and most of the crowd. The only ones not happy were the hopeful parents of the other children, who didn't want to see so much time wasted on the first two picked.

Cora, on the other hand, was having a ball. Whether it was the shared cigarette, the salty language, or the que sera, sera attitude, she considered Daphne a kindred spirit, and was getting a huge kick out of her antics. She dipped her spoon in the cereal, and held it out to the youngsters' parents with all the satanic glee of a dope peddler pushing her wares.

9

FREDDY FOSTERFIELD WAS WAITING when she got off. "Can I give you a ride?" he said when Cora emerged from the trailer.

Cora sucked in her breath. It was five-fifteen. Most everyone else had left. Sherry and Aaron had departed right before lunch, as had half of the crowd. Which had not surprised her—after all, how long can you watch kids eat cereal? The only ones there in the afternoon were the curiosity seekers who straggled by, and those who still hoped to get their kids on the air. By four Daphne had ordered a cutoff on anyone else signing up, and they'd shot the last kid by four forty-five. The production vehicles had taken off like a shot. Only the camper remained, and that was only because Cora had to change. The minute her feet hit the pavement, the impatient teamster slammed the door, hopped in the cab, and pulled out.

Leaving her alone with Freddy Fosterfield.

It was cold in the parking lot, and Freddy had pulled on a trench coat over his three-piece suit. Now he looked like a bald, chubby private eye.

"So, do you have plans for dinner?" Freddy asked.

"I plan to eat it." Cora brushed by Freddy, headed for her car.

Freddy tagged along. "Well, if you're going to eat here, you need a guide. Because some restaurants are good, and some of them are yucky."

"I have to get home."

"To Bakerhaven?"

"Yes."

"How come?"

"I have a dog."

"What kind?"

"The kind that eats. What difference does it make?" Cora said irritably. "I gotta feed my dog."

"I thought you lived with your niece." Freddy was nattering at her heels.

"Who told you that?"

"I read the gossip columns. Call your niece, tell her to feed the dog."

"She isn't home."

"Yes she is."

"How do you know?"

" 'Cuz I called her."

Cora stopped short. A cold chill shot down her spine. "You *called* her?"

"Asked her if you had plans. She had no idea what you were doing, didn't even know if you'd be home for supper. She didn't mention the dog, or I'd have asked her to feed it. But if she didn't know if you were coming home, she must have fed the dog."

Cora groaned. There it was, the same pedantic, methodical thinking that drove her nuts in high school. Cora couldn't talk to the man for as much as ten minutes without wanting to rap him upside the head, or launch a foot in the general direction of his chubby derriere. And here he was, the ultimate wet blanket, to rain on her parade. Just as she was congratulating herself on making it through her first day on location.

"Freddy. You remember in high school when you asked me to go out with you and I said no? The answer is still no."

Freddy didn't take offense. He smiled placidly. "Nonsense. This is not like asking you to go out in high school. This is a grown-up asking you out for a steak."

For just one second, Cora hesitated. Cora liked steak. If the truth be known, in the past there had been any number of otherwise thoroughly objectionable men she had allowed to buy her steak.

Then reason kicked in. "You're not buying me dinner, Freddy."

"Of course not. We'll go dutch treat. I know you're a big celebrity. I wouldn't want to presume."

"Get out of my way."

Freddy didn't budge. "Why don't you ride with me? I'll bring you back after we eat, you can pick up your car."

"I'm not going out to dinner. I'm tired. I'm going home."

Cora started around Freddy. Unexpectedly, he reached out, grabbed her arm. His grip was iron. It startled her. She would have imagined Freddy's hand to be weak and flabby. But, no, it was surprisingly strong.

Cora grabbed his thumb, pulled up. And—

It was like an icicle through her heart. Cold, sharp, horrifying.

Cora staggered, reeled. Then, as a rush of adrenaline kicked in, she dropped into a crouch, pivoted away.

Her purse swung like a pendulum, clipped Freddy on the shoulder. He winced, loosened his grip on her arm. Before he knew it, Cora was walking, not running, but walking rapidly away from him, toward her car.

Her hand fumbled for her keys in her purse, came up with the butt of her gun.

Cora glanced over her shoulder. Freddy was hurrying after her.

Would she have enough time to drop the gun, grab her keys, open the door, slam the door, lock the door?

Cora's hand came out of her purse. She leveled her gun at the astonished man.

Freddy screeched to a halt, like a cartoon character who realizes he's reached the edge of a cliff. Cora half expected to see his legs swivel and helplessly pedal the air. Instead, his mouth fell open, and his eyes bugged out of his head.

"Are you crazy?" he wailed. "I just asked you to have dinner."

"And I said no," Cora replied evenly. "Perhaps you didn't hear me."

Freddy's look of astounded incredulity dissolved into one of bemused admiration. "Wow! I'd heard you were a spitfire, but this is fantastic. I'm sorry we can't have dinner. Another time, perhaps."

Freddy turned on his heel and walked off.

Cora made sure he kept going before lowering the gun. She unlocked her car, put the key in the ignition with trembling fingers. She started the car, switched on the lights, backed up, and pulled out of the lot.

No one followed. Cora made sure of that. She drove figure eights before heading out of town. But even on the highway, she couldn't calm down.

In her mind, she kept seeing Freddy Fosterfield's right hand shooting out to grip her arm.

His fingernails were meticulously filed, just as she remembered, an annoying habit of an unappetizing man. But that wasn't the memory she fixated on.

It was the scratch. The scratch bisecting the angle of Freddy's thumb and forefinger. The scar with a long thin scab that had all but fallen off.

It could have been a paper cut. That would have been in keeping with Freddy's high school image, the one that featured the pocket protector with a host of pens.

But it also could have been from a knife blade, gripped too tightly between thumb and forefinger, while being hurled at a wooden door.

10

"YOU PULLED A GUN ON HIM?" Sherry said incredulously.

"It was either that or have dinner with him."

"Aunt Cora—"

"It worked remarkably well. I wish I'd had a gun back in high school."

"Nowadays, kids do."

"Yeah. I'm just ahead of my time. Where are you going?"

Sherry was putting on makeup in front of the bathroom mirror. She wore a terry-cloth robe, and had a towel around her head.

"It's Saturday night, Cora. I have a date."

"With Aaron?"

"You think I'm seeing someone else on the side?"

"I don't know why not. I always did."

"Cora, could you be a little less incorrigible?"

"Sorry. I'm upset."

"Right. You're being stalked by your high school sweetheart."

"He wasn't my sweetheart!"

"No, you were his."

"You're not helping, Sherry."

Sherry finished highlighting her eyes. She took the towel off her head, shook out her wet brown hair. It hung halfway down her neck. She combed it with her fingers. "What do you want me to do, ridicule the notion? Fine. It's a ridiculous notion. I don't think this nerd you used to know is throwing knives at your door. There. You feel better?"

"I should feel better because you're humoring me?"

"Well, what do you want?"

"Logic, Sherry. That's what you're good at. Tell me why he couldn't be the one."

"This guy must have really shaken you up, Cora. *I'm* not good at logic. *You're* good at logic. I'm good at words. So let me ask you. Did this guy ever show any proficiency in crossword-puzzle construction?"

"He's a nerd."

"Thanks a lot. Believe it or not, nerdiness and cruciverbalism don't necessarily go hand in hand. Did he ever show any aptitude for puzzles?"

"Not that I recall."

"What does he do for a living?"

"I don't know."

"You didn't ask?"

"I wasn't trying to date him. I was trying *not* to date him."

"So you pulled a gun on him. Fine. I assume he got the point."

Cora followed Sherry down the hall to her room. "If this were just a casual thing, I'd tend to agree with you."

"But you're going to obsess about it because the guy had a scratch on his hand."

"Go throw a knife at the door. See where your hand touches the blade."

Sherry's eyes widened incredulously. "Did you throw a knife at the door?"

"While you were in the shower."

Sherry stepped into a pair of panties, shrugged off the terry-cloth robe, and pulled on a sweater.

"You're not going to wear a bra?"

"Oh, look who's talking. You burned yours in college. Right after you drove what's-his-name wild with it. Till he went nuts and threw a knife at your front door."

"Right. It was umpteen years later, but still. . . ."

"That doesn't strike you as far-fetched?"

"That strikes me as downright stupid." Cora reached in her drawstring purse, pulled out a huge carving knife. "Granted, this is not exactly the same knife. The blade is longer and wider and the handle is lighter. So it's probably not as heavy. I bet you a nickel you can't stick it in the door."

"Cora—"

"First try, anyway. You can probably do it in five."

"Cora, please tell me you didn't wreck our door."

"I didn't wreck our door. I stood up a sheet of plywood in front of the garage."

"You stuck the knife in plywood?"

"On the third try. And on the fifth. Two out of five. If I can do two, you can do one."

"You're getting agitated over nothing."

"Nothing?" Cora held up her right hand, palm down. Between her thumb and her forefinger was a thin red line. "See? That's where the knife blade cuts the hand. Try it. You'll see."

Sherry sighed. "Cora. You're all wound up. You're taking this way too seriously. Look, why don't you come out with us to the movies."

"Yeah, right. Drag your old aunt along on a date."

"It's not a date. Aaron and I are going to the movies. It's no big deal."

"Of course not. You just showered, made up your face, and put on your slinky no-bra outfit. Who could possibly confuse that with an actual date?"

"Probably the same person who could confuse a high school crush with an actual threat."

"Touché! The wordsmith strikes back. Hey, look, I don't wanna cramp your young man's style. Not when you've prepared such a tempting package. So here's the deal. I won't horn in on your movie if you do me a favor first."

"What's that?"

"It's a little embarrassing."

"How could it be more embarrassing than what we've been talking about?"

"I got a fan letter."

"When? There was nothing in the mail today."

"This was a while ago. I forgot all about it. And it didn't come here. It went to the company. My publicist gave it to me."

"You have a publicist?"

"Don't start with me."

"So? What about it?"

"There was a crossword puzzle in it."

"So?"

"Could you solve it?"

"Why? What made you think of it now?"

"Freddie Fosterfield. Acting like an obsessed fan. It made me think, maybe the knife thrower's a fan."

"Where is this puzzle?"

"I stuck it in my purse. It's probably still there." Cora sat down on the couch, flopped her purse on the coffee table, and began pulling out an incredible assortment of junk. Cigarettes. Lighter. Matches. Compact. Eyeliner. Gun.

"Is that the gun you threatened him with?" Sherry asked.

"I only have one gun."

"I have *only* one gun."

"You have a gun?"

"No, you do. And you have only one."

"That's what I said."

"No it isn't. You said that one gun was the only thing you have."

Sherry indicated the array on the coffee table. "So none of this is yours."

"If I shot you with my only gun, it would be justifiable homicide." Cora pulled out the folded puzzle. "Here it is. Can you solve it?"

Sherry took the puzzle, unfolded it, looked it over. "Well, I should think so."

Cora frowned. "Why do you say it like that?"

Sherry handed Cora back the puzzle.

"Because it's the same one that was stuck in our door."

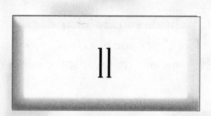

11

Quentin Burns was having a snit fit. The producer stood beneath the overhang of the entrance to the Stamford Food 4 Less, and watched the wind whip the driving rain along the pavement. The vast mall parking lot was deserted except for the production vehicles and the cars of the employees.

"Look at that!" he moaned. "Just look at that!"

Daphne was having none of it. "Oh, for God's sake," she told him. "It's April. It rains. Get over it."

"Well, I do hope people come," Morton Giles said. A slender man with a short crew cut, large round glasses, and a weak chin, the assistant manager of the Food 4 Less gave the impression that if people didn't, it would be entirely his fault. "We've had posters up all week. And the cashiers have been sticking flyers in the grocery bags. We expected a big turnout."

"What's the forecast?" Cora asked.

"It's going to rain all day," Morton said gloomily.

Cora knew that. She'd heard it on TV and called the producer to suggest they cancel the shoot. Quentin, of course, hadn't listened. Which was why she was rubbing it in.

"Yeah, that's what I heard," Daphne said. "If it were my schedule, I'd have had a rain date. But I don't run the zoo."

"Any time you're done fixing blame," Quentin said, "you want to figure out what we are going to do?"

"Whaddya think we're gonna do? We're gonna shoot inside. We're gonna set up a pyramid of cereal boxes and put a table in front of it. I would think a child of four could have figured that out."

"But there're no *people*," Quentin whined. "You can't shoot with no *people*."

"We've got Lance and Ginger. We can shoot them."

"*Inside?* What for? We've *got* shots of them *inside*. Put 'em in front of cereal boxes and they might as well be in the studio. What's the good of that?"

"If it's no good, we won't use it."

"Then why shoot it?"

"What do you do when it rains?" Daphne asked the assistant manager. "You close up? You go home?"

"Of course not."

"You do business?"

"Of course. Just not as much."

"How bad does business fall off?"

"It depends on the storm."

His remark was punctuated by a flash of lightning and a re-sounding crack of thunder. They were very close together, indicating the lightning was near.

The crew were standing around in rain slickers, waiting for the word. The cameraman shrugged his shoulders, spread his arms. "So?"

Quentin looked to Daphne.

"All right," she said. "We're shooting inside. Load in while we map out the set. You got a place she can change?"

"There's a women's room on the east wall," the assistant manager said.

"I didn't bring my compass, so somebody point her to it. Makeup and wardrobe set up around there. You, break open some cartons of cereal and help us make an arrangement."

"You can't dress a set," Pepe the property manager protested.

"We're not dressing a set. We're *arranging* props. That's your job."

"Inside? That sounds suspiciously like a set."

"It's a location. Inside or out, it's a location."

"I'm calling the union."

"Give them my regards."

The Food 4 Less was the size of a small third-world-nation, with probably ten times the food. Cora followed Lance, Ginger, and the makeup lady past a zillion cash registers, only three of which were open, to what presumably was the east side of the building.

Flo pushed a small metal coatrack on wheels from which the costumes hung. Her makeup kit was slung over her shoulder. It looked heavy. Neither Lance nor Ginger offered to help her. Cora was tempted to, just to shame them. But she figured it wouldn't work, and she'd wind up schlepping the damn thing.

When they reached the far wall, Cora grabbed her costume off the rack and plunged into the women's room. She hooked the hanger over the stall door, lit up a smoke, and glared at the young actress, Ginger, who came trailing in wetly behind her.

"Don't look at me like that. If we're going to be stuck in here all day, I've got to smoke. Besides, I saw you and what's-his-face lighting up."

Ginger was considerably older than the parts she played. She favored Cora with a world-weary sneer. "That was *pot*. You don't think we'd smoke *cigarettes,* do you? *Cigarettes* are bad for you. Of course, you wouldn't know that."

Cora was miffed. "Hey, I grew up in the '60s. I know both sides of your argument."

"What's that supposed to mean?"

"*Give peace a chance. Make love, not war.* In the '60s, a lot of people smoked anything they could get their hands on, good or bad. There weren't any value judgments." Cora grimaced. "Actually, there were plenty. We just pretended there weren't."

Ginger frowned, looked like a little girl again. "What are you talking about?"

"Just jabbering while I finish my cigarette. And you are going to be a good girl and not tell them I'm smoking in here."

"Hey, you're smoking in here," Flo scolded, coming in the door.

"It's not me, it's Ginger," Cora shot back, surreptitiously dropping the cigarette in the toilet.

Ginger looked positively stunned.

Cora flashed her a devilish look. "Better hurry up and get changed." She pulled her costume off the hanger. "Wouldn't wanna keep 'em waiting."

Cora, in full Puzzle Lady garb, hung her street clothes on the coatrack. She kept her purse. Her cigarettes, her wallet, and her gun were in it. Not the type of things to leave about.

Cora found her way to the front of the store, where Quentin was still arguing with the propman over who had the right to set up what. In the meantime, the electricians had erected arc lights on tripods, and the grips had anchored the bases with sandbags. Camera and sound were ready to shoot. The cameraman had aimed his camera, the soundman had loaded his tape recorder, and the boom man had plugged in the boom. All were sipping coffee and gobbling doughnuts from the Krispy Kreme next door. The sight of the pastries was almost enough to make Pepe cave in and let Quentin arrange the cereal.

The pyramid of boxes was to be set up at the end of the cereal aisle, on a rack made expressly for that purpose. Setting them up merely meant replacing boxes with pictures of Tony the Tiger with ones with pictures of the Puzzle Lady. Why this required a union waiver was beyond Cora, but what did she know?

Around Cora's table, and effectively blocking off two aisles, were stanchions and ropes designed to keep the crowd back. As there was no crowd, it was merely providing an arena for Quentin and the propman to duke it out.

Daphne, who couldn't have cared less, was sitting in a director's chair sipping coffee and reading the *New York Times*.

"Where'd you get the paper?" Cora asked.

"Starbucks."

"Oh?"

"They always have the *New York Times*." Daphne held out the Arts section. "You want to do the crossword puzzle?"

Cora repressed a shudder. "You got the Sports section?"

"Depends. You a Yankees fan?"

"Shh. Don't say that too loud. This is New England."

Cora sat with Daphne, shook out the Sports section, and settled in to read about George Steinbrenner's latest acquisitions.

"Hey," Cora said, "could be worse."

The lights went out.

12

It wasn't an absolute disaster. Power was restored. The rain, which never stopped, at least let up. Customers straggled in. Film was shot.

And not just with Ginger and Lance. Cora had actual children to work with. Unfortunately, none of them could act.

"What a bunch of stiffs," Daphne complained, as she and Cora took a bathroom break. Cora had tipped her off it was a good place to smoke, and now the two women were huddled like schoolgirls puffing on cigarettes.

"They're not actors," Cora pointed out.

"No, but they're human. Or they're supposed to be. What's so hard about eating a goddamned bowl of cereal?"

"Did you taste that stuff?"

Daphne's eyes widened. "Are you saying it's no good?"

"Absolutely not. You can quote me on that. I am *not* saying the cereal is no good."

"I don't care if it tastes like cow pies," Daphne said. "If a kid wants to be in a TV commercial, he can damn well eat it."

"You getting any footage at all? Not that I love this gig, but I'd hate to see them pull the plug."

"Relax. Quentin's too dumb to know if we're getting anything or not."

Cora was not too dumb, and in her opinion the whole day was a total washout. Not one child looked like he wasn't being given castor oil. A girl with pigtails and a gap-toothed smile looked promising, until she bit the spoon, cut her lip, and cried.

Cora was just recovering from that disappointment when a middle-aged woman in a tan raincoat approached the table. She was dragging a young lad with a duck umbrella. Cora liked the duck umbrella, the curved handle of which was the head and bill, and was about to ask Daphne if they could shoot it, when the woman said, "Cora Felton! I just *had* to come and see you!"

That set off instant alarm bells in Cora's head. This woman *didn't* have to come and see her. This woman didn't have to see her at all. Who the hell was she? Cora had no idea, but the woman had just become a definite liability, duck umbrella or no duck umbrella.

"You don't remember me, do you?" the woman went on, giving Cora one more reason to resent her. *Don't pull that on me,* Cora thought. *If you* really *think I don't know who you are,* tell me.

Instead, Cora smiled and asked, "You're not just a cereal lover?"

"Lord, no." The woman laughed. "We're porridge people."

The woman had chubby cheeks. So did her son. It occurred to Cora they must consume a lot of porridge. "So why are you here?"

"To see you, of course! Good lord, you really don't remember, do you?"

"Say that one more time and I'm calling Security," Cora said good-naturedly. One would have had to listen carefully to catch the edge in her voice.

"I'm Margaret."

This announcement was made as if it should clear up everything. In fact, it cleared up nothing. Cora's mind raced, trying to conjure up a Margaret of any kind who might be accosting her in a Connecticut supermarket with a chubby child.

"Margaret. My, my, my." Cora was totally at sea. Was there a Margaret at the Manhattan Bridge Club? Had she divested any of her ex-husbands of any first wives named Margaret?

"You found my earrings for me," Margaret gushed. "I will never forget you for that."

Cora felt a huge rush of relief. Of course. That trip to Mohonk her third husband, Frank, had insisted she go on. One of those mystery weekends where a bunch of actors staged a murder, and the guests had to figure it out. During the course of her stay, a woman's diamond earrings had been stolen. Cora had not only solved the murder, she had also solved the theft. At least, she had retrieved the earrings. The culprit had gotten away. Actually, Cora had felt sorry for the thief, and decided not to expose *him or her,* as she had worded her denouement, for anonymity's sake.

Ironically, while Cora had been finding the missing jewels, Frank had been finding a buxom young jewel of his own.

Cora wasn't happy with Margaret for eliciting the memory. She shot pictures with Margaret's pudgy child, none of which would ever make its way into a commercial. Not that the boy didn't like the cereal. He shoveled it down happily enough. It was just that the image it conjured up was someone spoon-feeding a pregnant sow.

Cora, trying hard to be a glass-is-half-full sort of gal, found herself working overtime with Margaret's kid. Cora had to remind herself that it wasn't the distraction of Margaret that had made Frank stray. Frank was the straying type. He would have found a way to wander regardless. Margaret was, therefore, not a reminder of Cora's failures, but of her triumphs.

Convincing herself was rough sledding. By the time she finally finished up with Margaret & Son, Cora couldn't help feeling somewhat shell-shocked.

What a day!

A hurricane, a blackout, and a blast from the past.

What could possibly go wrong next?

B

"WHERE'S MY WALLET!?"

The child actress, Ginger, exhibiting remarkable lung power for one so young, or one so small, or for anyone else, for that matter, nearly broke windows. Her furious shout reverberated through the recesses of the cavernous Food 4 Less, echoing off the walls, freezing shoppers in their tracks and cashiers at their scanners. One would have thought a firstborn child had been taken, rather than a wallet, considering the anger, anguish, distress, and consternation invested in that single ear-piercing yowl.

Cora Felton, smoking in the girls' room on a five-minute break, banged her head on the paper-towel dispenser. She flipped her cigarette in a toilet and plunged out of the bathroom to see who had been killed.

Ginger, clad in her little-girl outfit, was standing at the coatrack, holding a pair of blue jeans she had just removed from a hanger. The girl's wide eyes and empty hip pocket told the story: Someone had ripped her off during the shoot.

Of course, it occurred to Cora, if Ginger was stupid enough to leave her darned wallet lying around loose, the kid deserved what she got.

Ginger clearly didn't think so. At the moment she was glaring at the makeup and costume lady as if it were all her fault. As if there were any doubt as to her opinion, Ginger promptly dispelled it by hurling a dazzlingly inventive string of invectives at the poor woman, blaming her for the event, and wishing upon her positions not known in the *Kama Sutra.*

People came running from all directions. Lance came charging out of the men's room, half in costume, half in street clothes. There was really little difference. As a boy, he wore shorts, which didn't play, since he was filmed behind the table. In real life, he wore khaki pants. He had changed into those. He still wore his cute little-boy shirt. He didn't look cute, however. He looked like an appropriate prop might be a switchblade knife.

"What the hell happened?" he demanded. "Ginger, what's going on?"

"My wallet. Somebody swiped my wallet."

His eyes widened. "You mean—"

"I mean my *wallet,* dork. Whaddya think I mean?"

"Where was it?"

"In my pants."

"You left your wallet in your pants?"

"Don't start with me."

The crew had gathered around, along with half a dozen curious shoppers.

Morton Giles pushed his way through them. The assistant manager wore a look of utter consternation. This had happened on his watch. "What's the matter here?"

"Somebody stole my wallet," Ginger wailed.

"Oh, I don't think so. There's got to be some logical explanation. When you hung up your pants, the wallet fell out, someone kicked it across the floor."

"Are you brain-dead, or what? It's not on the floor! Somebody swiped it."

"I don't understand. We're still filming. Why were you changing your clothes?"

Ginger fixed the assistant manager with a look of concentrated contempt. "What the hell difference does *that* make? I've been *robbed*!"

"Lance and Ginger are finished for the day," Cora volunteered, since the girl was so rude. "We have enough other kids to shoot."

"I see, I see. Well, don't worry," Morton assured Ginger. "We'll do everything we can. First you can make out a report—"

"*I* have to make a report? *You* lost my wallet, and now *I* have to make a report? What kind of a place are you running here? You let them steal my wallet, and then you act like it's all my fault."

Cora restrained herself with great effort from pointing out whose fault it might be.

"Exactly where was your wallet?" Morton asked.

"Right there." Ginger pointed. "On the hook. In my pants pocket. Where I changed into my costume."

Cora noticed some of the electricians and grips whispering and giggling. She figured they were making lewd remarks about the young actress changing out there by the coatrack.

Quentin Burns came bustling up. "I called the police. They'll be right here."

"You called the cops?" Ginger screeched. "Who the hell asked you to call the cops?"

Quentin was stunned by the savagery of her tone. It was a moment before he recollected that he was the producer and wasn't about to be talked to in that manner by a child actress in his employ. "I called the police because I'm in charge, young lady. I called the police because we have theft insurance and it only covers us if we follow proper procedure. But mainly I called the police because it's the right thing to do. You, young lady, keep a civil tongue in your head and remember who you're working for, or you may wind up working somewhere else."

"Great!" Ginger fired back. "Can me for getting my wallet stolen. What a prince!"

The producer considered how that union grievance might play out. Clearly, he wasn't happy with the prospect. "Well, the fact is, the police are on their way and there's nothing we can do about that now."

"Can I go change?" Ginger whined.

"Let's wait for the police."

"Oh, for God's sake!"

They were still arguing when the first cop arrived, a Stamford policeman, who was, in Cora's humble opinion, way too youthful for the job. He had freckles and a turned-up nose and looked perfectly adorable in his yellow rain slicker.

The officer quickly sized up the situation. "You left your wallet hanging here?"

"That's right." Perhaps due to her prior questioning, Ginger said it rather defensively.

"And while it was hanging here, where was everybody else?"

"On the set."

"What set?"

"We're a film crew," Quentin volunteered. "Shooting a commercial. Over there in the front of the store, where the lights are set up."

"Who would have been free to come over here and take the wallet?"

"No one. We were working all day."

"Hah!" Daphne said.

"You disagree with that? And who are you?"

"Daphne Decker. I'm the director. You ever been on a film set? You know how much time there is between shots? It's not so bad when you're grabbing footage like this, but trust me, it's slow. There isn't a person on this crew who wouldn't have time to steal a wallet."

"Did you see anyone leave the set?"

Cora cleared her throat.

The cop looked at her. His eyes widened. "I know you! You're the Puzzle Lady. You're on TV. So this is that. Like they said in the ad. You're here with the new cereal."

"Yeah, yeah, right." Cora brushed it off. "The point is, these are the bathrooms, we've been here all day, probably everyone's been by. Not that I suspect anyone on the crew for a minute, but that's a fact. We also had a store full of customers, any one of whom could have taken the opportunity to swipe the wallet. For anyone going in or out of the bathrooms it was right there hanging on a hook with a sign saying STEAL ME."

Ginger, who had enough on the ball to realize that theory reflected on her, said, "Hey! Is that my fault? We got a wardrobe mistress on duty who's supposed to be looking out for that stuff."

It was Flo's turn to be offended. "Well, think again. I'm doing costumes and makeup. Where am I doing makeup? On the set, that's where. Now tell me how I can be in two places at once!"

The propman piped up in his shop steward mode. "She can't. Which is why we need two people for the jobs. I've pointed this out again and again."

The cop wasn't interested in the union dispute. "The fact is," he told the costume lady, "you weren't watching the clothes. You were over there on the set, so no one saw what happened."

The assistant manager cleared his throat. "Actually . . ."

"You mean you saw something?" the cop demanded instantly.

"I didn't. But we have video cameras throughout the store. They might have caught something."

"You're saying you might have the robbery on videotape?"

"It's possible." Morton pointed to a small camera mounted high on the wall above the entrance to the restrooms. "I can't tell from this angle, but that just might cover the coatrack."

"Is that camera filming?"

"It should be."

"Where's the monitor?"

"In my office."

The manager's office of the Food 4 Less turned out to be a glass-enclosed booth halfway up the side wall next to the row of cash registers. A staircase led to the small enclosure, which barely had room for a desk and chair. A floor safe, file cabinet, and TV monitor made it very cramped indeed.

"Okay," the young cop said. "We can't all come up here. You're the producer, right? You're the one in charge?"

"Yes, I am," Quentin said, pushing forward.

"Good. Then you can see that no one comes up here, because there's just no room." The cop turned to the assistant manager. "I assume you know how to run this thing?"

"I'm sure it will be no problem."

"Fine," the cop said. "You play it back. Miss Felton and I will check it out."

Cora's inclusion in the group was met with considerable grumbling.

"You're not making me real popular," Cora told the young policeman as they wedged into the booth.

"You want to wait with the others?"

"Hell, no."

"Then let's take a look."

Despite Morton's assurances that he could play back the tape, it took the assistant manager close to fifteen minutes to figure out how to get a particular angle up on the screen. There were twelve cameras mounted throughout the store, and eleven of them seemed to be running. For once, Murphy's Law was not in effect—the malfunctioning camera was not the one over the rest room door.

Once Morton got the tape rewound, Cora and the cop settled back to watch some of the most boring footage in the history of law enforcement. It was, at least, relatively fast. The surveillance camera was set on a ten-second capture. In other words, it took a still picture every ten seconds. As a result, images seemed to jump across the screen. Cora Felton could be seen approaching the clothes rack. In the next frame, Cora Felton could be seen entering the restroom with her costume in her hands. There was no intervening frame showing her taking the costume from the rack.

"Won't that be a problem?" Cora said. "If we spot the guy, but don't actually see him commit the crime?"

"Not for me," the cop said. He shrugged. "The prosecutor is another story."

Ginger jumped into frame, hung her pants on a hook, jumped out again.

"There we go," the cop said. "Now the wallet's in place."

"Really? Can you see it?"

"No. But that's where she said it was."

"Yes, she did. And I can't think of a reason why she'd lie. But you can't rule it out. Can you see the wallet?"

"It seems like there's a bulge in the hip pocket."

"Yes, it does. Let's see if it ever looks like there isn't."

The tape continued jumping ahead, but no one came near the wallet.

"Can you speed this up?" the cop asked Morton.

"I think so. I don't know what you can see at that speed."

"Try it. If there's any movement, slow it down."

Morton fast-forwarded the tape, slowed it to see Cora Felton pop out of the bathroom and take off toward the set in a series of jarring jump-cuts.

Ginger and Lance also headed for the set without going anywhere near the hanging pants.

Morton sped up the tape again. Hours whizzed by in minutes, slowing only as each crew member used the restroom. None showed any interest in Ginger's wallet. At least, not in the split second they were caught on tape.

An occasional customer wandered by, but none ventured close to the clothes rack.

Adding to the futility was the fact that it was so well documented. In the lower right-hand corner of the surveillance tape was a readout of the exact time, which jumped ten seconds with each frame. In fast-forward these numbers flashed by like the pictures in a nickelodeon. The seconds were just a blur, but the minutes streamed by, with the hours popping periodically.

It had just turned 3:00 when some movement necessitated a second look. Morton slowed the tape, backed it up.

A woman in a raincoat and a boy with a duck umbrella jumped into frame. At normal speed they passed through camera range in four stills, rather slow, to be sure, but they never ventured near the wallet.

Morton aimed the remote control to resume scanning.

The cop said, "Look!"

The boy with the duck umbrella had just come back into frame. His mother was nowhere in sight. A second later, he jumped to the coatrack. A second after that, he was running off after his mother with something in his hand.

"Stop!" the cop said. "Freeze that!"

Morton rewound, hit the PAUSE button, managed to freeze on the picture of the boy at the coatrack.

His hand was clearly up, reaching for the pants.

"Got him!" the cop said. "Can you advance it one frame?"

Morton could. He clicked the remote, froze on the picture of the young culprit walking away.

He was carrying a wallet.

Cora Felton sucked in her breath. Her flesh tingled.

But Cora wasn't looking at the pudgy young thief, trapped like a bug in amber.

In the upper left-hand corner of the screen, paying no attention to the crime, and proceeding calmly down the aisle as if he hadn't a care in the world, was her old classmate, Freddy Fosterfield.

14

CHIEF HARPER MADE A BIG SHOW OF dumping sugar in his coffee. It occurred to Cora he didn't want that much sugar, he was just buying time to think. "You sure you won't have some?" he inquired.

Cora politely but firmly demurred. She had tried the police station coffee before. It had taken days to get the taste out of her mouth. Cora followed the chief down the hall and back into his office.

"Now, then," he said, "where were we?"

"You know damn well where we are. I told you I was being stalked. You developed a sudden, insatiable craving for caffeine."

"That's hardly a fair assessment of the situation."

"Call it whatever you like. The guy's bugging me. I want help. What are you going to do about it?"

"This is where we run into a little problem."

"A little problem?"

"Actually, several. Stamford is slightly out of my jurisdiction. In fact, the number of calls I get to cooperate with the Stamford police is, at last count, let me see now . . . zero. So it would take some pretty strong evidence on my part to get the Stamford police interested. And what have I got? I've got a grocery store surveillance video of a customer in a store. Granted, this is a video of a crime, which would make it worthy of notice. But is the gentleman in question *committing* the crime? No, he is *not*. He is in the *background* of the video in which someone *else* is committing the crime. And what is the gentleman you are interested in doing? He is shopping. Shopping in a grocery store. I can see the Stamford police getting terribly interested in that. Yep, they'll just drop everything else and get right on it."

"That's not fair," Cora protested. "The guy's not from Stamford. He's from Danbury. He was at the store in Danbury. Now he's at the one in Stamford. And at the one in Stamford he kept in the background, didn't let me see him."

"Did you want to see him?"

"No."

"And had you made that clear?"

"I told you I did."

"So." Chief Harper set down his coffee, steepled his fingers. "The gentleman in question is someone you've told to leave you alone. He *did* leave you alone. And this bothers you because . . . ?"

"Don't be a horse's ass. The guy lives in Danbury. He could have left me alone by shopping there. Not driving umpteen miles to Stamford to go shopping in the very store where I'm giving a demonstration. The guy is *stalking* me. That's the word you're looking for. That's what you want to communicate to the Stamford police. I'm a celebrity, and I'm being *stalked*."

"Isn't there a reality show like that?"

"Very funny."

"Cora, you're making public appearances. It's not stalking to show up at public appearances. That's why public appearances are advertised. So they're *public*."

"At *two* breakfast cereal promotions? You couldn't pay me enough to get me to *one* breakfast cereal promotion."

"There's no law says you can't. That's the bottom line. No laws have been broken here."

"Are you forgetting the knife in my door?"

"You think this guy threw the knife?"

"He could have."

"What makes you think he did?"

"He had a cut on his hand."

"A cut?"

"Well, a scratch."

"The guy had a *scratch* on his hand?"

"Damn it, Chief, I'm not crazy. The guy had a scab between his thumb and first finger. Right where a knife would cut you if you threw it at a door."

"That's nice." Chief Harper sipped his coffee. "So what do you want from my life?"

"I'd like you to take this seriously."

"Oh, really? What about the alleged robbery?"

"It wasn't alleged. They caught the fat kid with the wallet."

"And what was the fat kid to you?"

"I beg your pardon?"

"Didn't you say you knew the mother? Wasn't she someone from your past?"

"So what?"

"I thought maybe that was why you were so upset."

Cora sucked in her breath. "You gonna help me or not?"

Chief Harper considered. "Did you tell the Stamford police? About the fact you think you're being stalked?"

"That's not the point."

"Why is that not the point?"

"I thought it would sound better coming from you."

"No you didn't. You thought it would sound like a *moron* coming from *you*. Well, guess what? It would sound like a moron coming from me."

"I don't think an idea can sound like a moron."

"Save your wordplay for someone who gives a damn. Look, if

you'll forgive me for saying so, this problem here is slight. You're doing grocery stores in broad daylight. If you're reasonably careful walking back to your car, you're not going to get hurt."

Cora sighed. "That's the problem."

"What?"

"We're going on the road."

"Oh?"

"We're doing a coastal swing. Connecticut, Rhode Island, all the way up to Boston."

"You're doing Boston?"

"No, somewhere near. We're not doing Boston, we're not doing New York. They're not folksy enough. We're doing the smaller cities with the local grocery stores, which are thrilled to death to get me."

"And who wouldn't be?"

"The point is, we're going to be stuck in hotels and motels in strange places and I want to feel safe."

"I can't come on the road with you, Cora."

"I'm not asking you to. I just want to go on record that I think my life might be in danger."

"Oh, you do, do you?"

"In case you might need to recall it at a later date."

Chief Harper frowned. "You still carrying that gun?"

"I've got a permit for it."

"I know you've got a permit for it. That's not the same as a hunting license. If the gentleman shows up dead, I wouldn't want you reporting this conversation as a justification for your actions."

"I wouldn't do that."

"The hell you wouldn't. If you shoot the sucker, you'll be in a tight spot. If you're in here laying the grounds for self-defense . . ."

"I don't need to do that, Chief. I got a throwaway gun to plant on the body."

Chief Harper grimaced. "I'm going to assume that was a joke. You show up with a corpse, he better not be carrying an untraceable weapon."

"Can I quote you on that, Chief? Are you telling me to ditch the guy's gun?"

"Any time you're through having fun . . ."

"This is not fun, Chief. How'd you like someone from your past stalking you?"

"I can't imagine that happening."

"Now you know how I feel. This absolutely, positively, should not be happening. Therefore, it warrants attention."

"Well, that's not entirely correct. I can't imagine it happening because I'm a cop. But you are a TV personality. Advertising public appearances. It is not unusual for someone to show up at public appearances. But we've covered that already, haven't we?"

"It's unusual for someone to show up at *all* of them."

Chief Harper sighed. "We're going around again. Just what is it you want me to do?"

"I don't want you to *do* anything. Just acknowledge the fact I've lodged a complaint. If this guy comes around again, I shouldn't have to argue with you that he's being unduly persistent."

"Fine, I won't argue the point. I hope you won't argue it's grounds for arrest."

"Fair enough."

"You got a picture of the guy?"

"Not a current one."

"Let's see it."

Cora fished in her drawstring bag. "You gotta understand, he doesn't look like this now."

"Why not?"

"Like I say, it's not a current picture."

"How uncurrent is it?"

"None of your damn business."

"I beg your pardon?"

Cora fished out a piece of paper, unfolded it, passed it over. It was a picture of a teenage boy, with thick, curly brown hair, black-framed glasses, and chubby cheeks.

Chief Harper frowned. "You're afraid of *this*?"

"He grew up."

"Into what? An insurance salesman? This is not the face of Jack the Ripper."

"No, it isn't. Tell me, Chief, do the neighbors of serial killers say, 'I always knew he was cutting people up,' or do they describe him as a quiet little guy who wouldn't hurt a fly?"

"You're making too much of this."

Cora got to her feet, shrugged the drawstring purse over her shoulder. "Maybe so, Chief. But hang on to that photo, willya?"

"You mind telling me why?"

"If I wind up dead, you'll know who did it."

15

AARON GRANT STUDIED THE YEARBOOK PHOTO. "He looks creepy."

"Oh, give me a break," Sherry said. "He's just a kid."

"A *creepy* kid. I'm telling you, something's not right."

"You're basing that on Cora. If you didn't know a thing about him, he's just another kid."

"Hey, I'm a newsman. I can spot these things." Aaron flipped the yearbook shut. "How come it's bound in contact paper?"

"So you can't see the year."

"Cora's really that sensitive about her age?"

"She doesn't want you printing it in the paper."

"She did this just for me?"

"No. It was like that."

Aaron flipped through the pages. "Somewhere it must say something about the class of such and such."

Sherry snuggled up against him on the couch. "Yeah, but you're not going to look for it. You're going to impress me with your wily newsman ways. Tell me how you know Freddy Fosterfield's a creep."

"Aw, piece of cake," Aaron said. "Look at the photo. Now, it's fifty or sixty years later—"

"Stop that."

"All right. It's whenever it is, and this guy is bald and chubby. Go on. Look at him and imagine him bald and chubby."

"He *is* chubby."

"Imagine him bald."

"Okay. So what?"

Aaron pointed. "He has those eyes. Those haunted eyes. Those depressed eyes. Those angry eyes. Those frustrated eyes. Those eyes of a teenager who isn't getting any."

"Do I hear experience speaking?"

"I don't know. Why don't you look in *my* eyes?"

"Not now, silly." Sherry giggled. "Where's your old yearbook photo?"

"I'm not sure I can find it. I covered the book with contact paper so you wouldn't know how old I am."

"It's no use. I know you're too young for me."

"I am not. Of course, you may be too old for me."

"Hey!"

"Well, you might be. Can I see your yearbook?"

"I don't have my yearbook."

"Why not?"

"I just don't."

There was an edge in Sherry's voice. It had gone from bantering to annoyed just like that.

"Hey, what's the matter?"

Sherry grimaced. "Dennis has it."

Aaron should have just said, "Oh." Sherry seldom talked about her abusive ex-husband, and the less said on the subject, the better. But Aaron's instincts as an investigative reporter betrayed him. "Why does Dennis have your yearbook?"

"I ran out on a drunk who was beating me, Aaron." Her voice was cold. "I didn't back up a moving van to the door."

Aaron put up his hands. "Sorry. Stupid question. That's what you get for going out with an insensitive jerk."

"No, it's what *you* get for dating an old divorcée."

"Fair enough." Aaron brightened. "Hey, does this count as a fight? Can we have makeup sex?"

"Makeup sex? How old is that? You know how long ago *Seinfeld* went off the air?"

"It's still in reruns."

Sherry smiled. "Nice try, newsboy. You ain't gettin' a matinee."

"It was worth a shot."

There came the sound of tires on gravel. Seconds later, the car door slammed with more than its usual force.

"Cora's home," Sherry said.

Aaron and Sherry went outside. Cora was leaning on the fender and lighting a cigarette.

"How'd it go?" Sherry called.

Cora blew out a puff of smoke. "Fabulous. Chief Harper thinks I'm a hysterical twit." She marched up the path, leveled her finger at Aaron. "There's a story for you: 'PUZZLE LADY HYSTERICAL TWIT. Suffers delusions of persecution, Police Chief says.' "

"You show the chief the picture?" Aaron asked.

"Picture? What picture? You been going through my yearbook?"

"Just the guy's picture," Aaron assured her. "Sherry wouldn't let me see anything else."

"You didn't show him the picture of me?" Cora demanded of her niece. "Gee, I looked good." She pushed through the door and bustled to the coffee table. She picked up the yearbook, flipped it open to the senior photo.

It was the picture of a young woman with curly dark hair and flashing eyes. Even then she had her trademark smile.

"Hey, you weren't kidding!" Aaron said. "You really did look good."

"Well, you don't have to sound so surprised." Cora turned to Sherry. "And I'll thank you not to take my personal items out of my room when I'm not there."

"You left it on the coffee table."

"Even so." Cora snapped the yearbook shut. "You using the computer?"

"No, I'm going downtown with Aaron."

"Good. I wanna check my e-mail."

"You're staying home?"

"Yeah."

"You mind if I take the car? Then Aaron won't have to drive me home."

"Separate cars? That's a hell of a date."

"It's not a date."

"Phooey. When you're young, everything's a date. Sure, go ahead, take the car. I'm not going anywhere. Till tomorrow. Then I'm going everywhere."

"You need anything for the trip?"

"I need to not go. I need a stay from the governor. A last-second reprieve."

"You'll be fine."

"Yeah, until I wring some fan's neck for asking for an autograph."

"What's wrong with asking for an autograph?"

"On a cereal box? How'd you like to sign your name on a carton of cornflakes?"

"Luckily, it's never come up."

"No, and it won't, either. 'Cause you've got me to do it. While you sit home and smirk."

"While I sit home and construct the crossword puzzles. Would you rather do that?"

"Not if you put a gun to my head. Go on, take the car, I'll be fine."

Cora went into the office, logged on to the Internet, and checked her e-mail. The only messages were computer-generated spam, several of which were obviously confused as to her gender.

Cora deleted her e-mail, and opened Netscape Navigator, one of Sherry's Web browsers. She clicked on BOOKMARKS, scrolled down.

Within minutes the impending promotional tour was forgotten, and she was happily checking out the bargains on eBay.

16

"It is kind of stupid taking two cars," Aaron said.

"You gotta work. There's no reason to drive me back."

"We could pull off the road and park."

"Like we were still in high school? Puh-lease."

"Just a hint," Aaron said, "but if you want to convince people you're not in high school, it would probably help if you didn't say 'puh-lease.'"

"Thanks for the tip."

Sherry got in Cora's red Toyota, backed around, sped down the driveway, and hung a right.

Aaron grinned. Sherry might be older than he was, but she still drove like a teenager. He spun his Honda around, hurried to catch up.

Before he reached the foot of the driveway, a blue Chevy Impala went by. Great. Aaron hated following someone with a car in between. And there was no safe place to pass, either. Aaron hoped Sherry would notice what had happened and slow down. She didn't, though. As he pulled out of the driveway he could see her up ahead flashing around a turn. If he got stuck behind a Sunday driver, he'd be in trouble.

He needn't have worried. The other car was going every bit as fast as Sherry. It was all Aaron could do to keep up.

Trees overhung the road, their branches casting long shadows in the late-afternoon sun. The three cars flashed in and out of the patterns, whizzed around the turns.

At the intersection Sherry turned left, toward the mall. They were stopping off on the way to town to buy Cora a gift for the trip. Sherry had been upset when Aaron had asked what. It occurred to him Sherry had been upset more than usual lately.

Two miles down the road Sherry turned into the mall. Aaron was glad he had her in his sights. The spacious parking lot was generally crowded, and today was no exception. If Sherry found a parking space, Aaron might have to circle for some time before he saw her.

Oncoming traffic prevented Aaron from making the left turn. It also prevented the blue Impala in front of him. There didn't seem to be any break in it. There was no traffic light at the mall entrance. The left-hand turn was a crap shoot. As Aaron watched, Cora's red Toyota turned down a row of cars. If he didn't get into the lot, he wouldn't know where Sherry went next.

Suddenly, the Chevy Impala sprang to life, shot across the oncoming traffic. An SUV hit the brakes and the horn, and was damn lucky not to hit the car. That set off a chain reaction, slowing the oncoming traffic to a crawl, making it bumper-to-bumper with no chance of getting through. Aaron, totally frustrated, could only sit and wait.

After what seemed an interminable stream of cars, there was finally a gap big enough for him to squeeze through.

Aaron circled the parking lot, scanning the rows. The first time around he missed her. The second time he spotted a car halfway down a row pulling into a space. All he could tell from a distance was that the car was red. That was good enough for Aaron. He gunned the engine, turned down the row.

Before he could get there, a car from the opposite direction drove by, blocking the red car from sight. To his surprise, Aaron noticed it was the Chevy Impala that had driven between them to the mall. It stopped, and the driver got out. He was a middle-aged man, bald and portly. He started around the front of his car, then stopped.

Looking past him, Aaron could see that Sherry had just gotten out of the red car. The man had seen her too. He got right back into his car and drove off.

Sherry hopped into Aaron's car, closed the door. "Come on, let's see if we can find another spot." She frowned. "What's the matter with you? You look like you just saw a ghost."

"The guy in the yearbook. I told you to imagine him pudgy and bald?"

"Yeah."

"I just saw him."

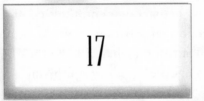

17

"You DIDN'T HAVE TO COME."

"Yeah, I did."

"I can take care of myself."

"I know you can."

"I think I'm pretty safe on this bus."

"I'm sure you are."

"Are you going to agree with everything I say?"

"Absolutely not."

Sherry and Cora were bouncing along Interstate 95 in the Granville Grains tour bus, a refurbished commercial coach clearly on its last wheels. It backfired frequently, and lost power on even the slightest inclines.

In theory, the suspension could handle a full bus. In practice, it could barely handle the ad agency's bare-bones skeleton crew, consisting of one cameraman, one soundman, one electrician, one grip, one propman, and the costume and makeup lady; the production staff, consisting of the producer, the director, and the publicity woman; and the talent, consisting of Cora and the two kids, Lance and Ginger.

Also on board was a teamster, whom the production could not do without. The teamster's job would have been to drive the bus, had the vehicle not been rented with a driver. The teamster was there not to drive the bus, but to collect his union salary for not driving the bus.

To Cora's great embarrassment, the side of the bus was decorated with a box of cereal and an immense caricature of her smiling face. Her portrait was somewhat distorted by the raised metal letters of the word BONANZA poking up through the paint. Underneath, was the logo, THE GRANVILLE GRAINS NEW AND IMPROVED CORN TOASTIES PUZZLE LADY PERSONAL APPEARANCE TOUR.

"That's a hell of a name for a tour," Cora groused. "Why couldn't we have something snappy like the Rolling Thunder Revue?"

"You want to be called the Rolling Thunder Revue?"

"That's an example, dummy. A little before your time."

"Believe it or not, I've heard of Bob Dylan."

"Oh, is that so, smarty-pants? How about the Rolling *Blunder* Review?"

"That would be Arlo Guthrie touring with his backup band Shenandoah."

"How in the world do you know that?" Cora demanded.

"Are you kidding me? *Arlo* is a crossword-puzzle staple, like *Ott* and *Orr*. It would help if you knew that."

"I know the words to 'Alice's Restaurant.' "

"For God's sake, don't sing."

Jennifer Blaylock came down the aisle, a perilous undertaking since the suspension was not good, and the bus had a tendency to bump and sway. The young publicist reached Sherry and Cora's seat, and knelt to talk to them. "I've been working out how to deal with you."

"What are you talking about?" Cora said. "How to deal with who?"

"Her. Your niece. How I explain her to the press."

"You don't have to explain Sherry to the press."

"Oh, but I do. I have to account for her presence."

"You have got to be kidding. Who could possibly care?"

"Some enterprising reporter. If he asks the question, we have to know what to say."

"Tell him to take a flying—"

The publicist put up her hand. "Miss Felton. I've warned you about your language."

"You see any reporters on this bus?"

"No, but if you get in the habit of saying whatever you like, you're apt to do it on camera."

"And then we edit it out."

"But you can't edit it out in the minds of your fans. Particularly if it gets picked up by the press."

"Fine. I won't tell them where they can stick their stupid questions, I'll just think it."

"Try not to think out loud." The publicist took a breath. "The thing is, we need to explain Miss Carter's presence."

"Why?"

"Two women traveling together. It doesn't look good."

"She's my niece."

"And that sounds like a bad lie."

"Oh, for goodness' sakes. You mean they're going to say I'm gay?"

"In the absence of any evidence to the contrary."

"How about my six or seven ex-husbands?"

"Six or seven?"

"Give or take a few. I never was much good at math."

"You really have six or seven ex-husbands?" The publicist frowned, wondering what *that* would do to Cora's image. She turned and slunk away.

"I'm surprised she gave up so quickly," Sherry said.

Cora peered down the aisle. "I think she just went for reinforcements. See how much trouble you're causing for me?"

"No, I don't. Who could possibly care?"

"I don't know, but the director's coming this way. Of course, she might be just headed for the can."

She wasn't. Daphne stopped at their seat and she, too, knelt in the aisle. "Jennifer says you blew her off."

"Oh?"

"About why you're not traveling alone."

"I'm not traveling alone because my niece decided to come along. Sherry Carter, this is Daphne Decker."

"Hi," Sherry said. "I saw you at the store in Danbury."

"That's fine. The point is, I can't afford an unhappy publicist, Cora. Because, God knows, you gotta meet the public. Why is beyond me, and I'd be perfectly happy if *she* weren't along. But since she is, I don't need her complaining to me."

"What did you tell her?"

"I told her I had nothing to do with it and she should speak to Quentin."

"Thanks a lot."

"My pleasure. Nice to meet you."

Daphne stood up and collided with Quentin, who was coming to take her place. The director and producer executed an impromptu do-si-do, after which Quentin knelt by Cora's seat.

"Hi, Quentin," Cora said. "This is my niece, Sherry Carter. She's going to stay in my room, and she can buy her own breakfast if Granville Grains is too cheap to let her eat with the crew."

"Actually, her meals would come out of the ad agency budget," Quentin said. "But that's not the point. Jennifer wants to know why she's here. In case anybody asks."

"You can't just say she likes cereal?"

"I know it's stupid."

"If you know it's stupid, why are you asking?"

"I have enough real hassles. I don't need anyone making up any."

"Oh, for goodness' sakes," Sherry said. "A guy's been following my aunt around ever since the first store, in Danbury. He showed up in Stamford, and he showed up at her house. It's a little creepy, and I don't want her traveling alone."

The producer seemed taken aback. "Oh. No, of course not. That makes sense. Who could argue with that? Thank you very much, Miss . . . ?"

"Carter."

"Yes. Miss Carter."

"There, that wasn't so bad," Sherry said, as Quentin made his way back down the aisle.

"That's what you think," Cora told her.

The publicist was back moments later. "You *cannot* tell that story!" she hissed. "What are you trying to do, turn this into the Puzzle Lady Stalker Tour?"

"Probably get you some ink," Cora observed cheerfully.

"Probably close us down. You think parents are going to want to bring their kids to meet someone who's being stalked? How are we going to build a campaign around *that*?"

Cora pantomimed holding up a box. "New and Improved Corn Toasties even withstands gunfire."

"You're joking. Please be joking."

"I'm joking. I don't really expect the cereal to repel bullets, and if someone starts shooting I'm grabbing the nearest kid and using him as a shield." Cora waved her hand at the aghast publicist. "Go away. I'm not going to blow your gig. On the other hand, I'm not dating anyone just for public relations. If anyone hassles me, I'm gonna tell 'em to take a hike."

"Well, that went well," Sherry observed as the publicist retreated.

"The truth is always a tough sell. No one wants to hear it."

"You mean I should have kept my mouth shut?"

"There's truth, and then there's truth. You could have come along to write my crossword puzzles for me."

"If you'd told her that, the tour would be over."

Cora shrugged. "What's the down side?"

18

Buddy shot out the front door and bolted down the drive.

Aaron Grant watched in horror as the tiny poodle skidded around the corner and vanished from sight. Aaron hesitated a moment, torn between hopping in his car or pursuing on foot. Choosing the latter, he sprinted down the driveway, yelling Buddy's name. By the time he reached the foot of the drive, the toy poodle was nowhere to be seen.

Uh-oh.

Aaron's life flashed before his eyes.

Cora would kill him. Sherry would kill him. They might even take turns killing him.

Aaron sprinted along the street. Damn it. Where the hell was he? Where the hell was the goddamned dog?

Just as Aaron had that thought, Buddy shot out of the woods and darted across the road.

An oncoming station wagon hit the brakes and fishtailed before driving on. The car never came close to the dog—still, the prospect was terrifying. Aaron was beginning to sweat. He plunged into the woods, yelling, "Buddy!" and went crashing through the under-brush in the direction he thought the dog had gone. After a few minutes he stopped, listened. Heard nothing. Saw nothing.

Aaron was a mess. He was hot, sweaty, his clothes torn by brambles.

And he still didn't have the dog.

"Buddy!"

There came a high-pitched yip in the distance.

Behind him.

Aaron blinked. Was it possible? Was he completely turned around?

It came again. It didn't matter which direction he was facing. That's where the dog was.

Aaron ran toward the sound. It seemed he was going deeper into the woods. The carpet of pine needles and maple leaves gave way to diverse vegetation, some of which looked suspiciously like poison ivy.

Aaron ran until he could run no farther. He slumped down, exhausted, at the base of a big oak tree.

Buddy sprang into his lap, trotted up his chest, and licked his chin.

"Buddy! Boy, is it good to see you! Do you happen to know the way home?"

Aaron didn't have a leash, so he had to carry Buddy out of the woods. This would have been easier if he had the faintest idea where he was going.

It was a while before he heard a car. Not that he hadn't been close enough to the road to hear one, there just weren't that many. Aaron zeroed in on the sound of the engine, and five minutes later he emerged from the woods into a small clearing.

When he reached the road, Aaron discovered he had indeed been backtracking. He was now a few hundred yards *up* the road from the driveway, in the opposite direction from where he had initially gone.

"Well, Buddy, they can't say you didn't get your exercise."

A car emerged from the driveway.

Aaron sucked in his breath. It was a blue Chevy Impala, exactly like the one he'd seen in the mall parking lot. What was it doing in Cora's driveway?

The car turned in his direction. Aaron shrank back in the brush to watch it go by. He wanted to get a good look at the driver. To see if it was the same guy. After all, there were a lot of blue Chevy Impalas. It didn't have to be the same guy.

It wasn't.

As the car went by, Aaron sucked in breath.

It wasn't Cora's stalker, Freddy Fosterfield.

It was Sherry Carter's ex-husband, Dennis Pride.

19

BECKY BALDWIN'S OFFICE SMELLED LIKE PEPPERONI. The law office was over the pizza parlor, and tended to take on the aroma of the daily special. Some days it was onions and peppers. Some days it was garlic and eggplant. Today, pepperoni seemed to be the pie of choice.

Becky Baldwin barely noticed, or at least did her best to give that impression. The lawyer was dressed, as usual, in a stylish business suit that could have passed muster in the most prestigious law firm in New York City. A stunning blonde with a fashion model face and girlish figure, Becky could charm one into forgetting her drab surroundings.

Aaron Grant was not charmed, however. "What is he doing here?" the newsman demanded.

"I have no idea."

"He's your client."

"You think I know where all my clients are?"

"This one is special."

"To you, maybe."

"Come on, Becky. Give me a break. We're talking about Sherry's ex-husband."

"I know who we're talking about."

"Don't be such a putz. What is the jerk doing here?"

"Did you just call me a putz?"

"I don't know. I wasn't paying attention. The jerk was at Sherry's house."

"What do you expect me to do about it? She's got a restraining order."

"Obviously it isn't working."

"That's not my fault."

"He's your client. You kept him out of jail. You want to see him go back?"

Becky shrugged. "Might be the best thing for him."

"Can I quote you on that?"

"No. And you can't put it in the paper, either."

"Damn it, Becky! Quit sparring with me. What's the deal with Dennis?"

"I really don't know, Aaron. I got him a suspended sentence. He's on probation."

"I know that. What's he up to now?"

"Last I heard he quit the band, married Brenda, and was working for her father."

"As what?"

"A traveling salesman."

"It's the traveling part that's the problem."

"Brenda's Sherry's friend. She could give her a call."

"It's an awkward situation."

"I understand. What do you want me to do about it?"

Aaron jerked his thumb. "Dennis is in the Wicker Basket. You might drop in, point out the error of his ways."

"Yeah, and I might not."

Aaron shrugged. "Well, that would be the tactful way to handle it. As opposed to my reporting the probation violation to Chief Harper."

Becky sighed. "Aw, hell."

The Wicker Basket was two blocks down from Becky's office. A popular family restaurant, it featured red-and-white-checkered tablecloths, and a homey atmosphere.

Dennis Pride wasn't there.

"You just missed him," the waitress informed them.

"See," Aaron told Becky. "If you hadn't argued with me—"

"*Me!*" Becky protested.

"Did you see which way he went?" Aaron asked the waitress.

"I think he drove off."

"Well, that settles it," Becky said. "Unless you think the situation warrants a high-speed car chase."

"I gotta get to work." Aaron looked at his watch. "Might as well grab lunch. Can you rustle me up a cheeseburg?"

"You got it."

"I'll have a tossed salad," Becky said. "Since you're buying lunch."

"Oh, now I'm buying lunch?"

"Well, you got me down here on false pretenses. You think a salad's out of line?"

They took a table by the window, ordered iced tea.

"So," Becky said. "I see hanging around the Puzzle Lady's beginning to wear off."

Aaron frowned. As far as he knew, Becky still thought Cora Felton was the Puzzle Lady. "What do you mean?"

"The wordplay. 'Rustle me up a cheeseburg.' I had visions of a mad cow being lassoed and slapped on a bun."

"Now, there's an image I'm bound to enjoy while I'm eating. How about little field greens with cartoon faces and high, squeaky voices saying, 'No, no, please don't eat me!' "

Becky smiled. "Doesn't have quite the same emotional wallop."

"Yeah. It'd be better if you had chicken in your salad."

"Yeah." After a pause, Becky said, "I miss you, Aaron."

"Becky."

"No, I'm not making trouble. I miss having lunch like this. It's not like we're strangers."

"No," Aaron agreed. "It's like you're my girlfriend's ex-husband's lawyer."

Becky made a face. "That was mean."

"Yeah, I know. I'm just upset seeing him around. Dennis used to hit her, Becky. How can you represent a guy like that?"

"Give me a break. Bleeding-heart-liberal newsman. Everyone's entitled to his day in court. Except Dennis Pride. Everyone's innocent until proven guilty. Except Dennis Pride. So maybe Dennis is not the most upstanding citizen in the world. I got news for you, Aaron. People charged with crimes often aren't. Last I checked they had the right to an attorney."

"That's not the point and you know it."

"What's the point?"

"I don't know. But you know what I mean."

Becky considered. "Yeah, I do."

They smiled at each other.

Aaron's mouth fell open. "There he is!"

"What?"

"Come on!"

Aaron sprang up and raced for the door. Becky followed. They brushed by the waitress, who was on her way to their table with their iced tea.

Outside, Aaron jumped into his car. After a moment's hesitation, Becky slid onto the front seat.

"What are you doing?" she demanded.

"He just went by."

"In a car?"

"Yeah. Blue Chevy Impala."

"If he's just driving by, what's the big deal?"

"He drove off. If he's driving by, he's back. I don't want him back. I want him gone."

Aaron spun his car out of the parking space, hung a U-turn, and tore off down the block.

"Hey, what do you think you're doing?"

"What does it look like?"

"Let me out, Aaron!"

"Jump if you want to. I'm not stopping."

"What are you gonna do, run him off the road?"

"If he hits the light at the bypass, I can pull alongside."

"You expect me to wave him over?"

"At least get him to roll down his window."

"That's not fair, Aaron. I—*Look out!*"

Aaron swerved around the station wagon that was backing out of a driveway. He straightened the car, flew down the street.

Up ahead the blue Impala was stopped at the light. Aaron gunned the engine, eased off the gas, pulled up alongside.

The driver wasn't Dennis. The car was being driven by a bald, middle-aged man.

The light changed and the Impala took off.

Becky turned to Aaron with an I-told-you-so look. "See? It wasn't him."

"Yeah." Aaron followed along behind.

"Hey! What are you doing? It wasn't him."

"Yes it was," Aaron said grimly.

20

"WELL, THIS IS MORE LIKE IT." Cora dug into her pan-seared swordfish.

Mystic, Connecticut, once a seaport and fishing village, now catered largely to the tourist trade, attracted by the Mystic Seaport Museum, the Mystic Aquarium, and the plethora of fashionable restaurants that lined the dock.

"You like your fish?" Sherry asked.

"Fish is fish. I like the view." Through the window in front of her, yachts and sailboats bobbed up and down in the harbor. "If we're gonna stay in a seaport, we ought to see the sea. I can't believe they booked a motel on the other side of the highway."

"Now, why do you suppose that was?"

"I *know* why that was. The dump was cheaper because it has a lovely view of the highway overpass. And Granville Grains are skinflints."

"Are you telling me we're paying for our own dinner?"

"*You're* paying for your own dinner. *I* have a per diem."

"Is it going to cover that fish?"

"Probably not. It certainly won't cover your lobster."

Sherry shrugged. "Hey, a girl's gotta live it up now and then."

"Here, here! Particularly the way they worked me."

The Granville Grains New and Improved Corn Toasties Tour had stopped and filmed at three supermarkets along the way.

"We need the money," Sherry said.

"Yeah, well, we're not getting the money. Not for this. They're only running local ads to fill the supermarkets. They won't go national until the tour is over."

"It's a good way to make sure you won't quit."

"You think they thought of that?"

"What, advertising people doing something devious? Surely you jest."

Cora, looking over Sherry's shoulder, said, "Oh, my God!"

"What? You forget to turn the gas off? No, you never cook."

Sherry turned to see Aaron Grant and Becky Baldwin come walking up.

Sherry was dumbfounded. That Aaron Grant was there was a surprise. That Becky Baldwin was with him was astounding. Sherry couldn't believe it.

Cora could. She cocked her head in a worldly-wise angle and demanded, "What the hell are you doing here?"

"We followed your boyfriend," Aaron replied.

Cora scowled. "What?"

"Freddy Fosterfield. He's hot on your trail. I came to warn you."

"And Becky came along for the ride?"

"Actually, he kidnapped me," Becky said.

"Did he really? How interesting!"

"Sherry—"

"No, Aaron. Tell me about kidnapping Becky." Sherry rolled her eyes at Cora. "I can't *wait* to hear this."

"I spotted Freddy Fosterfield skulking around town. I followed him here."

"Why did you bring Becky?"

"Becky was in my car."

"Ah, that's the interesting part," Cora said. "The part where Becky gets in his car."

"Do I need to be here for this?" Becky shrugged. "As long as you're going to talk about me instead of to me."

"You've already stated your position," Cora told her. "You were kidnapped. Now we're trying to find out why."

The other diners in the restaurant seemed to be taking more of an interest in the scene than in their food. At the next table, a woman with her neck craned had managed to paint a line of cocktail sauce down her cheek with a shrimp.

"You want to sit down?" Sherry observed. "Before we wind up in the local paper."

"Are you inviting us to join you? How nice." Becky slid gracefully into a chair. "Sit down, Aaron. Don't be such a nudge."

"Oh, for goodness' sakes." Aaron flopped down, said, "There's a perfectly simple explanation."

"What is it?"

"We thought he was Dennis."

"What!?"

Aaron told about going over to feed Buddy and seeing Dennis pull out of the driveway. "He was breaking his restraining order, so I complained to his attorney."

Becky smiled and waved.

"You didn't feed the dog?" Cora accused Aaron.

"I *did* feed the dog. I fed the dog. I let him out. I put him back. I went to town," Aaron declared. All of which was true. He just left out the part about losing the dog and thinking it had been run over. "The point is, I reported Dennis to Becky, asked her to talk to him. We followed a car I thought he was driving. It turned out to be Fosterfield, so we followed him here."

"So, where is he?" Cora asked.

"He checked into a motel on the other side of the highway. I assume it's yours, since there's a big bus with your picture on it out front."

"What happened to Dennis?" Sherry asked.

Aaron shrugged.

"He's working for Brenda's father as a traveling salesman," Becky explained. "His route must have taken him through town."

"You don't know?"

"No, I don't. Dennis is on probation, not house arrest. As long as he doesn't break the law, it's none of my business."

"Violating the restraining order doesn't count?"

"Of course it does. He can't come within a hundred yards of you. Aside from that, he can go anywhere he wants."

A waitress appeared with menus. "Are you two having dinner?"

Becky smiled. "I'd love to, but it just wouldn't work. Thanks all the same."

The waitress nodded uncomprehendingly, and moved off.

"What are *you two* going to do?" Cora asked. "Notice I use the words *you two* in a catty, insinuating manner, hoping to promote controversy."

"You can be quite a wordsmith when you want to be," Sherry observed.

Becky frowned. "What do you mean, when she wants to be?"

"Nothing." Sherry changed the subject. "I assume you're staying over, since it's too far to drive home now. Have you registered already? Perhaps as Mr. and Mrs. Grant?"

"Guys, we're losing sight of the main point," Aaron protested. "What are we going to do about Fosterfield?"

"There's nothing we *can* do," Becky said. "He's not breaking any laws either."

"He's stalking Cora," Sherry pointed out. "He's obsessed and he's insane."

"Hang on. Are you saying any man obsessed with me has to be insane?"

"Not if he understands the meaning of the word *no*. This guy doesn't. He's creepy."

"I can take care of myself."

"I'm sure you can," Aaron told Cora. "But won't it put a crimp in your ad campaign if you shoot a fan?"

"I think it would drive sales through the roof. Killer Corn Flakes? But our publicist's a bit of a stick in the mud."

"Oh?"

Cora's eyes widened. "Speak of the devil!" she muttered.

Jennifer Blaylock came swooping in. "Ah, so there you are. I knew I'd find you! Isn't this wonderful?" Taking in Becky and Aaron, she said, "How do you do? Are you Puzzle Lady fans?"

"Absolutely," Becky said.

"Actually," Aaron corrected, "we're friends from Bakerhaven."

Jennifer was amazed. "And you came all this way? Are you staying over?"

"We were just discussing that," Sherry said dryly.

Jennifer frowned.

"Oh, for goodness' sakes," Aaron said. "I'm Sherry's boyfriend. Becky's an old friend of ours, and we were just figuring out the sleeping arrangements. It's no big deal."

"Oh," Jennifer said. "Well, I just wanted to see if you have a bathrobe, Cora."

Cora stared at her. "I beg your pardon?"

Jennifer put up her hands. "The bus is parked outside the motel. With your picture on it. It occurred to me some enterprising reporter might try for a candid photo."

"You thought I might be running around *naked?*"

"Of course not. But if you were to come out of your room . . ."

"Oh, for Christ's sake!"

Jennifer looked around in horror. "And if you could stop saying *Christ!*" the publicist hissed.

"You got it." Cora picked up her fork. "Now, if you could let me eat my fish."

Jennifer said, "I'll get you a bathrobe," and scurried away.

Cora shook her head. "It's a good thing she doesn't know why you guys are here."

"Why don't you tell her?" Aaron suggested. "Let her take care of the guy."

"No way," Cora said. "Sherry suggested I was being stalked and young what's-her-name nearly had a cow."

"So what are we going to do about Fosterfield?"

"Where is Freddy now?"

"Back at the motel."

"He's still there?"

"Oh. Let me check." Aaron whipped out his cell phone, called the motel, asked for Freddy Fosterfield. The phone rang four times before voice mail picked up.

Fosterfield wasn't there.

21

HE WATCHED THEM THROUGH THE RESTAURANT WINDOW. *Not the front window, the big plate-glass window overlooking the harbor, but a side window, a latticework window, a window not designed to look out of, but merely to let in light.*

As if a traveling companion wasn't enough, now there were three people, three close friends, clustered around her.

Spoiling his fun.

It was infuriating, to have come all this way to find his plans thwarted by a surfeit of people. Surfeit. She'd like that. If she'd ever hear it. If he got to talk to her. Which seemed unlikely, with so many obstacles in the way.

He hadn't been able to get a room next to her at the motel. That officious desk clerk—what a jerk he was. Nine out of ten people would have fallen for the bait. "Hey, that's the Puzzle Lady's bus out there. Is she stayin' here?" But the smug son of a bitch strikes an attitude: "Well, I wouldn't say yes, and I wouldn't say no." Did the moron know what kind of a hick that made him sound like?

What a pain. He'd had to take the room offered so as not to appear suspicious. Which was too bad, since that film guy told him what room she was in, and it wasn't near his. Not that he could have gotten one of the rooms next door—those units were probably taken by the film crew. Even so, the manager should have told. He was tempted to go back and ask the clerk to change his room, just to see what the hick would do. But that would make the hick suspicious. He couldn't afford to make anyone suspicious.

    Not now.

    Not with what he had in mind.

22

"YOU STILL UPSET?" AARON ASKED.

Sherry said nothing. The two were sitting up in bed. The TV was on, but neither of them was watching. It was some reality show or other. The MUTE button was on. They were just waiting for the news.

The solution to the room problem was simple. Sherry was staying in Aaron's room. Becky was bunking with Cora.

"It was nice of Becky," Aaron said.

"Yeah."

Aaron took a breath. "Look, Sherry. What part of this am I not understanding? I know you're upset about Dennis. Why are you upset with me?"

"Why am I upset with you?" Sherry pursed her lips. "Let me see. Where should I begin?"

"Uh-oh."

"You saw Dennis at our house. The next thing you know, you and Becky are following him in your car. Only it isn't Dennis."

"Right. It was Fosterfield."

"How'd you and Becky come to be following him in your car?"

"I went to town and looked for Dennis. His car was in front of the Wicker Basket. I went and got Becky to go talk to him. It took me a while to talk her into it. But by the time we got to the Wicker Basket, Dennis was gone."

"How'd you wind up following Fosterfield?"

"Fosterfield has the same kind of car."

"I know that. How exactly did he enter the picture?"

"He drove by the window."

"Of the Wicker Basket?"

"Yes."

"And what were you doing at the time?"

"Having lunch."

"With Becky Baldwin?"

"Well, I dragged her down there."

"Yes, you did. So this was a business lunch? Not personal?"

"That's right."

"Becky didn't bring up old times?"

"Sherry—"

"And then Freddy Fosterfield drove by the window? And you ran out and followed him?"

"Yes. What's wrong with that?"

"There's nothing wrong with that. The only thing wrong with that is how careful you were to leave out having lunch with Becky when you told me about it."

"I wasn't *really* having lunch with Becky."

"Were you sitting at a table?"

"Yes."

"Were you eating food?"

"Actually, the food hadn't come yet—"

"Aaron—"

"It wasn't like we made a lunch date. We went there on business, it was late, we had to eat."

"Which you carefully avoided mentioning."

"It was an irrelevant detail that would have led the conversation in the wrong direction."

Sherry's eyes widened. "You consider Becky Baldwin the wrong direction?"

"Someone's stalking your aunt. Your ex-husband's stalking you. In light of that, I would consider Becky Baldwin beneath notice, and an annoyance at best."

"Well, when you put it that way."

There came a knock on the door.

Sherry raised her eyebrows. "Speak of the devil?"

It was Cora Felton in a pink bathrobe and matching slippers. Aaron grinned broadly.

Cora leveled a finger at him. "Don't start with me. This is what Goody Two-Shoes gave me to wear so I wouldn't go running around in my nightgown, in case there's press hanging out here hoping to get a picture of me in my skivvies. It's easier to wear it than argue. It's a long tour, I gotta choose my battles."

"You're in a no-smoking room?"

"It's a no-smoking *motel*! I gotta come out on the balcony and flick my ashes over the rail. Goody Two-Shoes wants me to look like Mary Poppins while I do."

"She'd probably rather you didn't smoke at all."

"Yeah, like that's gonna happen." Cora flopped into a chair. "I had to get out of there. That Becky Baldwin's gonna drive me nuts. You may have problems with Sherry, here, but, trust me, she's a saint. All Becky does is whine, whine, whine. She's got no clothes, she's got no makeup, she's got no hair dryer. Talk about roughing it! You'd think the girl was living in the woods."

"I thought she got some stuff at the drugstore."

"Yeah. Toothbrush and a comb. That leaves her without a hair dryer, shampoo, skin cream, and a couple of dozen other essentials you really need if you want your beauty to be a hundred percent natural. She's also got no change of clothes, and God forbid she should wear the same outfit twice. She rinsed out her underwear in the sink and hung her bra and panties from the shower rod. She hung her skirt on a hanger, and she's wearing her blouse as an extra-shortie nightgown."

Aaron Grant was struggling to maintain an absolutely neutral expression.

"I think that's *way* too much information," Sherry told Cora dryly.

"The point is," Cora persisted, "I'm not happy. I understand why you didn't want to spring for two more rooms, and I understand why you don't want Aaron bunking with Barbie Bare-Bottom. But I can't take more than one night of this. Tomorrow I want her out of there."

"She's going, she's going," Aaron assured her. "She'll be gone tomorrow. I just hate to have to take her back. Maybe we can put her on a train and I can stay."

"You don't have to stay. That's why Sherry came along."

"Sherry came along just in case. When you had no idea if the guy was going to show up. Now he's here. Someone ought to keep an eye on him."

"You're not keeping an eye on him," Cora pointed out. "You're just distracting the one who should."

"Oh, come on, Cora," Sherry protested.

"It's a lose-lose situation, Sherry. Aaron's monopolizing you, and I'm stuck with Becky Bare-Bottom."

"Not if we send her home," Aaron said. "Then Sherry moves back in with you. And I hang around and keep an eye on him."

"You can't," Cora reminded him. "You gotta walk the dog."

"Oh, right."

"So, first thing in the morning you take the naked lawyer lady home. Sherry won't mind, will you, sweetheart? I just gotta get rid of her." Cora shuddered. "She's the roommate from hell!"

23

BECKY BALDWIN FLICKED THE TV CHANNELS with increasing disgust. Sure enough, they went up to 22, then back to 2 again. Wouldn't you know it, they didn't have *Hardball.* Just the lousy local news, and how boring was that? Becky clicked back to channel 8, which was a good indication of just how bad things were, if Rick Reed, Channel 8's clueless, young, on-camera reporter was the best available choice.

How had she ever allowed herself to be talked into this? So an obsessive fan was stalking Cora. She'd seen the guy, and he was about as dangerous as a teddy bear. All right, so a lot of psychos looked normal. A lot of normal guys did too. This guy was clearly one of them. And even if he wasn't, Cora Felton could take him. In hand-to-hand combat, Becky would bet on Cora every time. Except she'd have no one to bet against, because everyone else would bet on Cora too.

A commercial came on. Becky got up, paced, looked in the bathroom mirror. Scowled. Cora said why buy cold cream, she had cold cream. Well, she did. If you wanted to dignify that jar of Crisco as a skin-care product. Cora obviously hadn't taken into account the vast difference in their ages. Becky didn't need a corrosive to eat away the ruins of time. Merely a gentle aloe to tend to the lightest touch of blush and mascara. She'd be better off with the washcloth and facial soap. If the motel didn't furnish such bathroom amenities generally not seen outside of a gym locker room.

Becky glowered at herself in the mirror, flounced back to the bed.

Then there was Aaron. Her high school sweetheart. In the motel room with Sherry. Granted, Aaron and Sherry had a long-standing relationship. Still, to drive her all the way here just to dump her for another woman . . . True, Becky had suggested the arrangement. But what else could she do? Insist on staying with Aaron? Insist on paying for her own room? Not given the current state of her law practice. No, staying with Cora was the only option. Even if it left Aaron in the room down the hall.

With Sherry.

The news returned from a commercial. Rick Reed was covering a fire in Hartford. Rick was always hitting on Becky. Pestering her. Offering to take her to dinner. Sometimes she went. The contrast between him and Aaron Grant seemed particularly cruel this evening.

There was a knock on the door. Cora must have forgotten her keys. Typical. Once again underlining the situation. Sherry had her little love nest. Becky was rooming with an aging dingbat.

Becky flopped out of bed to let her in.

Dennis Pride stood in the doorway. He wore a business suit. His white shirt was open at the neck, and his tie was loose. Otherwise, he could have come to sell her an encyclopedia.

Except for the expression on his face. Dennis could not have been more surprised had Becky answered the door stark naked. It occurred to Becky how little she was actually wearing. That took a few moments to kick in, for Becky was almost as shocked at seeing Sherry's ex-husband as he was at seeing her. They gawked at each other, speechless.

Becky recovered first. With amazing presence of mind, she said, absurdly enough, "I'm sorry, Dennis, but it's rather late. If you want an appointment, come by the office."

"What are you doing here?"

"What am I doing here? No, Dennis, I think the question is, what are *you* doing here? If you have an answer that doesn't violate probation, I'd love to hear it."

Dennis blinked. Having recovered from his initial astonishment, he seemed to see Becky for the first time. His eyes took in her bare legs, the shortness of her shirt.

Becky flushed, hopped behind the door, peeked out. "Damn it, Dennis. You can't be here."

"You don't understand."

"I understand perfectly. You thought Sherry was here."

"Becky—"

The door to the next unit swung open and the cameraman came out. He smiled at them as he went by.

"Damn it," Becky told Dennis. "We can't talk like this."

"Then let me in."

"Fat chance."

Becky slammed the door in his face. She hurried into the bathroom. As she feared, her bra and panties were too wet to put on. She grabbed her skirt off the hanger, stepped in, zipped it up. It seemed incredibly short. It never had before. She wondered if she was just imagining it. She looked in the full-length mirror on the closet door. Damn! It *was* incredibly short.

Becky sat on the edge of the bed, pulled on her shoes. Why did she have to be wearing heels? Well, no help for it now.

Becky hurried to the door and slipped out.

24

BECKY AND DENNIS STOOD AT THE END OF THE DOCK. Yachts and cabin cruisers bobbed nearby. None appeared occupied. At least no lights were on. They were, to all intents and purposes, alone.

Becky had forestalled conversation on the way, both to collect her thoughts and for fear of being heard. They'd left the motel, driven to the dock in Dennis's car—parking was no problem this time of night—and strode out on the empty pier.

"All right," Becky said. "I don't need to tell you how many different ways you shouldn't be here. Never mind violating a court order. You're blowing your chance and wrecking your marriage. Can you possibly see an upside in this?"

Dennis grinned. "You know, you're beautiful when you're angry."

The wind off the water was whipping up Becky's skirt. The moon seemed uncommonly bright.

Becky pushed the skirt down. "Damn it, Dennis. This isn't funny. What do you want?"

"I need to talk to Sherry."

"No you don't. That is the last thing in the world you need. You don't need to talk to Sherry, and Sherry certainly doesn't need to talk to you."

"You don't understand."

"You keep saying that. *What* don't I understand?"

"We haven't had a chance to talk."

"There's a reason for that."

"I don't care. I married her best friend. You can't just slough that off. Pretend it didn't happen. It's gotta be addressed."

"Even if that were so, there are proper ways to do things. Following someone around the country and accosting them in a motel at night isn't one of them."

Dennis grabbed Becky's wrist. "Just a damn minute. You're a lawyer, you can argue anything. That doesn't make it right. You bring up the motel like it was something illicit. Sherry's here with Cora. That's one hell of a chaperone. Or had you forgotten that?"

"That's not the point. Why are you here at all?"

Dennis shrugged. "I'm a salesman. I'm out on the road."

"So you just happened to be working near here?"

"That's right."

"Your job took you to Mystic?"

"Near enough."

"So you just swung by?"

"Yes. Nothing sinister about it."

"Why'd you wait till eleven o'clock at night? If you were working in the area, why come so late? Why didn't you swing by after work? Maybe ask Sherry out to dinner?"

"You want me to ask her out to dinner?"

"Not at all. I'm just wondering why you didn't. See, Dennis, your working-in-the-area story would have more credibility if any of your actions suggested you were actually *in* the area. But they don't. Where was your last appointment today?"

"What's that got to do with anything?"

"Did you *have* any appointments today?"

Dennis said nothing, looked out at the sea.

"I'm sure you did, because you're working for Brenda's father, and he's no dope. He's not going to send you out banging on doors. You have appointments set up for you. Set up by the company. A schedule you follow. Since you were in Bakerhaven this afternoon, I would assume today's appointments were around there."

Dennis stole a glance at Becky, then continued to gaze out over the ocean.

"You're probably wondering how I know that, what with me being here on the tour and all. You had appointments in the vicinity. Probably not in the *near* vicinity—Brenda's father wouldn't do that—but close enough to swing by. You went to Sherry's, but she wasn't there. So you nosed around downtown, found someone who knew that Sherry left with her aunt this morning on the Granville Grains tour. You checked out their itinerary, which couldn't have been that hard—it's a publicity tour, they're not exactly trying to keep it quiet. So you finished up your afternoon appointments and headed here. Which is why it took you so long." Becky shrugged. "Only thing is, Bakerhaven's pretty close to New York, so you'd have been driving back to the City. I wonder what excuse you gave Brenda for staying out on the road."

"That's none of your business!" Dennis snapped.

"Ah. Touched a nerve. I guess your excuse didn't go over well. What was your plan, assuming you found Sherry with Cora? Gonna spirit her out of there, bring her down here on the dock? Talk pretty in the moonlight?"

"Damn you."

"That's not the way to talk to your lawyer."

"You're my lawyer? It's hard to tell. You keep forgetting you're on my side."

"I did the best I could for you, Dennis. I worked damn hard for you. I'm working damn hard for you now."

"Oh, yeah?" Dennis turned, took her by the arms. "You know what it's like to be me? I quit that band. You know how hard that was? I was the lead singer. I gave it up. Put on a suit. Took this loser job."

"If that's the way you feel about it, why'd you do it?"

"Are you kidding me? It was a condition of probation."

"Getting married wasn't."

He sneered. "It was a condition of the *job*."

"That's a terrible thing to say."

He shrugged. "Is it? I suppose. Brenda's okay, but she's not Sherry. When you've been married to Sherry. When you've been the lead singer in a band."

"You feel entitled?"

She said it mockingly. He scowled. For a second Becky feared Dennis was going to hit her.

Instead, he pulled her to him and kissed her.

Becky was so startled it took her a second to react. Then she twisted away angrily. It took an effort to keep from slapping his face. She glared at him, said evenly, "Don't . . . ever . . . do . . . that . . . again."

His grin was mocking. "Oh, spitfire!"

"You creep. How long have you been married, a month?"

"Oh, poor Brenda," Dennis scoffed. "As if she has a clue."

Brenda Wallenstein Pride, crouching behind a sailboat in the shadows of the dockside marina, wasn't close enough to hear her husband's words. But from her vantage point Brenda could see Dennis and Becky silhouetted in the moonlight just fine.

25

BRENDA COULDN'T BELIEVE IT. Not that Dennis wouldn't deceive her, she'd long suspected that. That was why she'd installed the transmitter in his company car. Why she'd monitored it closely, especially today, when his work had taken him near Bakerhaven. She hadn't been particularly surprised when she'd seen his car heading for town.

Or when he'd called to say he was staying over. It occurred to Brenda that Dennis would make a good salesman. His story might have been plausible if it weren't for that side trip into Bakerhaven. In light of that she wasn't at all surprised when he asked to stay overnight.

Not asked. That sounded so awful. Told her he was staying overnight. She'd argued—if she hadn't, he'd have been suspicious—before giving in. She got out the car and the homing device, prepared to track Dennis to Sherry's and have it out with him once and for all.

Brenda was so sure of what Dennis was up to, she was nearly to Bakerhaven before he finished his last appointment. When he turned south, she couldn't believe it. It had to be a malfunction of the equipment. Or perhaps he had to go a few blocks south in order to get on the highway.

To her amazement, he continued south. Brenda hung a U-turn and tried to catch up, but he had too large a lead. When he turned east on Interstate 95 she was still a frustrating twenty miles behind. Brenda stepped on the gas, had managed to cut it to ten by the time he left the highway in Mystic. When she reached the exit, Dennis and Becky were headed for the dock. She caught up just in time to see the couple park the car and walk out onto the pier.

She could not have been more amazed.

Becky Baldwin?

Dennis was two-timing her with Becky Baldwin?

It couldn't be. It had to be some sort of horrible joke. She should stand up, walk out on the pier, demand to know what was going on.

Of course, she would have to explain why she was there. The bugging-the-car bit would not go down well. Brenda wouldn't care about that if it were Sherry, but this? She wasn't prepared for this. To have spied on Dennis to learn this. To have used electronic surveillance to catch him at it. Her mind was reeling.

Brenda slunk back into the shadows, crept away to her car. She slipped into the driver's seat, closed the door. Put the key in the ignition, and started the engine. Grabbed the steering wheel in both hands.

And began sobbing uncontrollably.

What was she to do?

Good heavens!

What was she to do?

Footsteps cut short Brenda's wretched deliberations.

Becky Baldwin strode up; Dennis was trailing behind. Evidently they'd had a fight. Becky stalked to the passenger door of Dennis's car, waited impatiently. Dennis didn't come around the car to help her in, just pressed the remote control on the key to unlock the door. They got in the car, and Dennis backed out and drove off.

Brenda followed at a discreet distance.

Dennis drove straight under the highway and turned into . . . a motel!

That was enough for Brenda. Kissing the woman was one thing. Taking her to a motel was another. She sped up. She'd turn into the parking lot and cut them off and then—

Only Dennis didn't pull up to a unit. He stopped in the driveway and Becky got out. She walked off toward the motel stairs, while Dennis pulled up at the office and went inside.

Brenda drove on by.

Reassessment time.

So they were staying at the motel. They'd had a fight. Becky had gone back to her room. Dennis had gone to the office to rent *another* room.

Served him right.

Next to the motel was a hardware store, closed of course at that hour. Brenda drove into the parking lot, killed the lights and motor, looked toward the motel.

Cora Felton smiled back at her from the side of the Granville Grains tour bus.

Oh, for pity's sake.

Were they *all* here?

While Brenda watched, Dennis came out of the motel office, drove his car up to one of the units. He took his briefcase from the backseat, unlocked the door to Room 212, and went in.

He didn't have an overnight bag. Unless it was already in Becky Baldwin's unit. Which didn't seem likely. So he hadn't planned on staying over. It was something that just came up.

So what should she do now?

Before Brenda could decide, Dennis came out again.

He was walking straight toward her. Instinctively, Brenda ducked her head. Which was silly. If he'd seen her, he'd seen her. There was no help for it. Nonetheless, she kept low, peered over the dash.

He hadn't seen her. He went walking down the row of cars. He stopped at a red Toyota, checked the license plate. He must not have found what he wanted, because he continued on down the row. When he got to the end he went back, checked the cars in the other direction. He stopped behind a nondescript Honda, checked the plate. He stood up, slammed his hand angrily against the fender.

There was a light on in the motel unit in front of the car. He walked up to the door, leaned his head, listened. Then he looked over at the window. The blinds were open a crack. Dennis walked slowly by, craning his neck to see, then stepped back into the parking lot.

There were two parking spaces in front of each unit, one for the ground floor, one for the unit above. Dennis raised his eyes to the balcony. The light in the upstairs unit was on.

Dennis looked around for the stairs. Spotted them at the end of the lot. He strode toward them. Once again, he was headed straight toward Brenda, but this time she knew she was safe. She watched in smoldering fury as her husband ascended the motel stairs. He reached the top, started down the row of rooms.

What was he up to? Was he going to pester Becky Baldwin again? Brenda doubted it.

She was right. He walked right by Becky's door and continued down the row to the room above the inspected car.

The door opened and Cora Felton came out.

They stopped.

Stared at each other.

For a second they were bugs in amber, suspended in time.

Then, to Brenda's amazement, Cora Felton grabbed Dennis by the throat, and slammed him up against the motel wall.

26

"WHAT THE HELL ARE YOU DOING HERE? No, never mind. I don't *care* what you're doing here! I want you gone! Get the hell out of here!"

Dennis, who'd recovered from the shock of having his teeth rattled, said, "You can't order me around."

Cora slammed him against the wall again. "Wrong answer."

The door to the adjoining unit opened and the gaffer stuck his head out. "Is everything all right?"

"Just fine," Cora told him. "This fan wanted an autograph. I was suggesting he come back tomorrow."

The electrician frowned, stared at them, then stepped back inside.

"Let go of me!" Dennis growled.

"Sure." Cora jerked him off the wall. "I'll let go of you. Just get in your car and drive off. Pretend this never happened. I won't call your wife, tell her she's got problems on her hands."

Dennis brushed this threat aside. "Where's Sherry?"

"I'm not gettin' through to you, Dennis. Are you looking for trouble?"

"She's with that reporter, isn't she? She's shacked up with that reporter. How's that gonna look? Young divorcée having a tryst in a motel?"

"You're a class act, Dennis. I can't imagine how Sherry ever let you go."

"Where are they?"

"I don't know. But if you knock on every door you might get lucky."

"They're in there, aren't they?"

"No, that's my room."

"No it's not. You're in the room down the hall."

Cora grinned. "Oh, you think so? Go knock on the door. I switched rooms with Becky Baldwin. You don't believe me, go check. I'm sure she'll be glad to see you."

"I talked to Becky."

Cora raised her eyebrows. "And she sent you to me? Remind me to rap her upside the head."

A door halfway down the row opened, and the makeup lady, Flo, came out. "You seen the soda machine? I know there's one on the ground floor, but that seems a hell of a long way." Her eyes lit on Dennis. "Well, hello, sweetie." She cocked her head at Cora Felton. "Talk about robbing the cradle. Any younger, we could use him in the shoot."

"Sorry, Flo, the infant's married. In fact, we were just discussing that now."

"I'll bet you were. So, no help with the soda machine? I'll just have to fend for myself."

Flo sashayed along the row, disappeared down the stairs.

Cora jabbed her finger in Dennis Pride's face. "Okay, kiddo. Here's the deal. You're not out of here in five minutes, I'm picking up the phone and calling your boss. Who happens to be your wife's father, in case you've forgotten. So you go down there, you get in your car, you drive back to New York. You do that, I won't cause you any grief."

"I can't do that. I told Brenda I had to stay over. I'm registered at the motel."

Cora regarded Dennis as one might observe a particularly loathsome tree slug. "Fine. You go back to your room and you go to sleep. You stick your head out the door once, I call your boss. You ring any other unit, I call your boss. You *snore* too loud, I call your boss. You got it?"

Dennis glared at Cora just long enough to show her he didn't give a damn about her threats, and could do anything he damn well felt like, then did exactly as she said.

27

HE FOUND IT ALL ANNOYING. *So many extraneous people. So many entrances and exits.*

So many witnesses.

There were too many people around her. That was the problem. And they kept changing. First she's in this room. Then she's in that. Then she's alone, but only temporarily. Why did the reporter have to show up? A reporter and a lawyer, what a combination. As if a movie crew wasn't enough.

How could he get close to her without being seen? Because it was important not to be seen. Not by her, of course, that was all right. But by anybody else. Anyone who might put two and two together.

He crouched behind the Dumpster in the hardware store parking lot, kept his eyes on the motel. He watched while the makeup lady purchased a Diet Coke from the machine on the ground floor. She fed in two bills, pushed her selection, fished out some change and a soda. Hard to tell at that distance, but most likely a twenty-ounce bottle for a dollar and a half. Not a bad deal. He might buy one himself if he got a chance.

Which wasn't likely. He'd never seen a motel with so much activity.

The makeup lady going upstairs again with her soda. And the young man who'd been manhandled on his way down. She saying something flirtatious to him, and he brushing right by, not even acknowledging her presence. And how must that make her feel.

And then the girl creeping out from behind the car. The one that drove into the hardware store's parking lot and made him hide. Creeping out now. Watching the young man return to his room.

She's the worst. She's the real headache. Watching the whole motel. Covering all the entrances and exits. Watching everything that's going on. Making it impossible to get close to the place without her knowing.

What a stroke of bad luck! In his wildest dreams he could not have envisioned a person inexplicably standing in the dark, keeping the motel under surveillance. Was she a private eye? She didn't look like a private eye. She looked like a jealous girlfriend. She appeared to be keeping tabs on a boyfriend spending the night alone. In spite of the allure of the attractive young woman he'd driven up with. It was inconceivable. You don't take a woman who looks like that to a motel, then stay in separate rooms.

The young woman walked across the sandy spit connecting the parking lots. Thank God. He thought he was going to be trapped behind the garbage bin forever.

He looked across the road. There were no houses on the other side, just marshy wetlands. He crouched in the tall grass, worked his way along the front of the motel.

The girl crept out across the parking lot to the unit where the young man had gone. She reached the window, peered inside. Withdrew her head. For a moment it appeared as if she was going to knock on the door. Then she turned and hurried away. Back through the parking lot. Back in the direction of the hardware store.

He heaved a sigh of relief. Thank goodness. It would have been a long way to come for nothing. Now, then. She got what she came for. Or she chickened out on getting what she came for. In any case, she had reached a decision. Now she could drive the hell off.

Only, she didn't. Lord! What was he dealing with here? Some insane, obsessed stalker. He chuckled at the idea. He wasn't a stalker. He was a friend, an equal, a kindred spirit.

That must be made clear.
He had to do something. Attract her attention.
There were only two things the Puzzle Lady liked.
Crossword puzzles.
And murder.
She hadn't responded to his crossword puzzles.
Guess it was time to up the ante.

28

DENNIS WOKE UP TO THE SOUND OF someone pounding on his door. He sat up in bed, disoriented. It took him a few moments to remember where he was. He looked over at the digital clock on the nightstand. Two-ten. Someone was knocking on his door at two-ten?

Becky? Becky wouldn't knock on his door at two in the morning. Sherry would.

His pulse quickened.

Sherry would wait until she was sure that damn reporter was asleep and then slip out of the room.

It had to be Sherry. It couldn't be anyone else.

Dennis hopped out of bed, opened the door.

Brenda said, "Hi, Dennis."

His thoughts whirled through a gamut of emotions. None seemed to be joy. "Brenda!" he blurted.

"Got it in one. Good. I was afraid you might have forgotten."

"What are you doing here?"

"Just thought I'd crash the party. Everyone else seems to be here.

Sherry. Aaron. Cora. Becky. I just hope I'm not too late to join the fun."

Dennis opened his mouth to speak, but couldn't think of a thing to say to his wife. "How did you know I was here?"

"Your car's right outside."

"I mean at the motel."

Brenda shook her head. "Oh, Dennis. You're so transparent. I would have figured out where you were. With or without a phone call."

"Who called you?"

"Did I say someone called me? Dennis. Please don't quote me on that. I wouldn't want to get anyone in trouble. The point is, I drove up from New York to see how you were." She smiled. "So, how are you, Dennis?"

"This isn't happening," Dennis groaned.

"Actually, it is. I suggest you let me in, Dennis. Unless you've got a girl hidden in there. Which I sincerely doubt. Even you couldn't be that stupid."

Brenda pushed Dennis into the room, slammed the door.

It had been worth it to Brenda, sitting outside for two and a half hours. Alluding to, but denying, a phone call tipping her off, a call that could have brought her driving up from New York. The nice thing was, there were at least two logical suspects who could have made that call: Cora and Becky. Either could have done it, so he wouldn't know which to blame. But trying to figure out who would totally obfuscate the real solution, that she had bugged his car.

Perfect.

Brenda smiled at Dennis, all wide-eyed and innocent. "So, what's up?"

29

CORA FELTON WAS HAVING A BAD DREAM. She was trapped in a gigantic maze and she couldn't escape. The maze was in the form of a crossword puzzle. Every potential alley of escape inevitably led to a black square. A dead end, where she would have to turn around, go back, and begin again.

Which she wouldn't have had to do if she had only filled in some of the crossword puzzle, if she only knew some of the answers, any answers, any at all. But she didn't, and she couldn't, and she wouldn't. And there was no chance that she ever would, for not only did she have no answers, but she also had no clues. Not one. Not a clue.

So she ran down row after row. Aisle after narrow aisle. With towering, constricting walls. Constructed entirely of breakfast cereal boxes piled end on end. Each with her own smiling, mocking face, telling her that she would never get out. Mocking and knocking and mocking and knocking and knocking and . . .

Cora sat up in bed. Someone was knocking on the door. Light was streaming through the rather inadequate motel room curtains.

Becky was sleeping soundly in the next bed. Well, that was a fine how-do-you-do. Falling asleep just when Cora needed her. Now, why did Cora need her? What the hell time was it?

The clock said seven-fifteen. *Seven-fifteen? Why the hell were they waking her up at seven-fifteen? Her call was for nine. She should give that officious assistant director what-for. Except he wasn't on the tour. The publicity director was helping out. Oh, was she going to get it!*

Cora staggered out of bed, flung the door open.

Two cops stood there. One old and one young. Both in uniform.

"Cora Felton?" the older one said.

"Yes."

"We need to talk to you. May we come in?"

Cora shot a glance over her shoulder. It was hot in the motel room, and Becky had thrown off the bedclothes and was sleeping on her stomach in her rather short blouse.

"You may not. I have a naked blonde in the other bed. You want to talk to me, you wait outside."

"It's rather urgent, ma'am."

"I'm sure it is."

Cora slammed the door in the cops' faces. She pulled on her pink bathrobe and slippers, padded over to the nightstand, grabbed her purse.

Becky raised her head from the pillow and moaned. "What's going on?"

"Some cops wanna see me."

"What'd you do?"

"Nothing. I've been sleeping. Go back to sleep."

The cops pounded on the door again.

"Oh, for goodness' sakes. Hold your horses!"

This time the younger cop was holding his hat in his hands. His brown hair had a cowlick, which made him seem younger still. "Got your story straight?" he asked Cora.

"I beg your pardon."

The older cop had a world-weary look. "He's joking. Jerry's always joking. Sometimes it's inappropriate."

"What's happened?" Cora asked.

For something clearly had. Below, in the parking lot, two police cars had their lights going. People, mostly movie crew, were hanging around and talking the way neighbors do after a robbery.

"You wanna come downstairs, ma'am? No, not that way. That way's blocked off."

A crime-scene ribbon had been strung across the balcony just to the right of her door.

"Uh-oh," Cora said.

The cop named Jerry nodded. "*Uh-oh* describes it nicely."

"Who's dead?"

The older cop fixed her with a steely glare. "How did you know someone was dead?"

"Give me a break, Officer. You got the entire Mystic police force here and a crime-scene ribbon up. I'd be a pretty dim bulb if I didn't think someone was dead."

The young cop grinned. "She got you there, Phil."

Cora fished her cigarettes out of her purse, lit one up.

"Smoking's a sign of nervousness."

"Actually, young man, it's a sign of nicotine addiction. But I am a little anxious to know who bought it. I got a lot of friends staying here."

"We don't have a positive ID. It's a young lady connected to your tour. But the crew didn't know her name. Twenty, brown hair, blue eyes— Hey!" the young policeman exclaimed as Cora pushed him aside and went pelting down the stairs.

The paramedics had just closed the ambulance doors.

"Where is she?" Cora cried.

"Relax, lady. We're taking her to the hospital."

"Is she dead?"

"Are you a relative?"

"Damn it, is she dead?"

A man in street clothes carrying a black bag came around the side of the ambulance. His expression said it all. Cora's face twisted in agony.

"Easy, ma'am. Do you think you know her?"

"Cora!"

Cora wheeled at the familiar voice, looked up at the balcony where Aaron Grant peered over the rail. "What's going on?" he called.

Cora opened her mouth to speak, but no words came. Her eyes misted over.

Sherry stepped out of the door, next to Aaron. "Aunt Cora. What's all the fuss?"

Cora let out a hysterical, relieved giggle.

"All right, Miss Felton," the cop named Phil said. "You mind telling us what you're up to?"

"She thinks it might be a relative," the doctor volunteered.

The older cop's face softened. "Is that right, Miss Felton?"

"No. The description fit my niece. But she's fine." Cora jerked her thumb at the closed ambulance door. "Want me to have a look? I must know her, if she's involved in the shoot."

The cop nodded to the doctor, who nodded to the paramedic. The paramedic, with no one to nod to, opened the ambulance door.

Cora looked in. "Is there a step?"

"I'll give you a hand."

The paramedic hopped up into the ambulance, pulled Cora up after him.

On the gurney was a pretty young woman with curly brown hair. Her beauty was marred by the gash on the top of her head, and the trail of blood down her cheek. Her eyes were glassy, staring. Her hair was sticky and matted.

"Do you recognize her?" the older cop asked.

"Yeah. It's Ginger."

"Who?"

"She's an actress. She looks young on film. We use her to play a child."

"You're kidding."

"Why do you say that?"

"Well, we won't know for sure till the tox screen's done, but she appears to have ingested quite a lot of drugs and alcohol."

"Which would be in keeping with how she died," Jerry said.

"Hey, blabbermouth!" Phil scolded him.

"Well, it's not like it's a big secret. She banged her head, right, Doc?"

"The preliminary indication is that she was killed by a blow to the head. How she sustained that blow is your job."

"She was drunk and she fell."

Cora looked up to the balcony where the crime-scene ribbon hung. A section of the wooden rail was broken, with the boards hanging down. Her eyes narrowed. "Is that the police theory of the case?"

"There *is* no police theory of the case," Phil said. "Which Jerry here doesn't understand because he's never *had* a case. Leastwise, he's never had an accidental death that didn't involve a motor vehicle."

Cora Felton frowned, mulled that over.

"Who'd you think it was?" the older cop asked. "When you came racing down here? You mentioned your niece?"

"The description fit. Then I saw her on the balcony. Here she comes now."

Sherry and Aaron, prevented by the crime-scene ribbon from taking the same stairs as Cora, came down the steps at the other end. They reached the ground just as Dennis and Brenda emerged from their unit. The two couples stopped short.

"Brenda!" Sherry exclaimed in surprise. She knew instantly it was a mistake. Brenda's face clouded over with suspicion. Sherry wasn't surprised to see Dennis. She *was* surprised to see Brenda.

Aaron and Dennis glared. The two men thrust out their jaws, stepped away from the women, circled each other like tomcats about to do battle over a female in heat.

Phil, regarding this, raised his eyebrows. "Who the hell are they?"

"Who the hell is *she*?" Jerry added, as Becky Baldwin, fresh from a quick shower and looking like a million bucks, came walking up.

Cora wondered where to begin.

"Well," she said, holding her thumb and forefinger about a millimeter apart. "It's a *little* complicated."

30

"Okay," the cop named Jerry said. "Let me see if I've got this straight. The one guy was married to two of the girls, but not the blond girl. The other guy is dating two of the girls, including Blondie, and barely knows the other one. The girl who was married to the one guy and is dating the other guy is your niece. The girl who is married to the one guy and barely knows the other guy is your niece's best friend. The guy who is dating your niece and used to go with the blond bombshell is a reporter. And the girl who looks like she just stepped out of a Victoria's Secret catalogue is a lawyer. Is that right?"

"Basically. I doubt if they'd appreciate being called girls, but that's their problem."

"And why are they here?" the cop named Phil asked. "How do they fit into the picture?"

"My niece came with me on the tour. The others tagged along." Cora hoped this minimalist explanation would suffice. Any more detailed speculation, she feared, would make the young officer's head spin.

Becky Baldwin also threatened to have that effect. Jerry grinned like an idiot every time Becky opened her mouth.

"Any trouble here, Officer?" Becky asked. "Am I right in assuming we're dealing with an accident and there is no cause for alarm?"

"You're a lawyer!" Jerry blurted.

Becky batted her eyelashes. "Is that a problem, Officer?"

Phil shot Jerry a look. "No, miss. But we need to ask some questions. You know how it is."

"Yes, I do. But, as your partner points out, I am an attorney. And before I let my clients answer any questions, I want to be certain they know their rights."

"Hold on, now, miss. Which of these people are your clients?"

"That depends. Which of them do you intend to charge?"

The older cop rolled his eyes. The young cop just grinned.

Jennifer Blaylock hurried up the driveway. The publicist looked as if the sky were falling, and she were the one entrusted to keep it up. "What's going on here?" she cried. "We can't have police cars in the parking lot. We can't have an ambulance. I'm sorry if one of the guests is sick, but could we *please* handle it with a little more decorum? We're at the Stop and Shop at ten-thirty sharp. That's our photo opportunity. Not this." She fixated on Cora Felton. "You, you in particular shouldn't be here. Could we please clear the parking lot before someone calls the press?"

"And who would you be?" the older policeman inquired.

"I'm Jennifer Blaylock. I'm the publicity director for the tour."

"*Publicity* director?"

"Yes."

"But you're filming? You have a film crew here?"

"That's right."

"Doesn't a film crew usually have a producer or director? Or both? How come they're not here?"

"Oh. They're staying at the other motel."

Cora Felton's ears pricked up. "Other motel?"

"They're at breakfast. They sent me to see how things are going. This is awful! What am I going to tell them?"

"Well, you can tell 'em their kid star is dead," Jerry said.

Phil frowned like Jerry just divulged the secret launch codes.

"Ginger? Ginger's dead?" Jennifer looked stricken. "Oh, my God! How did it happen?" She raised her eyes to the crime-scene ribbon. "She fell off the balcony?"

"That's what we're trying to determine, miss."

"I don't understand."

"That's all right, miss, that's not your job. Now, Miss Felton was telling us the young woman was an actress in your televison spots."

"That's right."

"Playing a child."

The publicist frowned. "Not so much playing a child as showing the children what to do. We're filming with amateurs. Young kids who haven't a clue. Sometimes it's necessary to show them what we want. Officer, can we please move this along?"

"Absolutely," the older cop said. "Miss, can you tell me why no one on your film crew happened to know this young woman's name?"

"I don't understand."

He jerked his thumb at the crew members hanging out in the parking lot. "These guys here. They knew she worked on the film. But they didn't know who she was."

Jennifer waved her hand airily. "Oh, that's just the crew." She flushed, lowered her voice. "What I mean is, on a shoot, there's production and there's crew. Crew members are technical people. They deal with objects: cameras, lights, props. Production people deal with actors. See what I mean?"

"Not entirely. But her name was Ginger?"

"Yes. Ginger Perkins."

"Her last name is Perkins? You know that for a fact?"

"It's the name on her résumé photo. It could be a stage name, but there's no reason to believe it's not real."

The cop looked like that was more than he wanted to deal with. "But the fact is, no one even knew her first name except Miss Felton here?"

"Well, what about Lance? He knew, for goodness' sakes."

"Who's Lance?"

"The other actor. Lance Griswald." Jennifer glanced around. "Say, where is he?"

The older cop frowned. "Wait a minute. There's another actor?" He looked at Cora. "You didn't tell us that."

"I didn't know it mattered. Officer, is there more to this than you're telling us?"

Becky Baldwin jumped in. "Just a minute. Are you accusing her of something?"

"I'm not accusing anyone of anything. I'm just trying to get the story. How many actors are there in this company?"

"Just three," Jennifer said. "Miss Felton and the two kids."

"This missing actor is a kid?"

"He's young. He's not a kid. He *plays* a kid. It's the same as with the girl. And I'm sure he's not missing."

"Where's he staying?"

The publicist flushed. "Officer, I don't want any trouble."

"I don't either, but someone's dead. Where's Lance?"

"You have to understand. We're on a shoestring budget. We're paying for the actors' rooms."

"Are you telling me Lance and Ginger were sharing a room?"

"They're over eighteen."

"I don't care if they're over forty. If the guy's sharing a room with her, I want to talk to him. How come he's not here?"

"I imagine he drank himself to sleep," Cora volunteered. "I bet you could tear up this whole parking lot with a jackhammer and he wouldn't notice." She took a breath. "There is someone missing you should check on."

"Miss Felton," Jennifer warned.

"Yes?" the policeman said. "You have some information?"

Becky Baldwin cleared her throat. "I would be very careful with my accusations, Cora. In particular, I'd be careful not to make one."

"Of course not. I'm just privy to certain facts I feel the police ought to know. Since the filming began I have been followed around the state by a rather persistent fan. He checked into the motel last night."

"And just who would that be?"

"Once again," Becky said, "I would point out that Cora is making no accusations."

"I'm delighted to hear it," Phil said dryly. "And just who is she *not* accusing?"

"What does it matter?" Jennifer said irritably. "This fan, whoever he is, had absolutely nothing to do with this poor young woman. Her acting partner is another matter. If it's a case of foul play, Lance is surely involved. A lover's spat. Something simple, tragic, and not particularly newsworthy. Nothing that is going to interfere with our tour."

"Isn't the death of an actress going to put a crimp in your tour?"

"We don't *need* her. We're shooting reality ads with real people. We don't need anyone except Cora here. Which is why I can't allow her to be your star witness in some ridiculous obsessed-fan theory. This was an accident, plain and simple. There is no reason to assume otherwise."

"Except for the fact he's not here," Cora said. "The guy follows me all over creation, then runs away when this girl gets killed? Is that just a coincidence?"

"It's not even a fact. It's just you using inflammatory language. And don't pretend you don't know it. You're a wordsmith. You know exactly what you're doing. You characterize it as 'running away'? How do you know he didn't just leave?"

Cora shrugged. "I would assume he didn't, because here he comes now."

Freddy Fosterfield came bustling up. Despite the early hour he was dressed, as always, in his three-piece suit. "What's going on here? Why are you talking to Miss Felton? I can assure you she didn't do anything. Cora, are these policemen bothering you?"

"No, they're not, Freddy," Cora said pointedly. "They happen to come from Mystic. They didn't drive across half the state of Connecticut to be here."

He smiled. "I'm a fan, I admit it. Come on, Officer, what happened?"

"A girl fell off the balcony. She's dead."

Freddy looked up at the shattered rail. "My God!"

Cora studied his expression. If he was acting, he was mighty good. She tried to think back to high school, to recall if Freddy Fosterfield had been in any student productions. "Damn it, Freddy, what are you doing here?"

"I came to see the filming, of course."

The cop said, "Where did you come from?"

"Danbury."

"You drove all the way from Danbury? That's a hundred miles."

"Actually, I drove by Bakerhaven first. I forgot where they were filming. I had to find out."

"Why didn't you just call?"

"I tried to call the company, but I just got a recording."

"We have a website," the publicist said.

"Good to know."

The older policeman had heard enough. He clearly didn't think much of Freddy Fosterfield as a suspect. "That's real nice. What about this Lance kid?"

"He's probably sleeping it off," Cora suggested.

"Which means he was drunk enough to do it. Let's have a talk with him. What's his room number?"

"I have no idea. You'd have to ask the manager."

The motel manager, a mousy little man who gave the impression he was afraid this would look bad on his record, was discovered skulking behind a burly teamster. Prodded, he allowed as how Lance and the dead girl had shared room 212, but protested that it wasn't his fault.

Two-one-two proved to be the unit just to the right of the broken rail. The cops went up and banged on the door. When they got no answer, the motel manager was dispatched for a key.

Cora, disobeying the directive that everyone stay put, tagged along. She didn't mean to make trouble for the police, but she was afraid of what they might find.

She was wrong.

Lance wasn't lying dead in a pool of blood just inside the motel door.

Lance was gone.

31

Dennis Pride was indignant. "How long are you going to hold us?" he griped. "I happen to have a one o'clock appointment."

Jerry, who was taking a witness statement from the unhappy motel manager, frowned at the interruption. "Relax, buddy. You got plenty of time."

"Oh, yeah? My appointment's in New Haven."

"Then what are you doing here?"

Brenda, at her husband's elbow, said, "Give him a break. He works for my father. We don't want to let Daddy down."

"Your father's a businessman?"

"Yes."

"Then he'd understand this is police business."

"But we'd have to explain what we're doing here."

"What *are* you doing here?"

"Nothing."

"I can see why that would be hard to explain."

"Look," Dennis said, "I don't know this dead girl, I never met this dead girl, I wouldn't know this dead girl if I saw her."

"In that case, you may well have seen her," the cop concluded, "and just don't know it."

"And that would aid your investigation how?" Dennis sneered back.

Jerry shrugged. "Maybe you saw her with someone. Someone you *could* identify."

"Oh, for Christ's sake!"

The young cop was conducting interviews in the parking lot with all of the people on the scene, who were waiting their turn with varying degrees of patience. Dennis represented one end of the spectrum. The teamster who had fallen asleep in the tour bus represented the other.

The cop had begun by questioning those who had actually seen the body. This consisted of the electrician, who found it; his roommate, the director of photography, who had run to tell; the grip and prop-man next door, who'd heard the commotion; and the motel manager, who'd called the police. This, in the policeman's point of view, seemed the natural order of things. So far only Dennis had seen fit to object.

Cora was close enough to eavesdrop. While her positioning was not exactly surreptitious, it was not exactly serendipitous, either. Cora had needed to smoke. In her considered opinion—and Cora was, after all, an expert on smoking—the only place to accomplish this just happened to be within earshot of the interrogation.

So far, she had heard nothing of interest, unless one counted the argument between Quentin and Daphne, who arrived shortly after the questioning began. The producer and director, who apparently knew absolutely nothing about the incident, each blamed the other for it. This was less than helpful to the young cop, who told each politely but firmly to shut up.

None of the other interrogations were much help either. No one had heard anything, no one had seen anything.

Freddy Fosterfield reported waking up around two in the morning to go to the bathroom. "And I never do that," he insisted. "So perhaps something woke me."

"Like the sound of a body falling?" Jerry suggested. He was unable to keep the ridicule out of his voice.

"I have no idea. I can only say that this was obviously an accident, and has nothing to do with Cora Felton and her tour."

That seemed an excellent opportunity for the young officer to grill Fosterfield on just what the hell he was doing there. Instead, he dismissed him and called on Dennis, who was seething with impatience. Cora figured the cop had kept Dennis waiting on purpose just for making such a fuss.

Freddy Fosterfield, released, looked around for Cora. Noting this, she scooted across the parking lot to where Aaron and Sherry stood with Becky Baldwin.

"Quick!" Cora hissed. "Talk to me about something. I'm avoiding my Number One Fan."

"What do you want to talk about?" Aaron asked.

"If it's the dead girl, we're all talked out," Sherry said.

"Nonsense," Becky scoffed. "I'm sure Cora can come up with a theory for everyone in the motel having murdered her."

"I wish you would," Aaron said. "If I ever get back to the paper, this is a very tame story to file."

"Did you call it in?" Cora asked.

"Sure I called it in. The editor'd like me to stick with it, come up with something good. A juicy sex killing is his first choice."

"That's fine," Becky said, "but if you're staying here, I gotta get back to Bakerhaven. Assuming none of you are charged with this crime."

"Hard to say until we're interrogated," Sherry said. "And who knows when that will be. We're rather peripheral and we aren't pushy. Basically, we haven't got a prayer."

"Not like Mr. and Mrs. Whiner," Aaron observed, jerking his thumb in the direction of Dennis and Brenda, who, having finally gotten to talk, were jabbering their heads off to the young cop. From Jerry's expression, their contribution was somewhat less than helpful.

"Anyway," Becky said, "if Aaron stays, I'm going to drive his car back. Assuming he's welcome on the bus."

"Well, we got more room now." Cora winced. "Sorry! Insensitive thing to say. I'm sure it's no problem. Aaron can—" Her eyes widened. "Buddy! Who's feeding the dog?"

Aaron's face was a picture of consternation.

"You mean Buddy hasn't been fed? You mean Buddy hasn't been *out*? Aaron, you gotta go back! You gotta go back and feed my dog!"

"You want me to tell the cop I have to feed a dog? He'll think I'm worse than the Whiners."

"Well, you can't let him pee on the rug," Becky said.

"Buddy wouldn't pee on the rug," Cora bragged. "But he's gotta go out, and he's gotta be fed. Aaron, what are you standing around for?"

"Don't be silly," Sherry said. "Just call someone."

"Sure," Cora scoffed. "I'll call Harper. 'Chief, a girl got bumped off and I need your help. Could you walk my dog?' "

"You might want to phrase that a tad more tactfully."

"You think?"

"Why don't you call Harvey Beerbaum?" Sherry suggested. "He'd be glad to do it."

Cora made a face.

"I'm not suggesting you marry the man, Cora, just let him walk your dog."

Freddy Fosterfield stuck his nose in. "You need someone to walk your dog?"

"Yeah, in Bakerhaven," Cora said sarcastically.

"Oh."

Cora could practically see Freddy weighing the brownie points he'd earn by making the drive. "No one's leaving here, Freddy. I'm trying to figure out who to call."

"Of course."

"The police wouldn't let you leave anyway," Aaron said. "With the investigation going on."

"But surely it's an accident," Freddy said.

"Yeah," Cora said flatly.

"Don't you think so?"

"I wouldn't bet my bottom on it."

Another police car pulled into the parking lot and drove right up to the interrogation. Phil got out, dragged Jerry off to the side, and conferred with him in low tones. Cora suppressed a smile. Jerry had been left alone to conduct the interviews, but apparently Dennis and Brenda had given the young officer so much grief that he had called for backup.

Cora was wrong.

Phil was there to expedite the interrogations because the medical examiner's preliminary finding was accidental death.

32

FREDDY FOSTERFIELD STAYED FOR THE FILMING. With Ginger Perkins's death deemed accidental, there were no grounds to exclude him. Unless Cora wanted to bring up the fact he'd been in Stamford without telling anybody. But he hadn't done anything in Stamford. Just been in the store. Which was creepy, but not illegal.

Neither was hanging around the filming. Not as long as he was doing it openly and making no attempt to harass Cora. Which he wasn't. Freddy kept his distance, never talked to her except in the presence of others. He was, to all intents and purposes, a model citizen. With a more than average interest in breakfast cereal.

Aaron and Becky had left. Aaron clearly hadn't wanted to, but his editor wasn't going to let him stick around and cover an accident. And with Fosterfield out in the open, there was no real need to keep an eye on him. Plus, someone had to feed the dog.

While Sherry wasn't happy sending Aaron off with Becky Baldwin, she had to be somewhat mollified by his obvious reluctance to go.

Cora wasn't mollified by anything. As far as Cora was concerned, this was the worst of all possible worlds. She was stuck with Freddy Fosterfield, and she was stuck selling breakfast cereal.

She was also stuck in the motel, which, it turned out, was THE GRANVILLE GRAINS NEW AND IMPROVED CORN TOASTIES PUZZLE LADY PERSONAL APPEARANCE TOUR home base for the first week of the shoot. Apparently—and Cora's eyes glazed over when Daphne tried to explain it to her—the union rules required only that the *primary* location be a certain distance from New York City, so by maintaining a home base in Mystic, the production company could get away with carrying the minimum skeleton crew, even when shooting at locations that were actually closer to Manhattan than Mystic.

It was all Greek to Cora, who had always considered a union to be a sacred bond between a man and a woman, until such time as the philandering lowlife revealed his true character in actions that could be documented in court.

Production resumed that afternoon at a mall on Route 95. Lance and Ginger were not missed. People noted their absence, they just weren't needed. As far as production was concerned, they were about as essential as the non-bus-driving teamster.

Filming was uneventful. If anyone had heard about the accident, no one alluded to it. Cora did her best to whip up enthusiasm from children who didn't care, for the benefit of parents who did.

On the plus side, it was sunny and bright, they could shoot outdoors, and there was little equipment to schlep. For Cora, who had to wait to go home until the crew had packed up the equipment truck, this was a major consideration. Freddy Fosterfield offered her a ride, which she refused. She might have accepted one from the producer, who, in addition to staying at a better motel, had seen fit to rent himself a car. But Quentin was driving Daphne and Jennifer, there was only room for one more, and Cora wouldn't go without Sherry.

Not that they had anything to say on the bus. Sherry brooded about Aaron. Cora brooded about the case. The whole accidental-death thing really bugged her. It was a mighty hasty medical finding. Cora wondered if the production company had pulled any strings. She doubted it. MGM, maybe, but Granville Grains? Even so, it bothered her. The girl was dead, the boy had vanished. If that wasn't cause and effect, what was it? If this was an accidental death, wouldn't the boy at the very least have to have contributed to the accident?

No, Cora couldn't believe the police were satisfied. The cops might have eased up on the interrogations, but their investigation was still ongoing.

So was Cora's.

And she knew just where to begin.

33

CORA FELTON KICKED THE MOTEL ROOM DOOR SHUT and wheeled to face the startled publicist.

"All right. Let's you and me have a little talk."

Jennifer Blaylock gasped. "Miss Felton. I'm sorry about the rooming arrangements. It had nothing to do with me. I assure you, if it's a problem—"

"Nice try. I could care less about the damn motel." Noticing the decor, Cora added, "Though, actually, this is a pretty nice spread." She waved her hand. "Never mind that. It's time you came clean."

"About what?"

"About the dead girl."

"Ginger?"

"Have we got more than one dead girl? My, my. Just how much are you covering up here?"

"I don't know what you're talking about."

"I'm talking about the killing that got ruled an accidental death so the tour could go on."

"It *was* an accidental death."

"Oh, really?"

"Yeah, really. What, you think I have some pull with the medical examiner?"

"Or slipped the cops twenty bucks to look the other way? No, of course not. On the other hand, I don't think you're above manipulating things to make that happen." Cora glanced around. "Is that a mini-fridge? I bet your TV gets HBO."

"I didn't assign the rooms. But if you want, I'll speak to Quentin."

"He assigned the rooms?"

"No, but he's in charge."

"Then who assigned the rooms?"

"Quentin said to cut down the rooming expenses."

"Who'd he say that to?"

"To the production manager."

"We have a production manager?"

"Not here. Back at the agency."

"The production manager made the rooming assignments?"

"He budgeted them."

"Who'd he give that budget to?"

"He gave it to Quentin."

"So Quentin made the rooming assignments?"

"He delegated them."

"Who'd he delegate them to?"

The publicist said nothing.

Cora smiled. "Ah. Well, it's a good thing I'm not concerned with rooming assignments, if Quentin delegated them to you. But I can see why you'd be in a good position to take up my cause. Say, is that an ashtray on the table? Does your motel actually have smoking rooms?"

Cora fished in her purse for her cigarettes and lighter.

"Miss Felton. What do you want?"

"I want you to come clean. Tell me the truth. It's your best option. I've been trying to give you time to come to that conclusion."

"I don't know what you mean."

Cora sucked in smoke, blew it out. "Want more time? Okay.

But when I finish this cigarette, your time is up. Tell me about finding the body."

The publicist's eyes bugged out of her head. "What?"

"It's your first gig on the road, but you sleep late, have a leisurely breakfast with the producer and director, then stroll over to check on the crew? I don't think so. You were up at the crack of dawn. Quentin and Daphne were snoring, but you were too psyched to go back to bed. You came by here to see if anyone was up. No one was, but you stumbled over a dead body in the parking lot.

"Which was the absolute worst thing that could have happened to you. Short of someone bumping me off—knock on wood. But it was bad enough. A murder investigation would shut down the shoot. An accident, you might just get by. But you *knew* it wasn't an accident. Now, how did you know that?"

"I didn't!"

"Yes, you did, or you would have called the cops. Instead of waiting for someone else to do it. And then showing up later with the innocent act."

"It wasn't an act. I never found the body."

"Oh, please." Cora waved her hand through a gale of cigarette smoke. "When the cop told you your kid star got killed, you said, 'Ginger?' Yes, it was Ginger. It also might have been Lance, but you knew better. Because you'd found her body. Now what else did you do?"

"I—I didn't do anything."

"Oh, now you found the body but you didn't do anything?"

Jennifer's eyes darted around.

Cora laughed. "That's the type of question that unless you come in with an answer right away, you might as well not bother. So, we can infer from your hesitation that you found the corpse. That must have been awful. You're young, you're scared, there's no one around, and there's a dead girl lying in the middle of the parking lot. So what would you do? You couldn't just run away. Letting someone else find the body would be the same as calling the police yourself. No, the only way it makes sense is if you did something. Something that

ACROSS

1 Mistake
6 "To ___ it may concern"
10 Box, but not for real
14 Fancy 9 Down
15 The Hawkeye State
16 Pueblo Indian
17 Dwelling place
18 Start of a message
20 "Amazin'" team
21 Hoses (down)
22 Beast of Borden
23 Hersey's "A Bell For ___"
25 High temperatures
26 Low stocking

29 "The Right Stuff" author Tom
31 Part 2 of message
33 Balloon filler
36 Fake fat
37 Italian port invaded during WW II
40 One little piggy ... later
41 Part 3 of message
43 Poverty-stricken
45 Fort Knox blocks
46 Dined at a deli
49 Damon and Lauer
51 Lesser
52 Lane who sang with Cugat
53 Dove's opposite
57 End of message

59	Really weird	24	What's owed
60	Swing around	25	Pet peeve?
61	Troubles	26	Minor hullabaloos
62	Like snail trail	27	___ contendere (court plea)
63	Omen interpreter	28	Was aware of
64	Alleviate	30	Unseat
65	Sounds of thunder	32	Unit of modem speed
		33	Guthrie who wrote "Alice's
	DOWN		Restaurant"
		34	Be ___ the finish
1	Dutch cheese	35	They go with reels
2	Judge's garb	38	Gave for a while
3	Unruly mob action	39	It's cracked by a chick
4	Veteran sailors	42	Representations
5	Bread or whiskey	43	Midday event
6	Make roomier, as a road	44	Foreign money
7	Night screecher	46	Out of kilter
8	Possesses	47	Book's name
9	Place ___ (table protector)	48	Follow
10	Put on the back burner	50	Treat like dirt
11	Deputized group	52	"Clan of the Cave Bear" heroine
12	"Open with ___ of jacks or	54	"Bess, You Is My Woman," e.g.
	better"	55	Cream puff
13	Takes the bus	56	Door openers
19	Squawk	58	7-7, e.g.
21	Hot tub spurter	59	Key above ~ on a PC

terrified you. Something you didn't want hanging over your head while you talked to the police. The answer is obvious. You tampered with the evidence. There was something that made it look like murder. You took it. Or you moved it. Or you planted something. But somehow, in some way, you altered the crime scene. Whatever you did, it scared you so much, you didn't dare talk to the cops. Which is not surprising. Tampering with evidence is a real serious offense. It would make you an accessory to murder."

The publicist sucked in her breath. She was trembling.

"See?" Cora said. "It's lucky you didn't talk to the police, because you stink at it. They'd wring you out like a sponge. Now, shall I turn you over to them, or do you want to tell me the score?"

Jennifer was white as a sheet. "No, no. No police."

"Fine. Then tell me what you did." Cora stubbed out her cigarette. "Last chance."

Silently, the publicist lifted the corner of the mattress, pulled out an envelope, handed it to Cora.

Cora scowled.

"I had to take it. I had no choice. We'd still be there." Jennifer pointed in the general direction of the other motel. "Answering questions. It would be the end of the tour."

Cora turned the envelope over. It wasn't sealed. The flap was merely folded in.

"Did you read this?"

"I looked at it."

"You looked at it?"

"I took it out."

Cora groaned. This was like pulling teeth. She reached in the envelope, pulled out the letter, and unfolded it.

It was a crossword puzzle.

34

SHERRY CARTER WAS INCREDULOUS. "You're covering up a murder?"

"I'm not covering up a murder," Cora protested.

"You certainly are. You're an accessory after the fact. And now you're trying to make me one."

"I would never do such a thing."

"I'm glad to hear it. That will be of some comfort to me while I'm rotting in jail."

"Sherry, you're my niece. I would never do anything to hurt you."

"You want me to solve this crossword puzzle?"

"You're good at puzzles. I'm not."

"That's not the point. You should take this straight to the police."

"They'll just ask me to solve it."

Sherry frowned.

"See, that wouldn't be good," Cora said. "On the other hand, if you solve it, I'm off the hook."

"And I'm on it."

"For what?"

"You know damn well for what. Tampering with evidence. Accessory after the fact. To murder."

"How do you know this is evidence?"

"You told me so."

"That's hearsay, Sherry. It would never stand up in court."

"That's not the point."

"That's *exactly* the point. If you're going to fling around words like *accessory,* you better know what they mean."

"That's a new one. You telling me what words mean."

"Right. Now, if I could teach you how to solve this crossword puzzle, I would, but I can't, so I won't. You gonna leave me in the lurch? And think about poor what's-her-face. The publicist. She's the one who tampered with evidence. She's the one in trouble. Are you suggesting I should turn her in?"

"Talk about loaded language. It's not a case of turning her in. The girl made a mistake."

"You realize you just called her a *girl?*"

"Well, I'm a little upset. This publicist woman, whose case you're championing, did a really stupid thing. Are we bound by her mistake?"

"No, but the girl has a point."

"Don't call her a girl."

"You did."

"I'm allowed to," Sherry said. "I'm a feminist. Your view of feminism is to marry as many men as possible."

"Oh, low blow. You must be losing the argument to resort to such tactics."

"This is not an argument, Cora. You have a piece of evidence in a murder case. *You* take it to the police."

"Fine. Just solve it first so they won't ask me to."

"And then you'll take it to the police?"

"Then I'll know if I should."

"Cora—"

"Well, the puzzle may be totally unconnected to the crime."

"It was found on the body."

"Yeah, but you don't know that."

"You told me so."

"I told you, the publicist told me. That's double hearsay. Or hearsay once removed. Or something. The publicist could be lying. I could be lying."

"Cora—"

"I absolutely agree with you. If this is evidence, it should go to the police. But think what that means. The publicist stole this because she was afraid it would shut down the tour. For once, what's-her-name's right. It *would* shut down the tour. Now, would you like a big, fat blemish on the Puzzle Lady's image?"

"Like the Puzzle Lady going to prison?"

"Sherry—"

"Give me the puzzle."

"Huh?"

"Give me the damn puzzle."

Sherry took the puzzle, grabbed a pencil, sat on the bed. "Okay. Simple, straightforward. No apparent tricks. There's a quote."

"Is that good?"

"No."

"What do you mean, no?"

Sherry's pencil was flying across the paper. "Hang on a sec. I'll show you."

Sherry finished the puzzle, turned it around to show Cora. "See the theme entries? 'Don't be sad, don't be blue. Just be glad it's not you.'"

ACROSS

1 Mistake
6 "To ___ it may concern"
10 Box, but not for real
14 Fancy 9 Down
15 The Hawkeye State
16 Pueblo Indian
17 Dwelling place
18 Start of a message
20 "Amazin'" team
21 Hoses (down)
22 Beast of Borden
23 Hersey's "A Bell For ___"
25 High temperatures
26 Low stocking

29 "The Right Stuff" author Tom
31 Part 2 of message
33 Balloon filler
36 Fake fat
37 Italian port invaded during WW II
40 One little piggy ... later
41 Part 3 of message
43 Poverty-stricken
45 Fort Knox blocks
46 Dined at a deli
49 Damon and Lauer
51 Lesser
52 Lane who sang with Cugat
53 Dove's opposite
57 End of message

59 Really weird
60 Swing around
61 Troubles
62 Like snail trail
63 Omen interpreter
64 Alleviate
65 Sounds of thunder

DOWN

1 Dutch cheese
2 Judge's garb
3 Unruly mob action
4 Veteran sailors
5 Bread or whiskey
6 Make roomier, as a road
7 Night screecher
8 Possesses
9 Place ___ (table protector)
10 Put on the back burner
11 Deputized group
12 "Open with ___ of jacks or better"
13 Takes the bus
19 Squawk
21 Hot tub spurter
24 What's owed
25 Pet peeve?
26 Minor hullabaloos
27 ___contendere (court plea)
28 Was aware of
30 Unseat
32 Unit of modem speed
33 Guthrie who wrote "Alice's Restaurant"
34 Be ___ the finish
35 They go with reels
38 Gave for a while
39 It's cracked by a chick
42 Representations
43 Midday event
44 Foreign money
46 Out of kilter
47 Book's name
48 Follow
50 Treat like dirt
52 "Clan of the Cave Bear" heroine
54 "Bess, You Is My Woman," e.g.
55 Cream puff
56 Door openers
58 7-7, e.g.
59 Key above ~ on a PC

35

THINGS WERE WORKING OUT. *He'd been upset when the publicist had taken the puzzle. After he'd gone to such pains to create it. After it had fit the situation so perfectly. What a stroke of luck. Well, not luck exactly. It had been a result of careful planning. To have such a puzzle. As a contingency. In case something went wrong.*

Or in case something went right!

What a rush it had been to actually do it! To move the game up a level, from the theoretical to the actual. From the murder game to the murder.

And then that damn girl steals the puzzle and the police are too dumb to catch on. So, instead of a murder investigation, you get what? Over, done, finished? The perfect crime?

Perfect, hell. How could it be perfect if no one knows it happened? It's as bad as if he slipped her poison and she died in her sleep. After all the trouble he went to to set the stage so beautifully. Arranging the body in the parking lot. Planting the puzzle. Smashing the balcony rail.

That had been the exciting part, the dangerous part, the part that could so easily have gone wrong. Standing up on the rickety rail, grip-

ping the overhang of the roof, stomping down hard with both feet. It had taken his full weight, smashing down like a battering ram on the weakest point, to break it. The rotten wood had snapped easily, barely made a sound. And yet it had taken considerable force. A thin girl, leaning on the rail, couldn't have done it, even if she'd been pushed.

If she had been, it still would have been murder. But the local cops hadn't a clue. Deemed it an accidental death. He wondered if they would have realized it was a murder even with the puzzle.

She would have. She'd have known right away. Hell, she'd known anyway. Refused to accept the police verdict. Set out snooping around on her own.

How did she get a line on the publicist? It wasn't as though she had stumbled over the publicist in the course of her investigations. No, she'd gone straight to her. Got the crossword. By now she would have solved it. By now she'd know.

Would she give it to the police?

It wouldn't matter if she did. They wouldn't know what to make of it. They wouldn't understand it. Most likely they'd brush her off as a dotty old woman, tilting at windmills. They'd nod and wink, humoring her. "Of course it's a murder," they'd say, and roll their eyes.

So whether she reported it or not, the result would be the same.

It was him versus her.

In this epic struggle, he had two considerable, if not insurmountable, advantages.

He knew who she was.

And she wasn't out to kill him.

36

FREDDY FOSTERFIELD SMILED AT CORA FELTON across the table for two. "It's so nice of you to ask me out."

Cora practically simpered. "Freddy, after the way I behaved when you asked me, it's a wonder you were willing to come."

"No, no. I quite understand. A woman in your position. You must have a hundred fans."

Cora hoped her smile was not too frozen. The thoughts, "No, just you" and "But you're my Number One Fan, you creep, you" sprang to mind. Cora shoved them back, glanced at the tabletop, wished there wasn't a candle on it.

The restaurant was tiny, dimly lit, and romantic. It had come highly recommended by the director of photography, whose sister-in-law lived in Weston. Cora wondered why his brother didn't live there, too, but it occurred to her for a woman with as many divorces as she had, that could be considered catty. At any rate, she planned to rap the DP upside the head. The place might boast the finest Italian seafood cuisine, but it was way too intimate for her taste.

Freddy Fosterfield seemed to like it. His eyes sparkled as he leaned over the table to light her cigarette. He snapped his silver lighter shut, watched her inhale.

"I didn't know you smoked," Cora said.

"I don't."

"Why do you have a lighter?"

"To light your cigarette."

Cora's flesh crawled.

Freddy Fosterfield had scrubbed himself to within an inch of his life. What was left of his hair was neatly trimmed. Not the faintest stub of a whisker could be seen on either rosy cheek. He wore a fresh, clean, three-piece suit—it occurred to Cora the man must have a suitcase of them. For the occasion he had a bright red bow tie around his chubby neck. He looked like the cherub from hell.

"Would you like a shrimp?" Freddy asked, extending a gigantic, cocktail sauce–dripping prawn.

"I have shrimp." Cora's was shrimp scampi. Belatedly, she said, "Would you like to try one of mine?"

He put up his hand. "Too much garlic. I have digestive problems."

Cora didn't want to hear about that. "Terrible about that young girl."

"Yes. Tragic."

"I take it you didn't hear anything when it happened?"

"No."

"But your room is downstairs?"

"Yes."

"She must have fallen right outside your window."

"Just about."

"That would have been awful. If you had woken up and looked outside."

"I doubt if I'd be having dinner at all," Freddy agreed.

"That's one way to look at it."

"I'm sorry. I didn't mean to be insensitive."

Cora waved it away. "When something like this happens, there's no right thing to say. Tell me, why are you here?"

"You invited me."

"No. On the tour, I mean."

"Oh. I'm enjoying it. I've never been a part of anything like this before. Not that I'm a part of it, but, well, you gotta understand. You live in New York City. Or you used to. People probably filmed on your block all the time. Doesn't *Law & Order* shoot there?"

"I'll say. They take up blocks and blocks with their trucks. Raises hell with alternate-side parking."

"You know how many movies get shot in Danbury, Connecticut? This is something special."

"It's just a cereal ad."

"But it's *your* cereal ad, Cora. Tell me something. Even with all the movies you see shot in New York, when you see them in the theater, don't you say, 'Hey, that's my street'?"

Cora had to admit that was true.

"Well, there you are. When this is on TV, I'll be saying, 'I remember when we shot that.' "

"You were there when we shot in Danbury. Isn't that enough?"

"You might not use the footage. Isn't that right? When the tour is over you'll edit the film. You won't know till then which store you'll use."

"You're going on the whole tour?" Cora was unable to keep the dismay out of her voice.

For a second, a shadow of annoyance crossed Freddy's face. Then he smiled. "I'm having fun."

"What about your job?"

"I took my vacation."

"Just like that?"

"I'm an assistant manager. I can call my own shots."

"Assistant manager where?"

"At Wal-Mart."

"Oh."

Once again, Cora's lack of enthusiasm registered.

"I'm in line for promotion. And it's not forever. There's lots of places I could go."

"Uh-huh," Cora said. "So when'd you decide to come along on the tour?"

"Sort of the spur of the moment. I realized how much fun I'd had, so I decided to go."

"How did you know where we were filming?"

"Actually, I didn't. I had to go to Bakerhaven to find out."

"Really? Who told you where we were?"

"I stopped in that muffin shop."

"Cushman's Bake Shop?"

"That's the one. They have wonderful muffins."

"They ought to. They truck 'em in from New York."

"Huh?"

"Mrs. Cushman can't bake a lick. She gets her stuff from the Silver Moon Bakery on Broadway and 105th Street. That's why her shop's so popular."

"Anyway, they knew where you were."

"Why didn't you ask me?"

"I didn't know where you lived. And your phone number isn't listed."

Cora nodded. "My niece had an abusive husband. When we moved in we got an unlisted number. We never had it changed."

"Would that be the young man in the parking lot? The one making such a scene?"

"Yes. How did you know?"

"The way he related to her. And he clearly had no interest in the other one. That's his current wife?"

"Yes, she is."

"Too bad."

Cora studied Fosterfield with interest. She had never known him to be a particularly perceptive judge of character. Of course, she had never known him as much of anything. There might be more to the man than she'd imagined. Cora found the thought unsettling.

"You got here last night?" she asked.

"Yes, I did."

"So you missed yesterday's filming?"

"I'm afraid so."

"What time did you get in?"

"Why do you ask?"

"I'm wondering why we didn't run into each other. I was in and out a lot."

"I was tired from all the driving. I just stayed in my room."

"Didn't you go out for dinner?"

"I ate on the road."

Cora wondered if that was true. She made a mental note to ask Aaron and Becky.

A busboy hovered, saw they were still picking at their appetizers, and left disappointed.

Cora, prompted, ate a shrimp. She had to force it down. She was more concerned with her dinner date.

"Ever been married, Freddy?" she ventured.

He seemed startled by the question. "Ah, no. I understand you have."

Cora smiled slightly at the understatement. "Yes. I'm not married at the moment, but yeah, I have been."

"Are you not married because of your work? I mean, your image, as the Puzzle Lady?"

"Good lord, no. These cereal people are bad enough. If they start telling me who I can date, that's the last straw."

"So you could marry again if you chose?"

Once again Cora felt that creepy feeling. "I could. Not that I have any intention of doing so."

"No, of course not," Fosterfield agreed, a little too quickly.

Cora was fed up with the toadying sycophant. "What do you mean, of course not? If I want to marry, I damn well will."

Fosterfield's face fell. "Of course. I mean . . ."

Cora laughed. "I'm kidding. Eat your shrimp, Freddy."

They munched in silence.

"So, tell me," Cora tried again. "This fascination with the

Puzzle Lady, is it just because you know me, or are you into cross-word puzzles?"

"I try. I'm not very good." His grin was sheepish.

"You try to solve them, or construct them?"

Freddy blinked. And for a second it was as if he were utterly transparent, as if his thoughts and feelings and emotions were there for all to see. Then he was smiling in an aw-shucks way. "Don't be silly. You're the puzzle whiz, Cora, not me."

He chewed a shrimp. Some of the color seeped back into his face.

As a busboy bore their plates away, Cora said, "Did you see her?"

"I beg your pardon?"

"The dead girl. Did you see her before they took her away?"

"I'm afraid I didn't."

"Did you see her here at all? Last night, for instance?"

"No."

"So you've never seen her?"

"I saw her at the filming. When you came to our store."

"That's the only time you've seen her?"

He frowned. "Why do you ask?"

"What about the boy? The one who's missing. Did you see him here?"

"No, I didn't."

"Do you know what he looks like?"

"Of course. He was at the filming too."

"And you didn't see him here?"

"No."

"Or anywhere else?"

"No. What are you getting at, Cora?"

"The boy is gone. If the girl's death was foul play, it could be him."

"That's obvious."

"There's another possibility. The killer killed the girl *and* the boy."

"So where's his body?"

"The killer dumped it to make it look like the boy did it."

"I think the other explanation is much more likely," Freddy said serenely.

"What's that?"

"The girl fell, the boy ran."

"Why?"

"He was drunk and scared."

"He'd have to sober up sometime."

"I suppose." Freddy reached for his water glass.

Cora said, "You cut your hand."

He stopped. Frowned. "Excuse me?"

"Right there. By your thumb. You cut yourself?"

"Oh." Freddy looked at his hand. "The cat scratched me."

"You have a cat?"

"I have two cats." Freddy beamed. "Sanford and Jeremiah."

Freddy seemed at ease. Cora couldn't tell if it was because he'd successfully deflected the question, or because he had nothing to hide. In either event, her attempt to grill him was turning out to be a total bust.

The waiter appeared with a gleaming tray and presented Cora with a lobster the size of a nuclear sub. On any other occasion she might have been pleased. Tonight, graced with Freddy Fosterfield's company, she wondered glumly how long it would take her to eat the damn crustacean.

37

"IT WAS MURDER," the young cop said. Jerry seemed rather happy with that pronouncement. "According to the medic, there was no way the head wound was the result of a fall. She was coshed with a two-by-four, sure as shooting."

"Could you keep your voice down!" the publicist hissed. "We have children here."

They certainly did. The good citizens of Westerly, Connecticut, had come out in force for the chance to get their kids in a national television commercial. It was a gorgeous day, and the Stop & Shop parking lot was jammed with a bunch of youngsters who, in Cora's humble opinion, would have been much happier at the seashore.

The young cop lowered his voice. "I don't mean to upset the children. But you understand what I'm saying. The Ginger Perkins case is a homicide. We have to approach it differently."

"I thought the medical examiner had ruled it an accidental death."

"That was the *preliminary* finding." Jerry tried not to sound defensive. Instead he sounded coached.

Cora suppressed a smile. "What do you want, Officer?" she said with all the solemnity she could muster.

"Thank you, ma'am. With accidental death ruled out, the whereabouts of the other actor takes on graver consequences. The kid's not here, is he?"

"Lance isn't back," Jennifer answered. "I doubt if any of the crew have seen him, but if you have to ask, could you please do it quietly?"

"I assure you I will, miss. I can also assure you every step is being taken to find him. We have his picture—his head shot, I think it's called—out to all officers. We're canvassing the hospitals and morgues, in case he's also met with foul play."

That seemed to alarm the young publicist even more. "Oh, I'm sure he hasn't! It seems perfectly obvious. The two had a drunken altercation, Lance hit Ginger and he ran away."

"It's certainly a possibility," the young cop said, "and one I'm sure we'll consider. If you'll excuse me, miss, I'd like to talk to your crew."

He did it quietly, discreetly, one at a time. Even so, it raised eyebrows. The accidental death of the girl had made the local news. Parents naturally assumed the connection. But that didn't stop them from pressing their children forward to film with the Puzzle Lady.

Sherry Carter pulled Cora aside between takes. "What's up?"

"Why? Hasn't young Kojak gotten to you yet?"

"I feel sort of slighted. Of course, I'm not actually on the crew. Do I understand it's a homicide?"

"According to Columbo."

"Your TV references are awfully old, Cora. Don't you watch any new shows?"

"They don't have cop names. *NYPD Blue. CSI. Without a Trace.* Where's a cop name, like *Baretta?*"

"*Judging Amy,*" Sherry ventured.

"That's a chick-flick show, and she's a judge. Besides, since when was *judging* a name? 'Lieutenant Columbo, this is Judging Amy.' "

"Cora—"

"You want me to call the cop Amy? I doubt if he'll like it."

"I know why you're joking."

"Who's joking?"

"If this is a murder, the cops need to have that puzzle."

"Absolutely not."

"Cora, that man threatened you."

"You're sure it's a man? That's rather sexist."

"I thought you thought it was Fosterfield."

"Shh. He's right over there."

"You don't think it's him anymore?"

"He didn't seem so bad at dinner."

"You had *dinner* with him?"

"You think I ate alone?"

"I don't know where you ate. You disappeared. I was worried sick."

"You were sound asleep when I got back."

"I figured you met a man."

"Sherry."

"If I waited up every time you stayed out late . . ."

"Let's not get catty."

"Catty? Cora, how did we get off the subject? You've got to turn that puzzle in."

"Sherry, let's think about that for a while. If I turn the puzzle in, we have a media circus, the tour is over, and we all go home. That isn't good for the cops. It just thwarts their investigation. But it's worse for me. If I go home, the killer stalks me there. Who knows when and where he'll hit? Here I'm surrounded by people. It's tougher to get at me."

"The killer had no problem getting at Ginger."

"Sure. She was young and stupid. And she was rooming with someone young and stupid. I'm rooming with you."

"Thanks a lot."

"And she wasn't carrying a gun."

"No, I suppose she wasn't. When you shoot this guy, try not to aim in my direction."

"You still insist it's a man. Interesting. Anyway, you won't be my roommate for long."

"Why not?"

"Aren't you going to call Clark Kent, tell him it's a homicide, and get his buns back here?"

"Oh."

"That's fine. I don't mind losing my roommate. But you read Aaron the riot act. He can't come unless he makes arrangements for my dog."

"Who should he ask?"

"That's his problem. It's his responsibility. He's passing it on, he better find someone responsible."

Sherry took a deep breath. "Cora, my head's spinning. How did we get so far away from the main point?"

"What main point?"

"The crossword puzzle."

"Phooey. You just think it's the main point because you *like* crossword puzzles. It really has very little to do with this."

"All right. Try this on for size. The boy is still missing. Suppose he's alive? Suppose there's a chance to find him before he's killed?"

"Are you writing a stand-alone thriller?"

"No."

"Or are you recycling a plot from one of those modern cop shows: *Law & Order: Kidnapped Actors Unit?*"

"Come on, Cora. What if Lance's in danger?"

"Sherry, that crossword puzzle doesn't threaten him, it threatens me."

"Even so."

"I promise you, if I thought there was the least chance it had anything to do with the kid, I'd give it to the police." Cora patted Sherry on the cheek. "Excuse me, I've got to talk to Little Mary Sunshine."

The publicist was smiling like a moron and doing her isn't-this-fun act for the kids. Cora hooked her arm and dragged her away.

"Don't do that!" Jennifer said.

"Don't do what?"

"I'm telling the children what a great person you are, and then you ignore them."

"I need to talk to you."

"Fine, but smile at the children. Is that so much to ask?"

"You want me to go back and smile at the kids?"

"I mean in general. I mean— You *know* what I mean. Stop giving me a hard time. As if I didn't have enough trouble."

"It is distressing, isn't it?" Cora agreed, sweetly. "With Ginger dead, and Lance missing, and the fuzz going nuts trying to find him."

"Yes, it is. So could you try to give me a break?"

"Give you a break? I haven't mentioned the puzzle. I haven't mentioned you finding the corpse. I think I've given you a break. Why don't you give *me* a break?"

Jennifer frowned. "What do you mean?"

"My niece is worried about Lance. She's concerned for his welfare. She's afraid that if I don't tell the police what I know, about the crossword puzzle and you finding the body, it will put his life in danger."

"That's absurd."

"I think so too. But Sherry's kind of upset. If you wouldn't mind, I'd like you to help me with Lance."

"Help you how?"

Cora shrugged. "Why don't you tell me where he is?"

38

LANCE GRISWALD'S HEAD WAS THROBBING. And it wasn't just the pint of whiskey he'd poured down his throat, though that certainly wasn't helping. His head kept going *bang, bang, bang.*

Lance was lying fully dressed on the bed watching TV. At least he had the TV on. But he wasn't really watching. And the volume was low. It couldn't be making the *bang, bang, bang.*

Lance's bleary eyes blinked through the layers of stale tobacco smoke. He needed a drink. But, no, the bottle was uncapped and on its side, the glass next to it containing only melted ice. No help for the incessant *bang, bang, bang.*

Lance groaned, rolled out of bed, stumbled to the door. He didn't open it, however. He leaned close, growled, "Yeah?"

"Housekeeping."

"Not now, not now," Lance muttered. He threw himself back on the bed.

Bang, bang, bang.

Good lord. Couldn't the woman hear?

Lance careened back in the general direction of the door. This time he actually leaned against it. "I'm not up! Come back later!"

"It's checkout time."

"I'm not checking out."

"Yes you are."

Good God! The chambermaid from hell!

Lance discovered the peephole in the door, put his eye to it. He blinked. Even through the distorted glass he could see the face of a totally gorgeous woman.

She banged on the door again.

"All right, all right," Lance muttered. He unlocked the door.

The blond goddess swept inside. She was not wearing a chambermaid's outfit, but a tan pantsuit. "Hello, Lance," she purred.

He gawked at her. "Who the hell are you?"

Cora Felton pushed Becky Baldwin aside, barged in, slammed the door. "She's your lawyer, you dumb cluck. You're lucky to have one. You're lucky on a lot of counts, you just don't know it yet."

Lance staggered back. "What the hell!"

"Well said." Cora flailed her arm at the air. "Jesus, open a window, willya? I smoke, and *I* can't stand it."

Becky pulled the curtain wide. Sunlight poured into the room.

Lance staggered back as if shot. "Hey, come on!"

"Oh, don't think too harshly of us," Cora told him. "The police are making a sweep of motels in the area. It won't be long before they get this far."

"The police?"

"Who'd you think investigates murders—the Boy Scouts? By the way, it's officially a murder now. No chance you accidentally pushed Ginger off the rail. She was deliberately coshed over the head."

"Oh, my God!"

"Yeah, puts you in a sticky spot. But things aren't all that bad. I got you a hell of a lawyer. Smart as a whip, and easy on the eyes. You'll thank me for it someday."

"I don't understand."

"Of course you don't. You're barely conscious. And you're not too clear on what happened. You're not even sure what you did. Let me fill you in.

"You and Ginger smoked some dope, drank some booze, maybe even tried some sex—though, if so, according to the medical examiner, you didn't succeed. Then you got totally wasted and passed out.

"You woke up to some rather bad news. Ginger was dead, and you couldn't remember a damn thing."

"How the hell do you know that?"

"How the hell do you think? How did you get here? You didn't fly, and you didn't take a bus, or they'd have found you by now. You got a ride from Little Miss Fix-It. Only she isn't really helping you. She's doing everything in her power to keep the shoot alive. Even if it means framing you."

"What are you talking about?"

"I'm sure you have no idea. Which is why you aren't going to say a word, Lance. You have a lawyer to say it for you. She will advise you not to talk. In the meantime, she'll put out this statement: You had drinks with the decedent and passed out; you woke up and discovered she was dead; you holed up in a motel while you tried to remember what happened."

Cora's eyes swept over the full ashtray and empty bottle and glass. "We'll gloss over the methods by which you attempted to remember. Just as you will leave out the means of transportation that brought you to this place. As well as any suggestions that might have prompted you to go. If you keep your mouth shut and do exactly as I say, we just might save you from the death penalty."

"Death penalty!"

"What'd you think they do to murderers, slap their hands?"

"But I didn't do anything!"

"Maybe not, but you can't remember. So you can't deny it. And flight is an indication of guilt."

"Oh, my God!"

"It will help a great deal if you surrender to the police before they catch you. But right now, it's a race against time. So splash some water on your face, and let's get the hell out of here before Sipowicz tracks you down."

"Sipowicz?"

Cora shrugged. "Well, I tried."

39

CORA GOT BACK TO THE MOTEL ROOM to find Sherry and Aaron watching TV in bed.

"Hi, Cora," Aaron said. "Afraid I stole your roommate. Don't worry, I brought you another."

Cora frowned. "I've got another roommate. She's down at the police station now."

Aaron sat up straight. "Police station?"

Before Cora could answer, there came an excited, "Yip! Yip! Yip!" and a toy poodle catapulted onto the bed and sprang into Cora's arms.

"Buddy!" Cora crooned. "What are you doing here?"

"Sherry read me the riot act. Said I was responsible for finding someone to take care of him. The only one I could find was you."

"For goodness' sakes."

"What's up at the police station? I've already filed my story. About it being a murder."

"There's been another development."

"What's that?"

"Police have made an arrest." Cora scratched the dog under the chin. "Hi, Buddy."

Aaron jumped out of bed. "My God! When'd it happen?"

"Just now."

"I gotta get down there."

"No need. He's not talking, and the police aren't giving anything out."

"Who's the suspect?"

"The kid. Lance."

"So they got him. How'd they do it?"

"Just lucky, I guess."

"Does Rick Reed have it?"

"Trust me, he hasn't got it."

On the TV, the Channel 8 anchorman said, *"We have breaking news, live, from Mystic, Connecticut. With a Channel 8 exclusive, here is Rick Reed."*

Rick Reed stood in front of the Mystic police station.

"Damn it, he's got it!" Aaron cried.

"This is Rick Reed, with another Channel 8 exclusive. Channel 8 has learned that the death of actress Ginger Perkins, of the Granville Grains Puzzle Lady publicity tour, has been ruled a homicide. Police have no comment other than to say that the death is suspicious, and the medical examiner has deemed it a homicide. This is Rick Reed, live on the scene, with breaking news from Mystic, Connecticut."

"See, he doesn't have a thing," Cora said. "He doesn't even know there's been an arrest."

"Lance's at the police station now?"

"Yeah."

Aaron headed for the door.

"Relax. The kid's not talking."

"Then I'll interview his lawyer."

"Feel free. She'll be along any minute."

"She?"

"Yeah. I told you, I got my old roommate back. Becky Baldwin. I think she's saying, 'No comment,' but if you wanna hang out a bit, you can hear her say it herself."

Aaron sat down on the bed. "All right. If it's not too much trouble, Cora, would you mind telling me what the hell is going on?"

40

THE SET WAS ABUZZ WITH THE NEWS.

Pepe, the propman, had the most to say, probably because Pepe had the least information. "They were having an affair. She thought it was serious. He thought it wasn't. The way men always do." Pepe allowed himself a slight swagger at the declaration.

Cora hid her expression behind a cough. There was no way she could keep a straight face at the thought of Pepe, the love-'em-and-leave-'em propman.

"She let him know this was no casual affair. He laughed at her. She made a scene. Things got rough."

"I can't believe it." The cameraman shook his head. "He was young. He had his whole life ahead of him."

"You don't think of that in the heat of passion," Pepe said sagely, as though he himself had committed a dozen murders. "Besides, he was drunk."

"Can they prove he was drunk?" Wayne ventured. The electrician, perhaps imagining his wife employing the expertise, seemed concerned by the prospect. "I mean, after all this time?"

"Hell, you saw him," Pepe said. "Did he look drunk to you?"

Wayne frowned. "Hey, do you mean I'm a witness?"

Pepe grinned. "We're all witnesses." He winked at the costume lady in the corner. "Ain't that right, Flo?"

Flo didn't reply. She seemed annoyed by the question. Cora wondered just what the relationship was between the two.

The crew was hiding out in the Price Chopper's employees' lounge so they wouldn't have to deal with the public. Whatever fears Jennifer Blaylock might have had about the murder putting a crimp in the tour, quite the opposite was in effect. The early shoots had been well attended. Today's was mobbed. This was perhaps the most exciting thing that had ever happened in southern Connecticut. The accident had become a front-page murder, and the police had a suspect in custody. It was positively delicious.

Rick Reed pushed his way in the door. The Channel 8 newsman looked around, spotted Cora. "There you are. What are you people hiding for? I can't bring my cameras in here. You should be out front. We can grab some interviews before you hawk your breakfast cereal."

"We're not filming interviews," Cora informed him. "In fact, I'm not sure we're filming the ad."

"Oh, I think you are. You got a couple of hundred stage moms out there ready to tear the place apart if little Lucy doesn't get her crack at fame. Come on, give me a tumble. I understand you're the one who ran the suspect down."

"Interview the kid's lawyer, did you?"

Rick shrugged. "I took Becky out to dinner. Purely social, of course." He turned, surveyed the room. "Anyone want to be on TV?"

Pepe looked like he might have volunteered, had not Quentin and Daphne showed up, ushered in by the publicist.

Quentin seemed horrified to find the crew there. "What's going on?" he demanded. "Why aren't you setting up?"

The propman, who seemed to square off against Quentin at any given opportunity, either because he was the union rep or because he just liked to, thrust out his chin. "We *are* set up. We've been set up for some time. I would like to point out, just in case we go into meal penalty, that the crew has been waiting on production."

Quentin seemed slightly off his game. He hesitated before saying sarcastically, "Right, it's all our fault, not the damn media's."

Rick Reed's ears pricked up. "Ooh! Could I get you to say that on camera?"

Quentin spotted the Channel 8 blazer and blushed.

"Don't be silly," Daphne interposed. "We're all just trying to get along in trying times."

Rick Reed beamed. "Could you say *that* on camera?"

"No one's saying anything on camera. We got kids out there. We're shooting a commercial, but our first thought is the kids."

The publicist pressed forward. "Let me handle this, Daphne." Her eyes sparkled at the newsman. "You're Rick Reed. Pleased to meet you. I'm Jennifer Blaylock. The tour publicist. If there's any way we can help the media, I want to make it happen." She linked her arm through his, walked him toward the door. "So let's put our heads together, see if we can work something out, okay?"

Quentin watched them go. "There's a gem. An absolute gem. Someone who puts the good of the shoot above personal gain. So, if we could all hop to it—" His eyes lit on Cora Felton. "Good lord, you look terrible! Why aren't you in makeup?"

Cora fixed him with an evil eye. "I *am* in makeup."

Quentin covered that blunder by turning his wrath on the costume lady. "You call that a makeup job? What, are you half asleep? I know we're all upset, but we can't let it affect our work! God, I hope at least you set the lights right."

With that, Quentin swooped out to inspect the set.

The cameraman and electrician, insulted, stalked along behind. Pepe trailed out after.

Daphne came over to appease Cora and the costume lady. "Don't mind him. He's just jumpy. Your makeup's perfectly okay." She leaned in, peered critically at Cora. "Put a little powder on, just to keep him happy. Maybe touch up the eyes a bit. Aw, hell, you know what to do. I gotta get out there before he offends anyone else."

As Daphne scooted off, Flo took out her makeup kit. She didn't look happy.

"Don't mind them," Cora said. "Everybody's jumpy."

"Yeah." Flo took Cora's chin in her hands, twisted her face around, squinted at it. Her manner was more brusque than usual.

"What's the matter?"

"Nothing."

"Then I'd hate to see you when the answer's 'something.'"

"Try not to twitch."

Cora reached up, grabbed the hand with the eyebrow pencil. "Something's bothering you. If it's personal, it's none of my business. But if it's about the murder, I need to know."

"Why?"

"What do you mean, why?"

"Well, you caught the boy. If he did it, what difference does it make?"

"What difference does what make?"

Before Flo could answer, Freddy Fosterfield popped in the door. Though excluded from the earlier employees'-lounge meeting, Freddy had been accepted as a hanger-on, and was sometimes used by the crew as an unofficial production assistant. "They want you!" He seemed proud of the announcement.

"Almost ready, Freddy," Cora said.

"You're fine," Flo said. "Ow!" she added, as Cora kicked her in the shin.

"Freddy, be an angel and tell them I'll be there in two minutes."

Freddy, eager to be an angel, nodded and ducked out.

The costume mistress was nursing her injured shin.

"All right," Cora said, "before I kick you in the other leg, stop screwing around, Flo, and tell me what you know."

41

JENNIFER BLAYLOCK HAD COMBED HER HAIR, lined her eyes, and powdered her shiny nose. Actually, most likely the TV people had done it for her, but the smile was her own. She practically simpered in the presence of Rick Reed.

"*That's right,*" Jennifer said. "*Our first thought is the children, and I want to assure every parent out there that every step will be taken to keep this unfortunate event from touching your children's lives. The tour is going forward, we're not canceling a single store. The Puzzle Lady will be there, of course. And we will use the utmost care to protect your children from this tragic event. And that assurance comes not just from us, but from the media as well.*"

Rick Reed joined Jennifer in the shot. "*That's right, Jennifer. Channel 8 News is proud to help. We're pleased to join you in assuring the parents that their children will not be inconvenienced in any way by our coverage of this event. The camera will be discreet and unobtrusive.*"

"Someone wrote that word for him," Cora grumbled.

"Shh," Aaron said. "I want to hear."

"*This is Rick Reed, live, from Mystic, Connecticut.*"

"Live, hell," Aaron said. "The sun's out. It's gotta be about noon."

"It was live when they taped it," Cora said. "How do you like that? The girl forbids us to talk to Rick Reed, then turns around and does it herself."

"What do you make of that?" Aaron said.

"She's ambitious. Even more than I gave her credit for."

"And that's important because . . . ?"

"I have no idea whether it's important. It's a fact. Couple it with other facts, and a pattern begins to emerge."

"You can't couple with more than one other fact," Sherry said. "Then you have more than a couple."

Cora shook her head. "I have to warn you, Aaron, she's rather tough to live with."

"I stand warned."

Cora yawned, stretched. "Well, I guess I'll get back to my room."

"Not that I'm complaining, mind," Aaron said. "But why did you choose to watch the news with us?"

"I'm sick of hearing Becky bitch about living with a poodle."

"You're going back to your room?" Sherry said.

"Absolutely."

"You're not thinking of calling on any publicists, asking them what the hell they're doing on camera after forbidding everyone else?"

"Hell, no, what do I care? Since when did I ever want to be on camera?"

"I thought you might be curious."

"You thought wrong. I have no intention of doing anything of the kind. Good night, kids."

"You're going straight home?"

"I might have a smoke on the balcony, so I don't offend my prissy roommate." Cora opened the door and slipped out.

"Think she's going home?" Sherry asked.

"I don't know." Aaron got up, headed for the door. "But I wouldn't bet on it."

42

HE COULDN'T BELIEVE IT. *The police thought they had the killer. Everyone said so. It was all that damn lawyer's fault. Typical shyster's trick, not letting the kid speak. What a bad move that was. The kid was so dumb, you could tell in a minute he didn't do it. He didn't have the guts. He didn't have the nerve. Hell, it was a wonder he'd had the spine enough to flee.*

Of course, he had help. And what was that all about? It was okay, as long as he was missing. He could be presumed dead, another victim. Bring him back and shut him up, it's like hanging a sign KILLER around his neck.

What a depressing state of affairs. And what a horrible way to undermine his achievement. To make it look like something a sniveling worm like Lance could accomplish. It really wasn't fair.

Which meant something had to be done. To correct this mess. To give credit where credit's due. Well, not where credit's due, but at least not where credit wasn't. Lance must be cleared. Too bad he was so worthless. Where was the Free Lance movement?

He chuckled to himself. It was a good thing he had a sense of humor.

Otherwise he would be angry. Since he really was angry. Angry at the police. Angry at that silly woman on TV. How manipulative she was. Especially considering her role in the matter. It occurred to him she really should get her comeuppance. Of course, these things were so hard to plan. You had to take what life would give you in the overall scheme of things.

No you didn't. That was just the defeatist attitude talking. You made your own breaks, that's what you did. You pressed forward. All you needed was a little courage. Even a little artificial courage.

He reached in his jacket pocket, took out the crossword puzzle, unfolded it.

Nodded approvingly.

Yeah, that was what he needed.

He stuck it back in his jacket pocket, signaled the bartender for another drink.

43

Quentin, fortified by a couple more drinks than usual, had trouble fitting his key in the lock. Finally succeeding, he clicked it open, stepped in, switched on the light, and closed the door. He turned around and stopped dead.

Cora Felton sat in the overstuffed armchair facing him.

"Gee, Quent, late night?"

"What are you doing in my room?" he demanded.

"I was admiring the decor. Not to mention the amenities. This chair is so much nicer than anything I have in my motel room. You could fall asleep in this chair. I almost did, as a matter of fact."

"How did you get in here?"

Cora dangled the room key in front of him, smiled. "I conned the desk clerk. Not that hard to do when your face is on breakfast cereal. One of the perks of the job."

"But—"

"Why don't you sit down before you fall down. Go ahead, there's another nice chair. It's just to your left, if you're having trouble getting your bearings."

"What are you doing here?"

"We're going to have a little conversation. I hope you're sober enough to appreciate it."

Quentin flopped into the chair. His collar was unbuttoned, and he wore no tie. His jacket was rumpled. His hair wasn't mussed, but that was only because he wore a wig. "This can't be happening."

"I quite agree. That's why it's important to separate the wheat from the chaff." Cora frowned. "You know where that expression comes from? I guess some guy had a lot of chaff in his wheat. I don't know. Anyway, I'm trying to figure out if you're important or just another distraction."

Quentin didn't answer, stroked his chin.

"Where were you when Ginger Perkins was killed?"

He stared at Cora, as if the question had abruptly sobered him up. "I beg your pardon?"

"I'm talking about the murder case against Lance. There are two possibilities. Lance killed Ginger, or Lance didn't kill Ginger. If Lance didn't kill Ginger, someone else did. Where were you when Ginger was killed?"

"I don't know when she was killed."

"Good answer. You must have been practicing it, to come right out with it even when you're drunk."

The producer scowled. Blinked his eyes. "Wait a minute. You're not the police. You're a goddamned actress. I *hired* you. You work for me."

"Well, I like to think of it as working for the greater good of children everywhere." That irony went right over his head. Cora continued, "However, you have a point. If I send you to jail, I probably lose my job. I'd hate that. Not that I love this commercial. I've just grown fond of cashing the paycheck."

"How can you joke?"

"Heartless, I know. But the girl's dead, nothing's going to bring her back, and I didn't kill her. Did you?"

"Don't be absurd."

"It's not as absurd as you think. Look around you. Nice room. I couldn't understand why you'd do that. Alienate the crew by choosing better accommodations, when our motel had empty rooms. It's such a bonehead move for a producer to make. There just had to be a reason why."

Quentin said nothing, glowered at her.

"The answer, of course, is mobility. To be able to come and go without being seen. To slip out, if you wanted, to spy on the crew. To keep an eye on what's going on. You're married, aren't you, Quent? Two point four kids. House in Scarsdale. Six-figure salary. Mercedes Benz. Be a shame to lose all that."

"What are you talking about?"

"You had your eye on Ginger Perkins. It's no secret. You're just lucky the police place Lance and her together right before the killing. Lance couldn't deny it because he wasn't here. Now he's back and isn't talking. If he were, he'd have to admit it was true. After all, he was rooming with her, and enough people had seen them together.

"The police haven't traced her movements earlier that night, at least not well, or they might have noticed she disappeared from the motel bar for a goodly stretch of time. Could that possibly have been to have a drink with someone at a higher-class motel? Someone who was staying at a higher-class motel just to afford her that opportunity. That would at least answer the question of why he would be stupid enough to miff the crew with the luxury digs. I assume you had a drink in the bar and got her back to your room. According to the medical examiner, she didn't put out. Which probably ticked you off, particularly when she went running back to Lance. I wonder if that ticked you off enough to tag along behind."

"You're crazy!"

"Well, I wouldn't spread that around. It doesn't reflect well on you, hiring a madwoman."

He said nothing, breathed deeply, continued to glare.

"There is another possibility. Wanna hear it? Suppose you *didn't* try to put the make on the girl."

"Damn right."

"Suppose you killed her for another reason. Suppose you killed her just because she was there."

"You're loco."

Cora shook her head, disapprovingly. "Too close to *you're crazy.* I know you're drunk, but you really need to vary your responses."

"God save me!"

"Better. Look here, you wouldn't be trying to kid me, now, would you? Suppose you left your motel, wandered over to mine, ran into the girl, and she got in your way."

"You're nuts."

"I had a feeling I was. You could do with a good thesaurus."

"When she got in the way of my doing what?"

"Ah, so you *do* hear what I say. I'm impressed. Try the concept. You're up to no good. The girl sees you, and has to be killed."

Quentin shook his head as if to clear it. Every hair stayed in place. The effect was oddly disconcerting. "I don't know what you're getting at, but you're wrong. I was nowhere near that motel. Anyone who says different is a liar. No one saw me there, did they? Of course not. You're just making it up."

"I'm just asking questions."

"Well, you're wasting your time. You know it, and I know it. Leave me alone. Let me get some sleep."

Quentin heaved himself out of the chair and flopped down on the bed. Jacket, shoes, and all.

Cora frowned.

Quentin seemed pretty confident about no one being able to place him at the motel.

She almost believed him.

44

SHERRY WAS GETTING CONCERNED. Aaron wasn't back yet. He'd followed Cora to her room to make sure she'd stayed put. Fat chance of that. Even so, he should have checked in. It wasn't like he'd run off to interview Becky Baldwin. Becky was back. She'd called Sherry to ask who the hell was going to walk the dog, and confirmed what Sherry already knew: that Cora and Aaron were nowhere to be seen.

Sherry was tempted to go after them. But she'd just miss them, and then they'd be back and she'd be gone. And she wasn't particularly keen on wandering around alone in the dark with a murderer on the loose. Not that she wasn't brave, just that it was the type of thing girls did in scary movies dumb enough to make people yell at the screen.

Even so, enough was enough. She couldn't just sit here.

There came a knock on the door. What a relief. Aaron had forgotten his keys. Wasn't that typical.

Sherry hopped out of bed, opened the door.

Dennis pushed his way into the room. His eyes were wide,

glassy. His hair was mussed. His suit jacket hung crooked, half off one shoulder. He had a crazed look on his face.

"Dennis!"

"You're alone. Good."

"Dennis! What are you doing here?"

"We need to talk."

"No we don't. You're married. To Brenda."

"Yeah. That's one of the things we need to talk about."

"You look strange. Are you on drugs?"

"No. Not really. A little."

"Dennis, you have to go."

"I gotta see you. It was so awkward the last time. We couldn't talk."

"Dennis—"

"You see what Brenda does? Stalks me? What kind of a marriage is that?"

"She stalked you because she thought you were coming here. I don't know why she would think that. Could it be because you were coming here?"

Dennis smiled. "Good to see you, Sherry."

He eyed her appreciatively. Sherry became aware of the fact she was in her nightgown. It had seemed perfectly adequate with Aaron and Cora in the room. With Dennis, it suddenly seemed skimpy. She slipped on her robe, pulled it around her. The damn thing was too short, the material transparent.

"Where does Brenda think you are now?"

Dennis frowned. "I'm at a salesmen's conference. Till tomorrow. In Cleveland. I put a DO NOT DISTURB sign on my door, and phoned in sick to my group. They think I just drank too much."

"You've been drinking too?"

"No, they just think that." Dennis scowled as she sniffed for whiskey. "Well, maybe a little. So where's the paperboy? Not that I miss him. I'm just curious. Or is that your own shirt?"

Sherry flushed slightly in spite of herself. "Aaron went to check on Cora. He should be back soon."

"Tell me, what do you see in him?"

"We are not discussing Aaron."

"*You* are not discussing Aaron. You are not discussing us. You got a lot of taboos."

"There's a restraining order, Dennis."

"That's just legal mumbo jumbo. Like wedding vows." Dennis reached in his jacket pocket, pulled out a piece of paper. "Some things are more important than vows. You know what this is? Guess what I been working on. Crossword puzzles. And not just solving them. I can construct them. Amazing what you can do with the right motivation. I constructed this one, just for you."

The motel door clicked open and Aaron came in. "What are you doing here?" He pointed to the paper. "What's that?"

Dennis shoved the paper into his pocket. "Come in, Aaron. We were just discussing you."

"What the hell?"

"We were doing no such thing," Sherry retorted. "Don't let him bait you, Aaron."

"What *were* you doing?"

"What do you think, Aaron?" Dennis said gleefully. With Aaron in the room, Dennis had slipped into his most mocking tone. He was also quite obviously ogling Sherry's bare legs.

Aaron scowled. "Dennis, I've had just about enough out of you. I don't know what you're doing here, and I don't much care. Get the hell out!"

"Or what?" Dennis sneered. "You'll throw me out?"

Aaron set his feet, clenched his fists. "Yeah."

Sherry rushed to Aaron, grabbed his arms. "No. That's not necessary. Dennis is leaving. Aren't you, Dennis? Or do I have to call your wife?"

Dennis's eyes faltered. He pulled himself up, brushed by Aaron, knocking the young reporter back a step.

Dennis turned in the doorway. "She never made that threat till you showed up and got all macho. What's the matter, Sherry? Just trying to save the paperboy from getting a licking?"

"I'm warning you, Dennis."

"Yeah, yeah. I stand warned."

Dennis stalked out and slammed the door.

"What the hell was he doing here?" Aaron demanded.

"What do you think? Is Cora back?"

"Yeah."

"Where'd she go?"

"To that motel. To see the producer. What's-his-name. Quentin something. Then she went back to her room."

"She know you were following her?"

"Not unless she's psychic. Sherry—"

"I didn't ask him, Aaron. I don't want him here, I didn't do anything to lure him here, I'm not happy that he's here. You want me to call the police, I'll call the police, but they're gonna get the wrong idea."

"How do you know it's the wrong idea?"

"Did Dennis kill that girl?"

"No."

"Then it's the wrong idea."

Aaron frowned. "What was that paper he didn't want me to see? The one he shoved in his pocket?"

Sherry sighed. "Would you believe a crossword puzzle?"

45

JENNIFER BLAYLOCK NEVER FELT SO HIGH. She'd never gotten publicity for herself before. What a rush! Coupled with what she'd done for her product, it was a publicist's dream. She was not only hyping the tour, she was hyping the *fact* that she was hyping the tour. She was boosting her career as much as she was boosting Granville Grains. Her next job wouldn't be for some dumb cereal company. Her next job would be for an actor or actress. Or for a *movie,* even. Or for a motion picture *studio.*

God, it was so exciting, she could barely stand it.

That on-camera reporter thought she was hot stuff. Taking her out to dinner. Lord, what was she going to do if he tried something? She had to be very careful with her image. Particularly with the media. Even if the media was buying.

Jennifer lifted her glass off the bar, realized she'd drained it. She was drinking Black Russians, not that she knew what they were, really, but she'd seen an actress drink them on TV. Cameron Diaz? She couldn't remember. But they were kind of sweet, and didn't make her gag like whiskey did. She doubted they had any alcohol in them at all.

Where was Rick? That was his name. It seemed like he went to the bathroom a long time ago. He should be back. It wasn't like they had a line in the men's room like they sometimes did in the ladies' room. Of course, not in a bar like this.

What did it matter? What was she thinking about? She wasn't sure. Maybe those things *did* have some alcohol.

So where *was* he?

It occurred to Jennifer he might have gone out to his van. She went to look.

He was such a gentleman. And so interested in her life. So many questions. About her. And her profession. And the shoot. Good thing she'd kept her wits about her. Hadn't told him anything.

Hey! The van was gone! It had to be. You couldn't miss it. It had a big CHANNEL 8 on the side. Rick had made a joke about it, how it wasn't a Mercedes Benz, but you could always find it. But she couldn't find it. It was gone.

It took a few moments for her to realize that meant Rick Reed was gone too.

Jennifer stood, blinking at the parking lot, first confused, then slightly angry. Now, why was she angry? What did she have to be angry about? Right. Here she was at a bar. Stranded. No way to get back to the motel. Now, why was that? Because she'd been *left* in the bar. By the reporter. The nice reporter, who'd asked so many questions, had left her in the bar.

All alone.

Jennifer stood there a few minutes while the realization she'd been ditched and the subsequent emotions swept over her. Like hurt. A tear ran down her cheek. She wiped it away. Snuffled her nose. Took a long leap toward sobriety.

She remembered. The bar was within walking distance of the motel. The only reason they'd taken the van was because they'd had dinner first. If they'd come from the motel they would have walked. The crew members had walked. She'd seen Pepe there earlier. And the light man. What the hell was his name? She really did need to know the names of the crew. It would help her in the long run.

Jennifer went back in and looked around the bar. There were none of the crew members left. She hadn't seen them go, but apparently they had. In fact, there weren't many people left in the bar at all. Just a few locals. She'd have to walk back alone.

With a killer at large.

Except he wasn't at large. He was in jail.

The thought comforted her for a moment before she remembered Lance wasn't the killer. At least, she had reason to believe that he wasn't. She had inside information that might cast doubt on his guilt.

As Jennifer wandered back outside, she didn't *quite* make the connection that in that case the real killer might still be on the loose.

So which way was the motel?

Jennifer found herself stumbling through the parking lot looking for a clue. She came to the mouth of the driveway. There were lights down the street to the right. Could that be it? Somehow it didn't seem like it. Down the street to the left the lights were farther in the distance, and they occasionally moved. Of course. The motel was on the other side of the highway.

Jennifer stumbled along the road, found she was on a sidewalk on a street of private homes. Frame beach houses that merely looked like looming shadows. Some had lights inside, but most were dark. How late was it?

A dark shadow loomed up ahead.

The highway.

The street passed under the highway.

A wide highway overpass, no problem in the daylight.

A jet-black tunnel now.

Jennifer didn't want to do it. She stopped, peered ahead. Considered the alternative: climbing the embankment, crossing Interstate 95. Not in her wildest dreams.

Her heart thumping, Jennifer pushed into the inky tunnel. Almost immediately, she could see the light on the other side. It wasn't that far away. It just seemed like it.

What were the night noises around her? Rats scurrying? Drunks sleeping it off? Muggers, and killers, and rapists, and murderers?

Jennifer tiptoed along.

Muggers and killers and rapists, oh my!

The first truck nearly blew her away, roaring overhead on 95 like a jet plane taking off. It took a moment for Jennifer to realize what it was. Even that was no comfort. She could imagine the overpass collapsing, the highway caving in, the truck crashing down.

She quickened her step.

Suddenly she was out. The highway and tunnel were behind her. The motel a few blocks up ahead.

Thank God.

Jennifer started for it.

Something moved!

Jennifer froze, terrified.

It was only a cat.

Jennifer let out a nervous giggle.

How foolish she felt. Afraid of a cat.

A shadow loomed up ahead. It seemed to come out of nowhere. Big, tall, menacing. This was no cat.

Jennifer shrank back in alarm.

"Hello, Jennifer."

Relief flowed through her. Not a killer. Someone who knew her name. A friend. But who? Rick Reed? It didn't sound like Rick.

The figure stepped out of the shadows, into the light.

Jennifer peered through the darkness.

Recognition poured over her. Relief. And then surprise. "What are you doing here?"

He took a step closer.

"Come here. I'll tell you."

If it hadn't been for the alcohol in the Black Russians, she might have noticed the slight catch in his voice, the suppressed, hysterical giggle of exhilaration.

46

CORA BARELY HEARD THE SCRATCHING ON THE DOOR. At first she thought it was Buddy, wanting to get out. But he was sleeping on the bed. As the scratching persisted he opened a bleary eye, closed it again.

"Some guard dog," Cora muttered.

She sighed and sat up. The room was dark, but there was light under the bathroom door and Becky's bed was unoccupied.

Cora grabbed her purse off the nightstand, reached in and pulled out her gun, went to the door. "Who is it?"

"It's me."

The voice was faint. Unrecognizable.

Cora clicked the safety off. Her fifth husband, Melvin, had advised her never to shoot anyone with the safety on. It was her only fond memory of Melvin.

Cora opened the door a crack, peered out.

The costume lady stood there.

Cora let out an ejaculation indicating Flo was a person of low IQ involved in romantic coupling illegal in several states. The woman, shocked and startled, gasped. Cora unobtrusively stuck the gun in the waistband of her pajama bottoms. She grabbed Flo by the arm, yanked her into the room, and slammed the door.

"All right, what the hell do you think you're doing?"

"I thought you might be up."

"So you scratched on my door?"

"I wasn't sure."

"You weren't sure what?"

"If you were up. If you weren't, I didn't want to wake you."

"Assume I'm up. What do you want?"

"I didn't want to leave you with the wrong impression. This afternoon. What I said about Quentin."

"I didn't get the wrong impression."

"But it seemed important. With the boy in jail."

Becky Baldwin came out of the bathroom drying her hair with a towel. "What seemed important?"

"Hell!" Cora said.

The costume mistress frowned. "And you are?"

"The boy's lawyer." Becky switched on the bedside lamp. "If you've got anything that seems important, I need to know."

"It's nothing, really. It's just earlier that night I saw the producer make a play for Ginger."

Cora rolled her eyes.

"You don't say!" Becky grinned. "That wraps up this case, thank you very much."

"Except for the fact that the killer's still on the loose," Cora said sarcastically.

"Not my job. If the police can't convict this pervert producer, it's none of my business."

"That's just it," Flo said. "I think you've got the wrong idea." She turned on Cora. "I didn't want to tell you what I did. You forced it out of me. It was a little fact. It bothered me, I know. But I don't for a moment think that Quentin did it."

Becky smiled. "Just as long as you don't mind if the jury gets the idea."

"Hell, I was almost in bed. In fact, I *was* in bed," Cora grumped. "Then you come scratching with your guilt trip. What the hell time is it anyway? One-fifteen. Wonderful. I bet nobody else is up."

"No, there was a man in the parking lot," Flo said.

"Great. It's one in the morning and you're running around with some strange man in the parking lot. Didn't you ever see any horror movies?"

"Not a stranger. The guy who was here the other day. With his wife."

Cora stopped dead. "With his wife? Now or the other day?"

Flo blinked. "He's here now. His wife was here the other day."

"You mean Dennis?" Becky asked.

"I don't know his name. Why are you so interested?"

"He happens to be my client."

"I thought Lance was your client."

"They both are."

"Fine. Can I go now? I don't mean to make trouble. I just didn't want you thinking that about Quentin. I mean, thinking *I* thought that about Quentin. That would be awful. People getting the wrong idea just because of me."

"No one's getting the wrong idea," Cora said. "Why don't you go back to sleep?"

"Now you got me worried about the man in the parking lot."

"I'll go with you," Becky volunteered.

"I was kidding. And you're not dressed."

"Big deal." Becky threw off her robe, pulled on a T-shirt, and hopped into a pair of shorts. Houdini never changed so quickly. "I'm ready."

"If you're interested in the guy in the parking lot, I think he left."

"Gee, those are the breaks." Becky stepped into a pair of sandals. "Come on, I'll walk you back to your room."

Cora grinned as Becky ushered her reasonable doubt out the door. "Just between you and me, Buddy, I think these people are nuts. You wanna go for a walk, or you wanna go to sleep?"

Buddy moved on the bed and curled up on a pillow.

"Good call. Let me freshen up, and I'll be right with you."

Cora went in the bathroom and brushed her teeth to get the sleepy taste out of her mouth. That was the worst of being woken up. Your mouth tasted bad.

Cora turned off the bathroom light and started back to bed. She stopped, looking at Becky's bedside lamp. "Whaddya think, Buddy? Should I leave that on so she can see her way back to bed, or turn it off so she breaks her damn neck?"

The poodle said nothing.

"Good call." Cora switched off Becky's light, groped her way over to the bed, and lay down.

Almost immediately, there came a knock on the door.

Great. Becky forgot her key.

Cora heaved herself out of bed, stubbed her toe, cursed herself for turning out the light. She switched it on, opened the door.

Sherry Carter came in. She was white as a sheet. She was trembling slightly, and appeared on the verge of hysterics.

"Sherry! What's the matter?"

"I had a fight with Aaron."

"About what?"

"About Dennis."

"You can't help how he's acting."

"Aaron doesn't see it that way."

Cora took Sherry's hands. "Come on, sit down, tell me about it."

Sherry pulled away. "I'm too upset to sit down."

"Where's Aaron?"

"I don't know."

"Oh?"

"He went out. He didn't come back."

"How long ago?"

"I don't know," Sherry snapped. "What difference does it make?" She pointed to the empty bed. "Where's Becky?"

"Talking to the costume lady."

"At one in the morning?"

"Yeah. Didn't you see her?"

"No, I didn't."

"What's the matter? You think she's with Aaron?"

"No, I don't think she's with Aaron," Sherry snapped. "Look, can we take a walk?"

"What?"

"I'm too nervous to stay still. I've got to move around."

"You want to take a walk?"

A high-pitched yip from the bed signified Buddy was ready to go. "Looks like you got a customer. Let me get his leash."

"Where is it?" Sherry glanced around.

"Let me see, where did I put it?"

"Come on, come on."

"Hold your horses. You're worse than the dog. Ah, there it is." Cora pointed to the closet doorknob.

Sherry grabbed the leash, called the dog.

Cora picked up her bathrobe from the chair, tugged it on. She slipped her motel key in the pocket, followed her niece out the door.

Sherry and Buddy were already on their way down the steps. Cora wasn't sure who was pulling who. Muttering to herself, she hurried to catch up.

The parking lot was empty. There was no sign of Aaron, Dennis, Becky, the costume lady, and whoever else was roaming around at that ungodly hour.

Buddy scampered across the lot, headed for an island of grass between the in and out driveways. Sherry stood impatiently looking around while Buddy lifted his leg, then yanked him off in the direction of the highway.

"Slow down! If you're going to drag that dog, give him to me." Cora hurried up, snatched the leash from Sherry's hand. "You think Aaron's out with Becky, is that it?"

"No."

"You think he went after Dennis?"

"I don't know."

"The costume lady saw Dennis in the parking lot. She didn't see Aaron."

Sherry didn't answer, set off down the street.

Cora followed at a slower pace, allowing Buddy to sniff.

The overpass to the highway loomed up ahead.

Cora found Buddy pulling her along. Keeping pace with the little dog, she caught up with Sherry.

"You know, Aaron's probably back in the room," Cora ventured.

"Yip!"

Buddy jerked the leash out of Cora's hands, darted into the shadow of the overpass.

"Buddy!"

Cora had an instant of panic while her brain processed the information that Buddy had darted *under* the highway, not across it. Instead of dodging eighteen-wheelers, he was safe under the overpass. Even so, she hurried into the shadows to corral him.

Cora could see the tuft of his tail wagging in the darkness ahead. She hurried up, bent to take the leash, and gasped.

Jennifer Blaylock lay on her back in a pile of rubble. Her head lolled, her eyes bulged. Her mouth hung open. Her right leg was straight, her left leg drawn up and bent sideways. Her hands were symmetrically folded across her stomach. The fingers were not intertwined. The hands seemed molded together as if holding an invisible flagpole.

Cora wheeled on Sherry. "Is this what you wanted me to see?"

Sherry said nothing, merely shivered.

"Damn it, Sherry! Did you know she was here?"

Headlights appeared on the far side of the underpass, hurtled toward them down the street. A police car whizzed under the highway and screeched to a stop, the headlights lighting up the body.

Jerry and Phil got out, followed by Aaron Grant.

"What are you doing here?" Aaron said.

"Stand back!" Phil ordered.

"Get that dog out of there!" Jerry cried.

Cora picked up Buddy, but held her ground.

The young cop whistled. "It's a homicide, all right." Jerry squinted at Aaron. "I thought you said she was holding something. A crossword puzzle, wasn't it?"

"That's right."

"So where is it?"

Sherry couldn't meet Cora's eyes.

Cora took a breath, stepped in front of her niece. "Officer, there's something you should know."

47

"You're sure you don't want a lawyer?" Apparently Jerry had seen too many cop shows about bad busts and cases thrown out of court, and was really paranoid about violating Cora's rights.

"I don't want a lawyer," Cora assured the cop.

"You have the right to an attorney. Just so you understand that—"

"I understand it. My roommate's an attorney. Unfortunately, she happens to represent everyone and his brother in this case. Unless you're dropping the charges against Lance, for instance, there would be a conflict of interest."

"You claim she's also representing Dennis Pride?"

"Yes."

"Isn't that a conflict of interest?"

"Not my problem. I just can't have her representing me."

The young cop frowned. "If you are unable to hire an attorney, an attorney can be appointed for you."

Cora's smile was maternal. "Sweetheart, does it look like I did this crime?"

"Aren't you about to confess to withholding evidence?"

Cora waved it away. "Oh, pooh."

"It's a serious charge."

"*If* you can make it stick. And you can't."

"Yes, I can. You're confessing, for goodness' sakes."

"I'm doing nothing of the sort. I'm telling you what happened."

"What happened is you obstructed justice."

"No, I didn't. But it's nice of you to say so."

The door to the interrogation room opened and a man in shirt-sleeves and gabardine pants came in. He was young, though not as young as the cop. His hair was uncombed. He looked like he'd probably been asleep. Which was not that surprising at two in the morning.

"Miss Felton, how do you do. I'm Samuel Dawson. I'm the district attorney."

"Pleased to meetya," Cora said. "You'll pardon me if I don't get up, but this young sharpshooter here just accused me of obstruction of justice, and I'd like to be able to say I took it sitting down."

The prosecutor frowned. "That's more than I can handle till I've had some coffee. Jerry, what's going on here?"

"This woman's confessing to withholding evidence. I told her she should have a lawyer, but she wouldn't listen."

D.A. Dawson flopped into a chair. "What's this evidence you're withholding?"

"I'm *not* withholding it. I'm *presenting* it, for what it's worth. It's a crossword puzzle, allegedly found on the body."

"And just where is this puzzle?"

"Sonny boy's got it in an evidence bag."

Jerry held up the bag for Dawson to see.

"It isn't solved?" the D.A. asked.

"No, but I have a solved xerox copy." Cora handed it over. "You can look at it if you like, but the long answers are all that matter. They say, in effect, 'This could have been you.' "

He nodded. "And you didn't think this was important enough to communicate to the police?"

"Well, now you're taking Junior's tack. And I thought we were going to get along."

"That was when you assured me you weren't withholding evidence."

"I'm not. As I was attempting to explain to young McCloud here, the puzzle was given to me by Jennifer Blaylock. She claimed to have found it on the body of the actress Ginger Perkins. But I had no way of knowing if that was true. Even less now."

"I'm beginning to sympathize with Jerry. Miss Felton, I believe a second body has been found."

"That's right."

"I understand you found it."

"Well, I wouldn't want to take all the credit. Aaron Grant found it first."

"And this second body just happens to be the woman you mentioned. The one who gave you the puzzle. Miss Jennifer Blaylock. And could you tell me how you came to find her body?"

"My niece had a fight with her boyfriend. She was upset. She came to my motel room. Our talking disturbed the dog, who wanted to go out."

"You have a dog in your motel room?"

"Don't tell the manager, will you? I'm in enough trouble as it is."

"Could you stick to the subject?"

"Well, you asked about the dog."

"Yeah, you did."

"Jerry, damn it!"

"Sorry, sir."

"You took your dog for a walk at one in the morning?"

"He had to go."

"A big dog?"

"A toy poodle."

"Then it would be no protection."

"I didn't bring the dog for protection."

"So you went walking around at one o'clock at night with a killer on the loose. Did you have a flashlight?"

"No. I had something better."

"Oh? What's that?"

Cora reached into her purse, dropped her gun on the table.

The prosecutor's mouth fell open. He wheeled on the young cop. "You let her bring a *gun* into the interrogation room?"

Jerry was mortified. "I had no idea!"

"How could you have no idea?"

"Well, I didn't frisk her. It's not like she was under arrest."

"Boys, boys," Cora said. "No big deal. I got a permit for the sucker. I didn't shoot anybody. If you wanna hold on to it until I leave, that's fine with me."

"You want me to check it in at the desk?" Jerry said.

"That's an excellent idea," Dawson told him. "Then go see if Phil needs any help."

"You don't need help here?"

"Oh, I think I'll be safe. Particularly if you have the gun. You don't have any *other* weapons, do you, Miss Felton?"

Cora frowned thoughtfully. "It's been so long since I cleaned out my purse. But, no, I think I'd remember that."

Jerry went out with the gun.

Dawson turned to Cora, smiled. "Now, then, Miss Felton. We have no witnesses, no one's taking this down, and it's somewhat past my bedtime. Would you care to expedite the situation?"

"I like the way you think. Unfortunately, I'm rather low on the totem pole of information."

"But you have the crossword puzzle that was found on the body."

"Yeah, but I didn't find it."

"I said we didn't need to be technical."

"And it wasn't on the body. At least not tonight's body. It was purportedly found on the first one."

"So you said. What about the crossword puzzle found on tonight's body?"

"I have no knowledge of that."

"Neither do I. I'm going on what people told me. Some guy

found the body and called it in. He said there was a crossword puzzle with the body. When he got back with the cops, it was gone."

"If you say so."

"Weren't you there when the cops arrived?"

"I was."

"Then you know the puzzle was gone."

"No, I don't."

"Yes, you do. You saw the body, didn't you?"

"Yeah. So?"

"Was the puzzle there?"

"No. There was no puzzle there."

"Then you know it was gone."

"No, I don't know it was *gone*. I know it wasn't *there*. But I have no knowledge of whether it was *ever* there. If I didn't know it was *there*, I can't know it was *gone*."

"You're splitting hairs with me, Miss Felton."

"No, I'm telling you the absolute truth. My niece and I went out with our dog. We found the body. There was no crossword puzzle on the body."

"Then the police showed up?"

"Yes."

"The young man was with them?"

"Yes."

"And he said there was a crossword puzzle on the body?"

"Actually, I believe the *police* said that he said that there was a crossword puzzle on the body. I'm not sure it matters whether you're dealing with second- or thirdhand hearsay."

"You never saw that puzzle?"

"That's right."

"How do you know it wasn't this crossword puzzle?"

"Because I had it in my purse."

"Could it have been the same puzzle?"

"I beg your pardon?"

"Could it have been a copy of the same puzzle? A duplicate? Could it have been that?"

"It could have been the Declaration of Independence for all I know. Anything's possible. I didn't see it, so I have no idea."

"And that puzzle there says it could have been you?"

"That's right."

"And the publicist found it. And then it *was* her? Is that what happened?"

"Ah . . . yes."

"You don't sound convinced."

"I'm sure those are the facts. I just don't agree with your inference. I don't think the puzzle was intended for the publicist. I think she just happened to find it. I think it was intended for me."

"So who do you think sent it?"

"I have no idea."

"You don't suspect anyone?"

Cora felt a flush of guilt. She suspected Freddy Fosterfield, but she didn't want to give him up. Cora wasn't sure whether she felt guilty about suspecting Freddy or about protecting him.

"What are you doing here?" she asked Dawson, changing the subject instead. "You're the prosecutor. You're not brought in until the police make an arrest."

Dawson smiled. "You underestimate your importance."

"Me? You're here for me?"

"Not entirely. But busting the Puzzle Lady isn't going to play well in the press. I got enough media trouble as it is."

"What do you mean?"

"Near as we can tell, last person to see the victim alive was Rick Reed of Channel 8 News."

"You've got to be kidding."

"I wish I were. I don't suspect the guy for a minute, but I can't give him a free pass just 'cause he's on TV. It's a hell of a situation. If I go after him, Channel 8 will crucify me. If I don't, all the other stations will make a stink."

"What's Rick say?"

"Not much. He bought the girl some drinks, pumped her for whatever information she had, and ditched her in the bar. I'd say that's probably true. If so, it's not criminal. It should be, but it isn't."

"Where's Rick now?"

"Right down the hall. We're holding him so no one can say we didn't."

"Did he see anything? In the bar, I mean. Anyone paying her undue attention?"

"He says he didn't notice. Of course, he wouldn't. Being a celebrity, and all that. So used to people gawking at him."

"Is that a direct quote?"

"Practically. So far, we've got no help."

"At least it gets Lance off the hook."

"Who?"

"The kid you tabbed for the first one. He couldn't have done this one while he was in jail."

"No, he couldn't. Unfortunately, his hotshot lawyer got him sprung."

"Really? Becky never mentioned it."

"Becky didn't do it. The kid called his mother. Mom rushed a high-powered New York attorney up here and raised hell. So the kid was out, and could have killed her just fine."

"Those big-city shysters always mess things up."

"Can I quote you on that? Anyway, the kid's not out of the woods. Lucky for him, we have a better suspect."

"Who's that?"

"Guy who shows up every time there's a killing." Dawson flipped his notebook open. "One Dennis Pride. Who, I understand, was married to your niece."

"So what? Dennis had absolutely no reason to kill either of these women."

"You're forgetting the crossword puzzle. *'It should have been you.'* If the murders were a warning, that's your motive right there."

Cora expressed her opinion of that theory in terms a sailor might use.

Dawson had a narrow escape from a blush. "What's wrong with that theory?"

"Give me a break. Dennis wouldn't be warning me."

"What if he's warning his ex-wife?"

"If he is, I'll buy you a pizza. I've been wooed a lot of ways in my day, but no one ever won my heart by dropping corpses in my lap. Trust me, your killer isn't Dennis."

"There's evidence against him. The crossword puzzle. The one that wasn't there. The one he showed your niece just before the commission of the crime."

"Sherry told you that?"

"No. She's been most uncooperative. But she told the reporter, and he told us."

"What does Dennis say?"

"Nothing. He skipped out. That's another strike against him."

"Where's Sherry now?"

"We let her go."

"Oh?"

"Her and the reporter. He told us all he knows. She hasn't told us anything. The lawyer lady was clamoring at us to spring 'em." Dawson shrugged. "So I let 'em go together. I thought it might be interesting."

"That's a hell of an understatement, Counselor."

48

"I CAN'T BELIEVE YOU DID THAT," Aaron Grant said from the backseat.

Sherry, sitting up front, stuck her nose in the air. "I haven't the faintest idea what you're talking about."

"Kids," Becky intervened, "try to hold it together until we get out of the parking lot. You never know who might be listening."

"It's two in the morning, Becky," Aaron pointed out.

"That's a news van right over there. Rick Reed may be in jail, but his crew's filming anything they can get."

"Why are they even here?"

"Are you kidding? They want to shoot Rick's release. And if they don't get him, they might just use footage of us. Smile at the camera, kids." Becky swung the car out of the police station parking lot, beaming.

"Damn it, Sherry," Aaron said. "You can't keep covering for Dennis."

"I am not covering for Dennis."

"Did you cooperate with the police?"

"That's not the point."

"Of course it's the point. Why wouldn't you cooperate with the police?"

"Do we have to have this conversation in front of Becky?"

"You want me to hop out?" Becky suggested. "I happen to be driving, but I could always pull over."

"I'm glad you think it's funny," Aaron said.

"I don't think it's funny. Dennis is my client. Why are you trying to make a case against him?"

"I'm not. I'm just reporting the facts."

"The facts you're reporting all have to do with Dennis. If you're not making a case against him, why are they important?"

"Hey! I got enough trouble with Sherry. If the two of you team up on me—"

"We're not teaming up on you," Sherry said. "Stop changing the subject. You went out of your way to tell the cops there was a cross-word puzzle on the body just because I told you Dennis had one."

"I didn't go out of my way. I reported it. It was a detail I happened to notice. I would have had to be blind not to. If I didn't report it, I would either be stupid or deliberately concealing evidence."

"It's not evidence."

"How do you know?"

"Come on, Aaron," Sherry said. "Do you really believe Dennis killed this woman and then stuck a crossword puzzle in her hands?"

"No, I don't."

"Then why would you want the police to think so?"

"Wait a minute," Aaron protested. "Why am I on the defensive here? What about the missing puzzle?"

"Are you making an accusation?"

"I'm asking a question."

"You want me to tell you in front of Becky?"

"I thought she was your lawyer."

"She's *everybody's* lawyer. What about it, Becky? Can I talk to you in front of Aaron?"

"Technically, no. The presence of a third party negates the attorney-client privilege. On the other hand, anything you tell him is fair game anyway."

"Wouldn't it be hearsay?" Aaron objected.

"Not if it's an admission against interest. They could put you on the stand and make you tell what she said."

"Couldn't I take the Fifth?"

"You can't refuse to answer on the grounds it might incriminate *me*," Sherry said. "You have to refuse on the grounds it might incriminate *you*."

"Is that right?" Aaron demanded.

"God save me!" Becky wheeled the car into the motel lot. "Okay, kids, everybody out."

"What about you?"

"I gotta go get Cora."

"The cops will drive her back."

"Assuming they let her out."

"They'll let her out," Aaron said. "Come on, Becky, you got me worried."

"What have you got to be worried about?"

"The missing puzzle. I saw it, and now it's gone, and Dennis had one."

"It's nice of you to be so concerned about Dennis," Sherry said, icily.

"Don't be dumb. I'm talking about you. If you took that puzzle, you're in a lot of trouble."

"Nice of you to say 'if.' "

"Damn it, I'm not kidding around. If the police decide to proceed against Sherry, would I have to testify against her?"

"Yes." Becky shrugged. "Unless you were married."

49

DENNIS PRIDE COULDN'T FIND A TUNE HE LIKED. He kept pressing the buttons on the radio from Z-100, to Classic Rock, to Lite FM, and every song seemed to grate. What was the matter with the bands these days? They just weren't playing like they used to. The stuff that passed for music. It was deplorable.

The fact that Dennis was sampling a range of songs from doo-wop to techno-pop did not occur to him. Nor did he notice the groups he was disparaging included the Beatles, the Stones, and the Grateful Dead. If the truth be known, Dennis's real concern with modern music was the fact that he wasn't playing it. Since quitting the band, all tunes seemed lacking.

That was the problem. The damn job. How could you be happy if you were doing something you didn't like?

How could you be happy?

His thoughts turned to Brenda. If he noticed any significance in the segue, Dennis didn't let himself admit it. Brenda would be asleep when he got home. At least, she'd *better* be asleep when he got home. She'd better not be in the car behind him, hurtling through Yonkers on the Cross County, heading for the Saw Mill Parkway South. But, no, it couldn't be her. There was no way she could hold her tongue that long. No way she wouldn't have run him off the road and beaten him into submission with the tire iron. And he couldn't do anything about it. Because of Daddy. It wasn't easy working for your father-in-law.

Dennis merged onto the Saw Mill, which quickly became the Henry Hudson. He whizzed through Riverdale, headed for the toll booth connecting the Bronx with the island of Manhattan. There were no cars on the bridge, no lines at the toll booths. He could have gone through the cash lane, but there was no need. As he pulled up to the booth, the light flashed GO EZ PASS, and the gate went up.

Too late, Dennis realized that toll would be on his monthly bill. Along with the time and the date. So if Brenda went over the charges, she would find a record of when he got back to the City tonight. And it would be just like her to go over the bill, and then nag him about where he'd been. Well, too late now. Dennis drove on through.

A police car parked just beyond the toll booth pulled out and tagged along behind. After a moment, the cop turned on his lights.

Dennis saw the red and blue flashing in his rearview mirror. His mind raced. Had he sped up to the toll? Probably. What was the limit on the damn bridge anyway? Who could possibly care at four in the morning? Some dumb-ass cop bent on making his quota. Of all the luck.

Dennis was in no mood for this. Why did it have to happen now?

He pulled the car off to the side of the road, sat seething as the cop came strolling up.

Dennis powered down his window.

The cop was a bullnecked man with no visible sense of humor. "Step out of the car, please."

Dennis's eyes closed. If he'd had a mantra, he would have re-cited it. He channeled all his energy into not screaming. It wasn't bad enough to get pulled over for speeding. He was going to have to prove he wasn't drunk.

Dennis got out of the car, turned to glare insolently at the officer, who was no doubt going to ask him to walk the line next.

The cop didn't. Instead, he said the last thing in the world Dennis expected him to say.

"Dennis Pride?"

50

BECKY BALDWIN PUSHED HER long blond hair out of her eyes, and said, "Run that by me again."

"Damn it," Dennis said. "Wake up and snap out of it. I'm in jail. The cops just gave me my one phone call. Don't tell me I should have called Pizza Hut."

"Dennis, what time is it?"

"It's five o'clock, why?"

"Believe it or not, I just got to bed."

Cora Felton switched on the nightstand lamp. "Who the hell is that?"

"Dennis. He's in jail."

"Good. Tell him to clam up on the cops and call you in the morning."

Becky waved at her to be quiet. "Where are you, Dennis?"

"I told you. I'm in jail."

"Yeah, but where?"

"New York. Some precinct in Manhattan. You really care which one? You thinking of dropping by?"

"How'd you get arrested?"

"How the hell should I know? I was driving home and the cops picked me up."

"You tell 'em anything?"

"Nothing important."

"What did you tell 'em?"

"It's no big deal," Dennis said. "One of them let it slip there'd been a murder, so I called you."

"Okay, you're not saying one word to them, and I'll see you in the morning. Where are you exactly?"

"I'm not sure."

"Put one of the cops on."

"Wait a minute. Here's the thing. They want the puzzle."

"What did you tell them about a puzzle?"

"Oh, hell!" Cora Felton swung her legs over the side of the bed.

"They asked me where my crossword puzzle was."

"What did you tell them?"

"I said, 'What crossword puzzle?' They said someone said I had a crossword puzzle. They didn't name names, but it had to be Aaron Grant."

"Dennis—"

"That son of a bitch is out to get me."

"Dennis, what did you tell them about the puzzle?"

"I told them I threw it away."

"Oh, sweet God in heaven!"

"What is it?" Cora demanded.

Becky waved her away. "Dennis, you shut up about the crossword puzzle."

"The cops want me to find it."

"I'll bet they do."

"No. You don't understand. They want me to take them where I threw it away."

"Well, you're not going to do that. In fact, you're not going to do anything until I talk to you."

"It may be too late."

"What do you mean?"

"They'll dump the garbage."

"What garbage?"

"Where I threw the puzzle. They'll dump the garbage, it'll be gone, I won't be able to prove it to the cops."

"What is he saying?" Cora was nearly hopping up and down with impatience.

Becky waved her away once more. "Dennis, where did you throw the puzzle?"

"He threw a puzzle?"

"Shut up."

"Becky?"

"Not you, Dennis. Where did you throw the puzzle?"

"In a trash can. At a service station on the Merritt Parkway."

"Becky, damn it! What's he saying?"

Becky covered the phone, turned to Cora in exasperation. "He told the police he threw the puzzle in a trash can on the Merritt Parkway."

"The hell!" Cora flung herself off the bed and grabbed the phone. "Dennis, you moron, you listen to me and you listen good. Believe it or not, I'd like to save your sorry ass. Not that I like you, but I don't want Sherry to have to watch you go down. So listen up. Do the cops know you're talking to me, or do they think it's still Becky on the phone?"

After a moment, Dennis said, "Go on, Becky."

"Tell me something. The place where you threw the puzzle. Is it closer to you, or closer to me? What I mean is, which of us could get there quicker?"

"I could."

"Okay. Here's some advice your lawyer can't give you, but I will. If you're lying about the puzzle, stall. Be uncooperative, drag your feet, draw things out. Do everything you can to make sure there's enough time for that garbage to get picked up before the cops take you out there to sift through it.

"That's if you're lying. But if you're telling the truth, if that puzzle exists, if you really did throw it in the trash, get out there *now*. Get to the service station *now*. Get your hands on that damn puzzle before anything happens to it."

Dennis started to reply before he realized Cora had slammed down the phone.

51

Sherry Carter was incensed. "I'm not going to marry you."

"Why not?"

"What do you mean, why not? Why are you asking me?"

"I'm asking you because I love you."

"And . . . ?"

"What do you mean, and?"

"You love me and what? What's the other reason?"

"I want to help you."

"Yeah." Sherry slammed the pillow. "That tears it. This may surprise you, Aaron Grant, but I don't *want* to get married to someone who's trying to help me."

"That's not why I want to marry you."

"Yes it is. You know it and I know it. You're asking me because Becky said you wouldn't have to testify against me if we were married. And there's another thing. You think I want to get married because Becky thinks it would be a good idea?"

"That wasn't Becky talking, that was a lawyer."

"You're digging your own grave."

"Come on, Sherry. Cut me a little slack. You're tampering with evidence to protect your ex-husband. And you fault me for taking legal advice from my ex-girlfriend?"

"So, you admit the whole thing is a legal ploy?"

Aaron took a breath, blew it out. "This was not how I envisioned proposing marriage."

"No kidding. This is not how I envisioned being proposed to."

"Well, at least you've had some experience at it."

Sherry's mouth fell open.

Aaron put up his hands. "Sorry! I'm stressed out, and I'm losing it. But there is the little matter of the missing puzzle."

"I wouldn't know anything about that."

There came a knock on the door.

"Oh, for God's sake!" Aaron snarled.

"Well," Sherry said, "we weren't going to get any sleep anyway. I'd just as soon have this conversation interrupted."

Aaron went to the door and let Cora in.

"The cops have Dennis. They picked him up on his way into Manhattan. They're holding him now."

"What's his story?"

"He's not talking, under advice of counsel." Cora grimaced. "Before he *got* that advice, he told the cops about throwing a crossword puzzle in the trash on the Merritt Parkway."

"You're kidding!" Aaron exclaimed.

"Not at all. And you know what that means?"

"It means I don't have to get married," Sherry said.

Cora gave her a look.

"Never mind," Sherry told her. "What about Dennis?"

"His lawyer told him not to talk. On the other hand, I told him if he's telling the truth about the puzzle, get the hell out there and get ahold of it before someone picks up the trash."

"Oh," Sherry said.

"Which is an empty gesture if it isn't there." Cora studied

Sherry narrowly. "On the other hand, if it *is* there, if Dennis *can* prove that he still had his puzzle after the murder, then the puzzle found on the body takes on enormous importance."

Sherry bit her lip. "I see."

"I certainly hope it hasn't been destroyed. Tell me, Aaron, is there anything you can remember about the puzzle that will allow us to identify it?"

"It was printed on a plain piece of paper. It seemed to be standard size. The puzzle, I mean. What is that, fifteen by fifteen?"

"That's standard size, isn't it, Sherry?" Cora asked.

"Even you know that."

"What did Dennis's puzzle look like?"

"I didn't get a good look at it."

"He took it out of his jacket pocket?"

"Yes."

"Folded?"

"Yes."

"How?"

"Like a letter. In thirds."

"What about the one you found on the body, Aaron? Was it folded?"

"No. But it was creased. Like it had *been* folded."

"In thirds?"

"Yeah."

"Interesting. So, Sherry," Cora said. "What do you want to bet me Dennis doesn't find his puzzle?"

Sherry bit her lip.

Cora nodded grimly. "That's what I thought."

52

"I THINK THAT'S THE ONE."

Dennis pointed across the divider to a service station on the southbound side of the Merritt Parkway.

"Of course," the driver said in his most put-upon voice. "It would be on the wrong side." Pudgy and lazy, the cop took everything as a great imposition.

His partner shrugged. "It had to be if he was going south."

"So how do we get there?"

"There's probably a crossover at the next exit."

"Where's that? Hartford?"

A road sign proclaimed: EXIT 38 — NEW CAANAN AVE, 1 MILE.

"There you go."

The cops passed the sign ENTERING NORWALK, got off at the exit, and drove under the Merritt, where another sign offered 15 SOUTH TO NEW YORK CITY.

"Is 15 South the Merritt?" the driver asked.

"What else could it be?"

Immediately a sign told them they were in New Caanan.

"Too bad. I enjoyed Norwalk."

The police car drove south. Dawn was breaking, and it was too early for rush hour. There was no commercial traffic on the Merritt, so there was only an occasional car.

The cops pulled into the service area. A single row of Mobil gas pumps on one side said SELF, on the other said FULL. None was occupied. Next to the pumps was a convenience-store-restroom-gas-station building. Beyond was a long, narrow parking lot with head-in spaces facing away from the highway, all nearly empty because of the hour. Down this row, at regular intervals, were square brown trash receptacles.

The cop drove by the pumps and stopped at the head of the parking lot. "Okay, which one?"

Dennis peered out the window from the backseat. "I don't know. It was dark. There were cars. It doesn't look exactly the same."

"Show us the can."

"I think it's the third one."

"I hope it is, for your sake." The cop drove up next to the trash can. "Okay, do your stuff."

The cops let Dennis out of the back of the car. He peered into the trash can. The top had a cover with a hole in the middle. It was dark. He couldn't see inside.

"Come on, come on," the cranky cop said. "There's no one on the road this time of day. It should be right on top."

Dennis lifted the cover off the can. Inside was an unappealing collection of paper cups, plastic bottles, baby diapers, and half-eaten food. There was no crossword puzzle to be seen.

"Farther down?" the cop said mockingly. "If you want to dig, we'll wait."

"It might not have been this can."

"Well, which one was it?"

"Let's try the next one."

The contents of the next can looked very much the same, except someone had apparently been carsick.

"So maybe the next one?" the cop suggested.

Dennis shook his head. "It wasn't that far down. Let's try the one closer to the station. That could be it."

It wasn't. Which was abundantly clear after Dennis moved the copy of the *New York Post* someone had used to clean up after her dog.

"Look," the driver said. "I wouldn't want to tell you your business, but it probably wasn't a good idea making a claim you couldn't prove. Dragging us all the way out here on a wild-goose chase to buck up your phony story. Not the way to make friends on the force, you know what I mean?"

The cops shoved Dennis into the backseat and slammed the door. They got in, started the car.

Dennis leaned up against the mesh divider. "Maybe it wasn't this one. The service stations on this road all look alike."

"You said the other one we passed wasn't it."

"It wasn't. That's the last one on the Merritt. I know it wasn't the last one on the Merritt."

"Now you know it wasn't the *next* to the last one on the Merritt."

"There's another station fairly close. It's gotta be there."

The driver scowled. "You mean farther *north*?"

"Yeah."

"We're headed *south*."

"So?"

"We gotta turn around. Then we'll be going *north*. Then the station will be on the south side, so we won't be able to get to it. We'll have to turn around *again*."

"Think it's not worth doing?" his partner asked.

The driver turned around in his seat. "How about it, kid? Is it worth doing? Or are you just stringing us along?"

"No. I had it. I threw it away. I swear."

The cop sighed. Dennis sounded just like every other lying punk he'd ever arrested. They never gave up their story, even though it wouldn't check out. They'd hang on to it till hell froze over. Even if it meant drag-racing up and down the Merritt Parkway.

Muttering to himself, the cop swung out of the parking lot and floored it.

53

CORA FLAILED HER ARMS through a confusion of blankets, sheets, and toy poodle, and groped for the receiver.

Becky beat her to it. "Hello?"

"Cora Felton?" a deep voice growled.

"No, this is Becky Baldwin."

"Yeah, you're next. Give me the other one."

"I beg your pardon?"

"I need to speak to Miss Felton. Then I need to speak to you. Would you put her on, please?"

"What's this all about?"

"You're the attorney for Dennis Pride?"

"That's right."

"Pride's under arrest. I need to speak to you about that. First I want Miss Felton. Put her on."

"Who is it?" Cora demanded.

"Some cop doing a macho act." Becky handed over the phone.

"Hello? This is Cora Felton."

"Miss Felton, this is Detective Draybeck, NYPD. We have Dennis Pride in custody with regard to a homicide in Mystic, Connecticut."

"Never mind the sweet talk. What do you want?"

"Mr. Pride has a crossword puzzle. He claims he wrote it. But it's not solved. We want you to solve it for us."

"You what?"

"You're the Puzzle Lady, right? You solve puzzles. We'd like you to solve this one."

"Wait a minute. Are you telling me Dennis found the puzzle he threw away on the highway?"

"That's right. And we want you to solve it."

"Oh, my God!"

"Now, there's a few legal points to be ironed out, but as soon as they're squared away, we'll fax a copy of the puzzle to the Mystic PD for you to solve. Be available, and be ready to cooperate with them on this matter. Can you do that, ma'am?"

"I have no idea."

"Me, neither. Put the lawyer on the phone and we'll try to work it out."

Cora thrust the phone at Becky. "Here. Deal with this."

"What's he want?"

Cora was already out the door.

Aaron and Sherry were wide-awake, and didn't look happy. To put it mildly. They looked as if they were barely speaking.

"Sorry, kids, we got trouble. Dennis found his puzzle."

"What?!" Aaron said incredulously.

"Yeah. In a garbage can on the highway, right where he said it was. At the moment the police are arguing with Becky Baldwin for the right to send a copy down here, rub my nose in it, and demand I solve it. Never mind how we're going to handle that. The point is, if Dennis has his puzzle, where the hell's the one you saw on the body?"

"Dennis has his puzzle?" Sherry repeated.

"That's right. The one you pilfered off the body was another one entirely. I suggest you stretch your memory of where that puzzle might be. And then when Becky gets off the phone we put our heads together and figure out some legal way of handing it over to the cops that doesn't get us all thrown in jail."

54

"ARE YOU SURE ABOUT THIS?" Sherry said anxiously, as Cora followed her out of the motel parking lot.

"No, I'm not sure about this. I have only the word of the cop on the phone. The whole thing could be an elaborate double-bluff to trick us into thinking Dennis has his puzzle. So we'll come up with the *real* puzzle they don't know we pilfered. That's too convoluted for a devious mystery writer, let alone a cop. If they say Dennis has his puzzle, trust me, Dennis has his puzzle. It couldn't be a trick."

"It *could* be a trick," Sherry insisted.

"Yeah. And the earth could stop spinning on its axis and tumble into the sun. You can't prepare for every eventuality."

"God, you're good with words when you're sarcastic." Sherry headed down the street toward the highway overpass.

"How come you wouldn't let Aaron come with us?" Cora asked. "You guys still fighting?"

"No. Well, yes, but that's not it. He has some macho idea that he's the one who got me in trouble so he has to defy the cops and refuse to talk."

"That's stupid."

"No kidding."

"*You're* the one who has to defy the cops and refuse to talk."

"Cora!"

"Don't worry. I'll keep you out of it. So will Aaron. So will Becky Baldwin. Between the three of us, they'll be so damn many people keeping you out of it, the cops will never get to you."

"Among."

"Huh?"

"*Between* means two. More than two is *among*."

"I'm sorry, Little Miss Know-It-All. Let me rephrase that. Becky and Aaron and I will be attempting to keep the police from placing you *among* the horde of defendants waiting to go on trial."

"I know what you're doing. You're kidding me to keep my spirits up."

"No. I'm kidding you to keep from strangling you. You have an ex-husband who beat you senseless, married your best friend, and chases you around the country. You hate his guts, but in order to protect him you're willing to commit a crime. One that endangers not just you, but everyone you know."

"All right, Smarty-pants, what would you have done?"

"My first choice would be to hide the evidence, and drag you out there to make sure that you're involved. I'd throw in waking you out of a sound sleep, but I wouldn't want to push my luck." Cora stomped along after Sherry, who was heading for the highway. "Where *is* this damn puzzle? Don't tell me you hid it at the scene of the crime."

"I didn't do that," Sherry said, but she kept on walking. Moments later the shadow from the overpass blotted out the sun.

"You could have fooled me. My sense of direction's not great, but I could have sworn this was the spot. But maybe I'm being influenced by those CRIME SCENE ribbons the police put up."

They passed the pile of garbage where poor Jennifer's body had lain.

"Got it," Cora said. "You didn't want to hide the puzzle between here and the motel, so you went farther instead of back. Am I right?"

"Almost."

As she emerged from the overpass Sherry turned off the street and hopped over the low guardrail at the base of the embankment.

"You're kidding . . ." Cora said.

Sherry said nothing, began scrambling up the bank. After a moment, Cora followed.

The embankment had a scattering of long grass, but was mostly dirt and rock. Cora's floppy drawstring purse banged along the ground behind her. It occurred to her it would serve them right if the gun went off and shot them both.

They reached the top of the embankment. In front of them cars and trucks rushed by on Interstate 95.

"Don't tell me we have to cross the highway," Cora said.

Sherry looked around. There was an exit sign about fifty yards south. She set out for it, with Cora tagging along behind. It was a typical exit sign, a huge metal panel on two metal poles. The back of the sign faced them. It was framed with pipes, which attached to the poles. The pipes were hollow. Sherry stuck her fingers into the end of the bottom crosspiece, and pulled out the end of some rolled-up paper.

"Hang on!" Cora said. "Good God! I didn't mean touch it!"

Cora reached in her drawstring purse, came out with a plastic evidence bag. She took a handkerchief, eased the paper out. Unrolled, it proved to be a single sheet, folded in thirds.

"Is this the way you found it?"

"It was unfolded when I found it."

"You folded it?"

"I *let* it fold. It was creased like this. It had been folded and then unfolded. I let it fold up again."

Cora unfolded the paper. It was, indeed, a crossword puzzle. Cora slid the flattened paper into the evidence bag.

Cora studied the puzzle, then turned it over, looked at the back of the page.

The grid (numbered cells):

Row 1: 1 2 3 4 ■ 5 6 7 8 9 ■ 10 11 12 13
Row 2: 14 ■ 15 ■ 16
Row 3: 17 ■ 18 19
Row 4: 20 21 ■ 22
Row 5: ■ 23 ■ 24 ■
Row 6: 25 26 27 ■ 28 ■ 29 30 31
Row 7: 32 33 ■ 34
Row 8: 35 ■ 36 ■ 37
Row 9: 38 ■ 39 40
Row 10: 41 ■ 42 ■ 43
Row 11: ■ 44 ■ 45 ■
Row 12: 46 47 48 ■ 49 50 51 52
Row 13: 53 54 ■ 55
Row 14: 56 ■ 57 58
Row 15: 59 ■ 60 61

ACROSS

1 Writes quickly, with "down"
5 Scammer's decoy
10 Bar in the bathroom
14 "I know! I know!"
15 Belly button type
16 Native Andean
17 Prefix on a bank credit card
18 Start of a message
20 Deny to
22 Mountain pass-through
23 Lawyer Dershowitz
24 Bottom lines
25 Tropical squeezer
28 Lost Labrador retriever?
29 Professor's assts.
32 Part 2 of message
34 Old Persian ruler
35 Trojan War epic
36 Bill, the science guy
37 New Olds, in 1999
38 Transport on runners
39 Part 3 of message
41 Heave-___ (rejections)
42 Small animals, to 25-Across
43 Don't have to
44 Dry ink?
45 "Modern Maturity" org.
46 Root for
49 Each and every kind
53 End of message

55 Quiet corner
56 "C'mon, be ___" ("Help me out")
57 Beneath
58 ___ 500 race
59 Actress Lamarr
60 Doesn't exist, quaintly
61 Santa Fe Trail town

DOWN

1 Nerd's opposite
2 "___ From Muskogee"
3 Carryall
4 Advance two grades in a year, e.g.
5 High voice range
6 Great Lakes lake
7 Entry in a list
8 Turned on, as a lamp
9 Caesar salad, mostly
10 YIELD and STOP
11 Getting ___ years (aging)
12 Big lot
13 ___ Mall (London street)
19 City in Arizona
21 Pink ___ (rock band)

24 Salesman's patter
25 Engage in on-line fraud, slangily
26 Mello ___ (Coca-Cola brand)
27 Makes an effort
28 In a foxy way
29 "___ never believe me!"
30 Golden calf maker, in Exodus
31 Whoop or holler
33 Still for rent
34 "Let me know tomorrow"
37 Asserts
39 Resolve
40 Ready for trouble
42 Gambit
44 ___ dancer
45 Invader from Mars, e.g.
46 "Jeopardy!" winner Jennings's home
47 Ready to eat
48 Pleased as punch
49 Throws in
50 "Class Reunion" author Jaffe
51 Brouhaha
52 "The ___ the limit!"
54 Introduction to sex?

"Uh-oh!"

"What?"

Cora showed Sherry. "It's a bloody fingerprint. I don't suppose you happened to see that."

"Oh."

"Is that your fingerprint?"

"I don't think so."

"You don't think so?"

"I mean, no. I hadn't touched anything bloody."

"That you know of."

"I didn't touch anything bloody," Sherry said irritably. "That's not my print."

A tractor trailer zoomed by on the interstate, leaving the two women in a cloud of sand and dirt.

Cora cursed after the speeding vehicle. "Any trucks go by when you hid the damn thing?"

"One or two," Sherry admitted grudgingly.

Cora sighed. "Let's get the hell out of here."

55

D.A. Dawson was not happy. And it wasn't just that he had been roused out of bed after very little sleep. He didn't like what he was hearing. He also didn't like the fact the attractive blond attorney who was presenting him with the disquieting information had brought along someone else to do most of the talking. Cora Felton wasn't a lawyer. Cora Felton was an actress and the Puzzle Lady and a celebrity and a major pain in the ass. On one hand, she had no legal bearing whatsoever. On the other, she had all the pertinent information. Or so the lawyer assured him. He had no way of knowing if it was true.

"You want to give me something?" he asked Cora.

"Yes, I do."

"And you need a lawyer along with you to do it?"

"I don't *need* a lawyer. She insisted on coming."

"The point is, she's here. And you haven't given me anything yet."

"Of course not. We haven't made a deal."

"And why should we make a deal?"

"Why shouldn't we?" Cora asked innocently. "We're on the same side."

"That's not what I mean." The prosecutor summoned up his patience and persevered. "Why is it *necessary* for us to make a deal?"

"In order to prevent any misunderstanding." Cora smiled her engaging, breakfast-cereal-selling smile. "We wouldn't want to have any misunderstanding, now, would we?"

"We certainly wouldn't. So why don't you tell me what you came to tell me and we'll take it from there?"

"That's an *excellent* idea. Becky, is there any reason why I shouldn't cooperate with this nice gentleman?"

"Not as long as you talk in hypotheticals."

D.A. Dawson stared. "Hypotheticals?"

"Yes, of course," Becky said. "Unless you'd care to offer immunity."

"What?!"

"If you'd care to offer immunity to any legal infraction, technical or otherwise, by any or all parties involved, which might be revealed in the course of this conversation, then there would be no problem. But as long as such offer is not forthcoming, I would advise my client to speak only in hypotheticals."

The prosecutor considered that and regarded Cora. "You have something for me?"

"I might," Cora said.

"You are aware that Dennis Pride has produced a crossword puzzle. Therefore not the one that was seen on the body, which subsequently disappeared." In the belief that he was dealing with a wordsmith, he added, "The puzzle, not the body."

"I'm glad to hear it," Cora said. "I hate it when the body disappears."

"I'm wondering if what you want to give me might not be a crossword puzzle."

"Any chance Dennis Pride might have found his puzzle on the body?"

"Not if the reporter's telling the truth. Pride would have left Mystic before the guy saw it on the decedent."

"Well, that's very interesting. Meanwhile, I'd like to give you this." Cora reached in her floppy drawstring purse, pulled out a plastic evidence bag. "Here's a crossword puzzle. It's not solved." She took out a paper and unfolded it. "Here's a photocopy. You can touch it all you like because it has no evidentiary value. On the other hand, it *is* solved, which makes it a lot easier to read."

The prosecutor's eyes bugged out of his head. "Where did you get this?"

"It wasn't hard. I used a copy machine."

"I mean *this* one!" He pointed to the puzzle in the evidence bag. "Where did you get the original?"

Cora waggled her fingers. "Well, there's where we get into a tricky legal situation. First off, how do we *know* this is the original? It could also be a copy. In fact, it looks like a xerox to me. Either that or a computer printout. The problem is, if it's a xerox of a computer printout, it's hard to tell the difference."

"I don't care what you *call* it. Where did you *get* it?"

Cora smiled. "Now, this is that gray area that might require a hypothetical. In lieu of immunity, of course. You're not promising immunity, are you?"

"I'm not promising a damn thing!" Dawson snarled. "Miss Felton, there's a fingerprint on this puzzle! In what appears to be blood!"

"It certainly does," Cora agreed, sweetly. "You'll know more when you test it."

"Right now I want an answer. Is that the puzzle found on the body by the reporter Aaron Grant?"

"Did he mention a bloody fingerprint? I don't recall if he did. Of course, the police haven't been very forthcoming with their information."

"Miss Felton—"

"Call me Cora."

"Damn it, *we* don't give *you* information. *You* give *us* information."

"Absolutely. That's what I'm trying to do. I wish you wouldn't make it so hard."

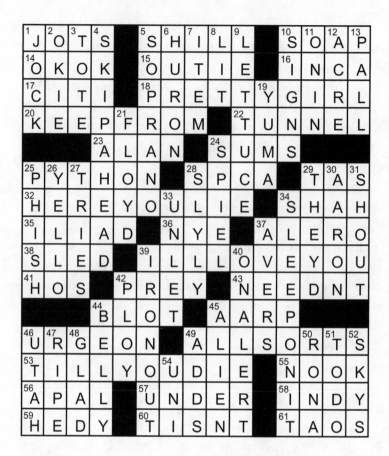

J¹	O²	T³	S⁴	■	S⁵	H⁶	I⁷	L⁸	L⁹	■	S¹⁰	O¹¹	A¹²	P¹³
O¹⁴	K	O	K	■	O¹⁵	U	T	I	E	■	I¹⁶	N	C	A
C¹⁷	I	T	I	■	P¹⁸	R	E	T	T	Y¹⁹	G	I	R	L
K²⁰	E	E	P	F²¹	R	O	M	■	T²²	U	N	N	E	L
■	■	A²³	L	A	N	■	S²⁴	U	M	S	■	■	■	■
P²⁵	Y²⁶	T²⁷	H	O	N	■	S²⁸	P	C	A	■	T²⁹	A³⁰	S³¹
H³²	E	R	E	Y	O	U³³	L	I	E	■	S³⁴	H	A	H
I³⁵	L	I	A	D	■	N³⁶	Y	E	■	A³⁷	L	E	R	O
S³⁸	L	E	D	■	I³⁹	L	L	L⁴⁰	O	V	E	Y	O	U
H⁴¹	O	S	■	P⁴²	R	E	Y	■	N⁴³	E	E	D	N	T
■	■	B⁴⁴	L	O	T	■	A⁴⁵	A	R	P	■	■	■	■
U⁴⁶	R⁴⁷	G⁴⁸	E	O	N	■	A⁴⁹	L	L	S	O	R⁵⁰	T⁵¹	S⁵²
T⁵³	I	L	L	Y	O	U⁵⁴	D	I	E	■	N⁵⁵	O	O	K
A⁵⁶	P	A	L	■	U⁵⁷	N	D	E	R	■	I⁵⁸	N	D	Y
H⁵⁹	E	D	Y	■	T⁶⁰	I	S	N	T	■	T⁶¹	A	O	S

ACROSS

1 Writes quickly, with "down"
5 Scammer's decoy
10 Bar in the bathroom
14 "I know! I know!"
15 Belly button type
16 Native Andean
17 Prefix on a bank credit card
18 Start of a message
20 Deny to
22 Mountain pass-through
23 Lawyer Dershowitz
24 Bottom lines
25 Tropical squeezer
28 Lost Labrador retriever?

29 Professor's assts.
32 Part 2 of message
34 Old Persian ruler
35 Trojan War epic
36 Bill, the science guy
37 New Olds, in 1999
38 Transport on runners
39 Part 3 of message
41 Heave-___ (rejections)
42 Small animals, to 25-Across
43 Don't have to
44 Dry ink?
45 "Modern Maturity" org.
46 Root for
49 Each and every kind
53 End of message

55 Quiet corner
56 "C'mon, be ___ " ("Help me out")
57 Beneath
58 ___ 500 race
59 Actress Lamarr
60 Doesn't exist, quaintly
61 Santa Fe Trail town

DOWN

1 Nerd's opposite
2 "___ From Muskogee"
3 Carryall
4 Advance two grades in a year, e.g.
5 High voice range
6 Great Lakes lake
7 Entry in a list
8 Turned on, as a lamp
9 Caesar salad, mostly
10 YIELD and STOP
11 Getting ___ years (aging)
12 Big lot
13 ___ Mall (London street)
19 City in Arizona
21 Pink ___ (rock band)

24 Salesman's patter
25 Engage in on-line fraud, slangily
26 Mello ___ (Coca-Cola brand)
27 Makes an effort
28 In a foxy way
29 "___ never believe me!"
30 Golden calf maker, in Exodus
31 Whoop or holler
33 Still for rent
34 "Let me know tomorrow"
37 Asserts
39 Resolve
40 Ready for trouble
42 Gambit
44 ___ dancer
45 Invader from Mars, e.g.
46 "Jeopardy!" winner Jennings's home
47 Ready to eat
48 Pleased as punch
49 Throws in
50 "Class Reunion" author Jaffe
51 Brouhaha
52 "The ___ the limit!"
54 Introduction to sex?

D.A. Dawson opened his mouth, snapped it shut.

"Where's the other puzzle?" Cora asked. "The one Dennis Pride had. The one you want solved."

"The New York cops have it. They're faxing us a copy. For you to solve."

"We'll drive off that bridge when we come to it," Cora said. "Right now, why don't you take a look at this one? *Pretty girl, here you lie. I'll love you till you die.*' Rather significant, wouldn't you think?"

"I certainly would. Where did you get that puzzle?"

"I took it out of my purse."

"That's not what I mean. Where did you find it? Or do you claim you created it?"

"I think I can safely say that I didn't. Once again, we have stepped into the realm of the hypothetical. Suppose, for the sake of argument, that I found it somewhere?"

"I am supposing that very thing. Just where might that be?"

"Suppose I found it not too far from the crime scene, secreted in a road sign?"

"Are you saying that you did?"

"Absolutely not. I'm exploring the possibilities that might develop if that were the case."

"And how did you come to find this road sign?"

"I went out to walk my dog."

"Hypothetically?"

"No, it's a real dog. He really had to go, so I took him. And the question is, if Buddy and I came up with this evidence, do I have your assurance that no one's going to get into trouble over it? With the exception of the killer, of course."

"I'm not in a position to promise you immunity."

"Well, let's suppose, hypothetically, that you *were* in a position to promise me immunity. What would you want to know then?"

Dawson blinked. "We're now dealing with hypothetical immunity?"

"Hypothetically."

"Someone shoot me!" The prosecutor turned to the cop. "Get that reporter in here."

Ushered in, Aaron Grant glanced at Becky and hastily averted his eyes. He did not look happy.

"Now, then, young man. When you found the body, you reported there was a crossword puzzle on it. Is this the puzzle?"

Aaron barely glanced at the evidence bag. "I really couldn't say."

"Look carefully. Take your time."

Grudgingly, Aaron looked.

"Well, is it the puzzle?"

"I don't know."

"You don't know?" D.A. Dawson said incredulously. "What do you mean, you don't know? You saw it, didn't you?"

"I saw it, but I didn't pay that much attention to it."

"Why not? Didn't you think it was an important clue?"

"I was a little distracted by the dead body," Aaron said sarcastically. "I thought it was something the police might be interested in, so I went to tell them. Was that wrong?"

"No, but it's certainly glib. May I ask if this young lady is your attorney?"

"Which young lady?"

The prosecutor turned to find Cora and Becky smiling at him. He started to say, "The blonde," realized that would get him in trouble. In fact, he decided, practically anything he said would get him in trouble. "Never mind. Are you telling me you can't identify this as the puzzle you found on the body?"

"I can't make a positive identification, no."

"You notice the fingerprint in blood?"

"Yes."

"Did the puzzle you found have a fingerprint in blood?"

"I can't say."

"Is that because you don't know, or because you aren't at liberty to say?"

"Now who's being glib?"

"Now who's evading the question?"

"Not me. The answer is, I don't know."

"How can you not know? It either did or it didn't."

"I would say that was a fair assessment of the situation."

"Thank you. Did you see the fingerprint?"

"I can't say."

"Then you didn't see it."

"I can't say that either. I can't say there was a bloody fingerprint, and I can't say there wasn't."

"Uh-huh," Dawson said. "Well, did you see anything on the puzzle that *might* have been the fingerprint?"

Aaron hesitated. "I think I should talk to counsel."

"I think I should talk to a psychiatrist!" Cora exclaimed. "For goodness' sakes, what is this, *I've Got a Secret?*" She sized up the prosecutor. "You're too young for that, but trust me, it was a fun show. And, trust me, you couldn't hold a candle to Kitty Carlisle. Anyway, hypothetical, schmypothetical. *Assume* this is the puzzle found on the body. *Assume* this fingerprint is therefore valuable, and the message in the puzzle is therefore valuable. *Assume* the only thing keeping these assumptions from being more than just a hypothetical is your stubborn unwillingness to grant immunity to innocent people."

"Why do innocent people need immunity?"

"Oh, bite me!"

"Cora!" Becky warned.

"No, damn it. I'm sick of this bozo missing the point. The point is, *this* is the puzzle found on the body. And this is *not* Dennis Pride's puzzle. Dennis Pride *has* his puzzle. So this puzzle doesn't *implicate* Dennis Pride, it *exonerates* Dennis Pride." Cora threw her hands in the air. "If you can't understand that, I give up!"

An officer stuck his head in the door.

"Not now," Dawson grumbled.

"Sorry, sir. The fax came through."

"Oh. Give it here." The prosecutor snatched the fax from the officer, took a look. "Excellent. All right, Miss Felton, do your stuff."

"My stuff?"

"Yes, of course. You're the Puzzle Lady, aren't you? Crack the puzzle."

Cora smiled. "Don't be silly. No one cares what Dennis Pride's puzzle says. Dennis Pride's puzzle has nothing to do with anything. You don't have to solve his puzzle. All you have to do is compare it with the one found on the body to prove that they're different."

"Oh, now you're *admitting* this puzzle was found on the body?"

"No." Cora waggled her hand. "It's still *hypothetically* found on the body. And it *hypothetically* proves Dennis Pride's puzzle wasn't. So I *hypothetically* don't have to solve Dennis Pride's puzzle. So I'm damned if I will."

Cora smiled at the exasperated district attorney.

D.A. Dawson controlled himself with effort. "Fine. So would you please point out to me where the two puzzles are different?"

"You could do that yourself. But just to show I'm a good sport." Cora took the xerox of the puzzle Sherry found on the body and the fax of Dennis Pride's puzzle and held them up together. "In the first place, the clues are different. For instance, in clue number one on Dennis Pride's puzzle . . ."

Cora's voice trailed off as her eyes wandered back and forth from paper to paper.

The puzzles were identical.

56

By the time Dennis Pride hit town there were TV crews on hand. One included Rick Reed, whom the police could no longer hold now that they had a better suspect. Luckily, it was the Channel 8 attorney who had negotiated this, otherwise Becky Baldwin would have had a genuine conflict of interest, arguing for the release of one client on the basis of the evidence against another.

Dennis arrived in the back of a Connecticut State Police car, which was a blow to the news teams, since the Connecticut State Police cars are all unmarked. Still, they got a great shot of Becky Baldwin in her bright red business suit, leaping into the fray to protect her client. She managed to elbow Rick Reed aside with the kind of shove usually not applied to someone who has bought you dinner. She reached the police car just as a beefy cop wrestled Dennis Pride from the backseat.

Dennis looked a fright. He was unshaven and his hair was uncombed. His white shirt was smeared with garbage, as were his hands and face. His bloodshot eyes looked like road maps for hell.

Becky leaped in front of him, hogging the camera time. "All right, everybody. This is my client, Dennis Pride. I am his attorney, Becky Baldwin. He's not talking. Direct your questions to me."

"Miss Baldwin. What do the police have on your client?"

"No comment."

"Why did the police arrest him?"

"No comment."

"When are you going to make a statement?"

"No comment."

Cora Felton pushed in front of the cameras. "Well, I've got a comment. Dennis Pride is the third man arrested for these crimes. First they arrested Lance Griswald. Then they arrested you." She clapped Rick Reed on the shoulder, while the camera crews filmed gleefully. Even the Channel 8 team caught the action. "I'd say the fact that the police arrested Dennis is a huge point in his favor, since everyone the police arrest seems to be innocent." She side-spied slyly up at Rick. "Unless, of course, you did it."

Before the press could ask any more questions, the police hustled Dennis Pride into the station. Becky followed along behind.

Cora declined further interviews and joined Aaron and Sherry on the edge of the crowd.

"Now what?" Sherry said.

"Now he tells Becky his story and we find out what's what."

"I'd like to be there," Sherry said.

Aaron snorted in disgust, turned angrily away.

"Hey," Cora said. "You want to take your squabble elsewhere? We got bigger things at stake here."

"We certainly do," Sherry said. "We put the noose around his neck. You, me, and Aaron."

"Wouldn't that be you, Aaron, and I?"

Sherry glared at her. "I am not in the mood. I hate the creep. I hope he gets what's coming to him. But this isn't it."

"Oh, for Christ's sake!" Aaron said.

"What, you think he killed those girls?"

"Of course not. And the evidence will show that."

"Not if we tamper with it. I did something stupid and put his neck in the noose. Can't you understand why that upsets me?"

"You did something stupid when you thought he was guilty," Aaron shot back. "Don't you see why that upsets me?"

"I *didn't* think he was guilty."

"I can't *begin* to tell you how many reasons there are why you shouldn't be having this conversation here," Cora cautioned them. "As far as the cops are concerned, I'm the one who had the puzzle. Now shut the hell up before you start attracting attention."

"We already have." Aaron nodded in the direction of a cop bearing down on them from the police station.

Cora summed up her feelings on policemen, men in general, the current situation, and the ironies of fate with a brief, pungent comment.

If the officer heard he took no notice, merely walked up to them with the inexorable tread of impending doom. "Cora Felton?"

"Yes."

He jerked his head in the direction of the police station. "They want you."

57

THE PROSECUTOR LOOKED LIKE he'd been dining on a bucket of roofing nails. "This is most irregular."

Becky smiled. "I quite agree."

"Your client's not willing to make a statement."

"That's right."

"He's not willing to talk to us at all."

"I believe he asked to use the men's room."

"Don't be cute. I'm way beyond cute. The fact is, Pride's not willing to make a statement, and you're not willing to make a statement either."

"Only that my client's innocent."

"That's less than helpful. On the other hand, he would like to talk to Miss Felton here."

"He was married to her niece. They have a bond."

"I'm happy for them. Miss Felton is not an attorney. Anything your client tells her is *not* privileged information. We could compel her to talk."

"Well, you'd certainly be welcome to try," Becky said, sweetly.

"The image of you attempting to toss the beloved Puzzle Lady in jail probably won't play well with your local constituents. Isn't this an election year?"

The prosecutor scowled, and ushered Cora and Becky into a small interrogation room. On his way out he recollected, and extended his hand. "The purse, if you don't mind."

Cora handed over her drawstring purse. "I wasn't about to bust him out, but I understand the sentiment."

The prosecutor went out and slammed the door.

"What's going on?" Cora asked Becky, even before the echoes died away.

"Dennis wouldn't talk. He wanted you."

"Why?"

"How the hell should I know?" Becky said irritably. "My client won't talk to me."

"That must be annoying," Cora said, innocently.

Becky glared at her.

Dennis, still handcuffed, was ushered in. The cops sat him at the table, across from the two women, and withdrew.

"All right, Dennis. What's up?" Cora said.

Dennis looked at Becky. "You gonna stay?"

Becky's eyes widened. "I'm your *lawyer*. Of course I'm gonna stay."

"You gotta understand, you can't use this. You're not gonna feed it to the press."

"Why would I do that?"

"To taint the jury pool. Make me look innocent."

"Dennis. What have you done?"

"I didn't do anything."

"Then why are we here?"

Dennis said nothing, sulked.

"What do you want, Dennis?" Becky persisted.

"I want to talk to Cora."

"Why?"

"Because I can't talk to Sherry."

Becky looked at Cora.

Cora said, "What do you want to tell Sherry?"

"I just want to explain."

"Explain what?"

"It sounds so bad," Dennis groaned.

"It's a murder charge, Dennis," Becky said. "You expect it to sound good?"

Cora shot her a warning glance. "What did you do, Dennis? I know you didn't kill that girl."

"Of course not."

"But she had your crossword puzzle."

"I know."

"How did that happen?"

"That's the bad part."

Cora resisted the urge to point out the grossness of the under-statement. "How did that happen, Dennis?"

"I have no idea."

"Then I guess we can't help you."

Cora got up.

Dennis waved his hands, a bit of a feat with the cuffs on. "No, no! That's not what I mean."

"What do you mean, Dennis?"

"I don't know how that puzzle could have got on her body."

"You didn't put it there?"

"Of course not."

"You didn't know the body was there?"

"I didn't know anyone had been killed. I was on my way home."

"When the cops stopped you?"

"Yeah."

"You didn't know what they wanted?"

"No."

"So you did a little talking?"

Dennis turned to Becky. "Hey, what's she trying to do?"

"My job," Becky said. "Since you won't let me."

"Don't be brain-dead," Cora said. "You've already told the cops too much. You had a puzzle, you threw it away. You went to look, and, miracle of miracles, you found it. Which would have been real nice if it wasn't the same one that was found on the body. It would have cleared you. As it is, it fries your ass. Now, you wanna explain how that happened?"

"I wanted to tell Sherry myself."

"That avenue is no longer open to you."

"I know." Dennis took a breath. "I came to see Sherry. That reporter was with her. I didn't want to bust in on them. I was angry, upset. I went to the bar. To have a drink, think it over."

"I thought you weren't drinking, Dennis."

"I'm not. Like I say, I was upset. I had all this pent up inside me. And I couldn't talk to Sherry. Just like I can't now. So I'm talking about it. Telling the guy on the stool next to me the story. Not with names or anything. But it's like we're in a different town. Nobody knows me. Nobody knows her. I can talk. Like guys will in a bar. You know what I mean?"

"Do I ever. My fourth husband Henry—"

Becky coughed.

Cora sighed. "Go on. You're talking to this guy."

"He asked me what she likes. I said she likes crossword puzzles."

"What?" Becky exclaimed.

It was Cora's turn for a warning cough. "Go on."

"He reaches in his jacket pocket, brings out a folded paper. He says, 'Here. Give her this.' I unfold it, it's a puzzle. I'm feeling light-headed, and it's not just the drink. I tell him Sherry likes crossword puzzles and he whips one out."

"*Sherry* likes crossword puzzles?" Becky said.

Dennis looked at her in surprise, then realized tardily she didn't know Sherry was the real Puzzle Lady. Not that he gave a damn about keeping Sherry's secret. He just didn't want the conversation to go off on that tangent. "He said, 'It's a Valentine's message. Got a love poem in it. Give it to her and say you wrote it.' "

"A love poem?"

"Yeah."

"Did this guy tell you what it was?"

"No."

"Didn't you ask him?"

"Of course I asked him. He excused himself just then. I thought he was going to the men's room. He never came back."

"Didn't you think that was odd?"

"Hey, I didn't *know* he wasn't coming back. I sat at the bar. I had some drinks. After a while I realized he wasn't there."

"Why do you think he left?"

"I don't know. It was right when a bunch of movie people came in."

"Which movie people?"

"I don't know. People I'd seen at the motel. I don't remember which ones."

"Try to remember, Dennis. It could be important."

"Yeah, but I didn't know that. So I don't know if that's why he left. I don't even know *when* he left. I just know he never came back."

"Had you ever seen him before?"

"No."

"So what did he look like?"

"I knew you were going to ask me that. He was just a guy. I wasn't paying that much attention. It wasn't like I was looking at him. He was sitting next to me at the bar."

"He listened to your story. He gave you a puzzle."

"Yeah. That's what I was concerned with. The puzzle and Sherry. Not the guy. If something hadn't happened, I wouldn't have thought of him at all."

Behind his back, Becky Baldwin rolled her eyes.

"You must have some impression. What did the guy look like?"

"Average."

"Tall, thin, short, fat?"

"He was on a bar stool."

"Black, white, yellow, tan?"

"The stool?"

"His skin."

"Oh. He was a white guy."

"Was he wearing glasses?"

"I don't think so."

"You don't *think* so?" Cora's contempt was ill concealed. Becky shot her another withering glance.

"Dennis," Cora practically pleaded, "do you remember *anything* about this man? Anything at *all*?"

Dennis frowned, thinking hard. "His hair."

"His hair? What color was his hair?"

"I don't remember."

"Well, what *do* you remember? Long, short, curly, what?"

"I'm not sure. It was just an impression I got. Like I say, I wasn't really paying attention."

"So, what about his hair?"

Dennis grimaced. Shook his head. Shrugged. "It might have been a wig."

<table><tr><td>58</td></tr></table>

BECKY AND CORA CONFERENCED IN THE HALL.

"All right," Cora said. "This is a little tricky with you not letting him talk. Is there any way you can let Dennis see our producer? Quentin Burns?"

"Why?"

"Quentin wears a toupee."

"Oh. But Dennis would know him, wouldn't he? He'd have recognized him in the bar."

"*You* wouldn't have."

"Yes I would."

"You didn't know he wore a toupee."

"Yes I did. I didn't make the connection because I didn't know what you were driving at. I didn't know what you were driving at because I didn't think your producer could be the person in the bar because Dennis would have recognized him."

"Dennis wasn't exactly paying close attention. He wasn't even sure it was a toupee."

"Which proves my point. That's a really obvious toupee."

"But what if he was wearing another one?"

"Huh?"

"He wears a wig. He takes it off. He puts on a different one. He goes in the men's room, switches toupees, and as far as any casual observer is concerned, he's another person."

"You've been reading too many mystery novels."

"Maybe so. The point is, Dennis should see Quentin. He's your client. If I were you, I'd make it happen."

"Anything else you'd do if you were me?"

Cora swept her eyes over Becky's figure and sighed. "Sweetheart, you have no idea."

Becky flushed slightly, said, "Any more suggestions?"

"Yeah. Let Dennis get a look at Freddy Fosterfield."

"Who?"

"The dweeb who followed me here. My Number One Fan."

"Why?"

"He's bald. Slap a wig on him and he might look entirely different."

"You're grasping at straws."

"Hey, it's your client's neck. But if I were you—"

"Keep it clean."

"I'd get Freddy's fingerprints and compare 'em to the one on the puzzle."

59

BRENDA WAS HYSTERICAL. "You have to let me in there! I'm his wife!"

The policeman on the front steps of the station fancied himself stolid and impassive, but he could barely conceal his delight at barring the door. "Sorry, ma'am. No one gets in."

"But I have to talk to my husband!"

The cop shook his head. "No one's talking to your husband just now."

The Channel 8 news crew was lurking, tape rolling. Rick Reed, mike in hand, sprang into the fray. "His lawyer's in there," Rick volunteered. "He's talking to *her*."

"You hear that?" Brenda told the cop. "How about that?"

"Of course he's talking to his lawyer. He has a right to an attorney. I don't suppose you're a lawyer too?"

"*I'm his wife.*"

"Not the same thing. See, the Miranda warning doesn't go, 'You have the right to a wife. If you cannot afford a wife, one will be appointed for you.' " The cop chuckled at his own wit. The camera was rolling. Maybe he'd wind up on TV.

Reed's eyes twinkled. "Cora Felton's in there too," he told Brenda.

"What?" Brenda said ominously. "Is that true, Officer?"

"He asked to see her," the officer said defensively.

"And you *had* to let him," Brenda said sarcastically. "Because it's his right. How does it go, now? 'You have the right to a Puzzle Lady. If you cannot afford a Puzzle Lady, a Puzzle Lady will be appointed for you.' "

The officer, now sincerely hoping this footage *didn't* get on the air, muttered, "There were special circumstances. . . ."

"Like what?"

Sherry pushed through the crowd. "Brenda, I'm so sorry."

Brenda's eyes blazed. "You ought to be!"

Sherry stopped cold. "I beg your pardon?"

"This is all your fault. Luring Dennis here, seducing him with crazy crossword puzzles."

The news crews zoomed in gleefully. The words *cat fight* reverberated among the cameramen.

"Hang on, Brenda!" Now Aaron Grant pressed forward. "None of this is Sherry's fault."

"I can fight my own battles, Aaron."

"You shouldn't have to, Sherry, with your best friend. Come on, Brenda, give the girl a break."

Cora breezed out the front door. The news crews sprang forward.

"Cora!" Brenda cried. "How is he? Did you talk to him?"

"He's dandy. He didn't do anything. This is all a big mistake."

"Then why is he here?"

"The police brought him here."

"I mean before. Why was he here *before*?" Brenda insisted.

"He's talking to his lawyer. All that will be straightened out."

"I need to see him."

"Not right now."

"You saw him. Why was that?"

"Oh. About the puzzle. I had to see him about the puzzle."

"Give me a break. Since when did Dennis ever write a puzzle?"

"My point exactly. Clearly the police have the wrong idea." Cora turned to Aaron. "Can you give me a ride to the motel?"

"Now?"

"Yeah. Sherry, come with us to the motel." Cora lowered her voice. "Unless you'd rather stay and talk to Brenda."

Sherry considered that option. "Let's get the hell out of here!" she told Cora.

60

Aaron Grant pulled into the motel parking lot and stopped the car. Without a word, Sherry got out and headed for her room.

"If I were you, I'd follow her," Cora suggested.

Aaron exhaled noisily. Then he jerked open the driver's-side door.

"You might want to park the car."

Aaron slammed the door, drove into a parking space. Cora watched him follow Sherry up to the room. She sighed, shook her head. Wondered if lovers were always so stupid. Of course, hers always had been.

On the far side of the parking lot, the crew members were breaking down equipment and stowing it away in the van. Quentin seemed to be arguing with them. His face was red, accentuating the line of his wig, which was slightly askew. Cora wandered over, listened in.

"We are *not* going home," Quentin declared with all the authority of one who was holding things together with Scotch tape. "This is a hiatus, not a shutdown. You have your motel rooms and you're on per diem. We're merely waiting for the police to give us the okay to go ahead."

Pepe, the cranky shop steward, waggled his finger. "A hiatus? I never heard such a thing. In all my years in the union, I never heard such a thing. I'll tell you what we're on. We're on salary. We're on salary, *plus* per diem. *Plus* room. *Plus* meals. *Plus* average daily overtime computed from the beginning of the shoot."

"That's outrageous!"

"No, that's union rules."

"I'm not prepared to pay that."

"Then we're going home."

The producer scowled.

Cora bustled up to them. "Quentin?"

He saw her and his eyes narrowed. He stepped away from the crew, just out of earshot. "What do *you* want?"

"Now, don't be like that," Cora remonstrated. "I want to help you."

"Is that so?"

"You know the police have a suspect in custody for Jennifer's murder."

"Of course. That young man who's been hanging around."

"Then you've seen him?"

"What do you mean, I've seen him?"

"Around the set. You've seen him around the set."

"What are you talking about?"

"I'm talking about the young man. You've seen him before. You know who he is."

"Of course I know who he is."

"Fine. Then you can make the identification."

"Identification?"

"Yes. You can identify him as the young man who's been hanging around the set."

"Are you nuts? I thought this was your niece's ex-husband. Isn't that who he is?"

"That's right."

"Then I don't have to identify him. *She* can identify him."

"She can identify him as her ex-husband. But she's not officially with the crew. See what I mean? You're the producer. You're the one in charge. You're the one whose word they're going to take."

"This is most irregular."

"No, it's absolutely routine. What you need to do is go down to the police station, tell 'em to get a message to Becky Baldwin. That's the guy's lawyer. Say you want to talk to her."

"Wait a minute. The guy's lawyer? Why would she want me to identify him?"

Cora, tap dancing fast, said, "She's cooperating with the police. She knows her guy didn't do it, she just wants to straighten everything out. Talk to her, she'll fix you right up."

Quentin, utterly baffled, said, "I don't see how I can help."

"We're all on the same side here. We want to clear this up and go back to shooting." Cora jerked her thumb at the crew. "Before these guys go home or run up the national debt. It's a great opportunity for you to point that out to the police. That they're dragging their feet and costing you money. So when this *does* start costing you money, you'll be on record as having warned everyone." She lowered her voice conspiratorially, jerked her thumb at the crew. "You argue with these guys, you're just going to lose. Wrong tack to take. Show 'em you're on their side, and you're going to fight for their rights."

Quentin frowned, considered that.

"What the hell is going on here?"

Daphne Decker came striding across the parking lot. "Did someone call off the shoot when I wasn't looking? I wish you'd told me. I wouldn't have bothered to stick around."

Quentin reached an abrupt decision. "We're shooting," he announced. "Cora's on board. All systems are go. I'm on my way to the police station to tell them our intention. This crew has too much invested in this production to quit now. We're shooting ten o'clock tomorrow morning, on location, as scheduled. Why don't you come along? You can make the TV announcement while I'm talking to the cops."

Daphne smiled and waved at the men. Out of the side of her mouth she said, "Suppose they won't let us shoot?"

"Then it will be the cops spoiling the fun, not us."

"Sounds good. Come on, let's go."

As Quentin and Daphne went off to get the car, Freddy Fosterfield hurried up. It occurred to Cora he hadn't been around all day. She felt a slight pang of guilt that she hadn't even noticed.

Freddy seemed preoccupied. "I hear they arrested someone. Is it true?"

"Yes. He's in custody."

"So the danger's over?"

"I wouldn't say that."

"Why not?"

"They haven't got the right man."

"How do you know?"

"How do I know anything? Trust me, it's the wrong guy."

"But isn't there evidence against him? A crossword puzzle, something like that?"

"I thought you didn't know anything about it."

"I was making small talk. I heard the police arrested someone. I heard a few details."

"Is that right?" Cora wasn't sure the bit about the puzzle had been made public. "Listen, Freddy, there's something you can do for me."

"Name it."

"The guy they arrested is my niece's ex-husband. You happen to hear that detail?"

"Actually, yes. That is, I'm not sure whether I heard it or I just know it." He grimaced. "That sounds stupid. I mean, I heard they arrested this guy Dennis. I happen to know he's Sherry's ex-husband, so I'm not sure whether I heard that or not. In connection with the arrest, I mean."

"Anyway, Dennis's lawyer's Becky Baldwin. My roommate."

"Wasn't she the other guy's lawyer?"

"She gets around. The point is, she's down there at the police station and she could really use some help."

Freddy frowned. "With what?"

"Clearing the guy. He didn't do it, but that's hard to prove. Anyway, she's stuck out here in the middle of nowhere, she doesn't have anyone to do her legwork."

"You mean . . ."

"Like a private investigator. If you went down there, told her I sent you to see if she needed help, she might have you check out a few leads. Maybe even talk to her client, see if you have any insight."

"You think she'd do that?"

"She's desperate." Cora grimaced. "I don't mean that like it sounds."

"Yeah. Okay." Freddy seemed dubious.

"You got a car. You could zoom right down there."

"Yeah, sure." Freddy fidgeted, checked his watch. "Sure thing, that's what I'll do."

Freddy headed for his car. He didn't get in, however. While Cora watched, he walked right by it and went in his motel room door.

Cora didn't like it. By rights, Freddy should have jumped all over the chance to play private detective.

Cora had maneuvered a meeting between Dennis Pride and the two men who were most likely to have worn a wig and slipped him a crossword puzzle in the bar.

One of them was on his way down to the police station to meet him.

The other one wasn't.

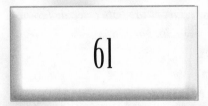

61

THIS WAS NO GOOD. *He hadn't planned on so much police activity. The second murder was a mistake. The first murder hadn't attracted that much attention. Life went on as normal. Routines were observed.*

But this . . .

This was a disaster. There were cops everywhere. Cops and newsmen. And then the damn suspect. That had worked like a charm, framing the son of a bitch. With the guy refusing to tell his story, not that they'd believe him anyway, but still. Talk about killing two birds with one stone. The guy clams up, so the cops never hear about the guy in the bar, plus they hold the poor sap in jail, so there's no chance the dumb schmuck will get out and accidentally run into him.

Not that he hadn't disguised himself well enough. The moron probably couldn't pick him out of a lineup. But it was nice not to have to worry about it.

Except for the cops. They were everywhere, spoiling the game. How could he play Puzzle, Puzzle, Who's Got the Puzzle? with the cops all around. He'd have to single her out of the herd. Which hadn't been his plan. Which might not be easy to do. And he might not have much time.

The tour might get shut down. It was hard to imagine it wouldn't, particularly now that they no longer had a publicist to give it a positive spin. Which would be difficult, under the circumstances: "Aside from the two murders, it's going very well."

It would ruin everything if the tour was over. Not that it would end the game. He'd still have to play it out, of course. But on a different playing field. Without so many suspects to spread suspicion around. Which would be necessary if the police decided to hold what's-his-name. Hard to frame the guy while he's in jail.

No help for that.

The game must go on.

No rain checks in murder.

No ties, either.

Each game had a loser.

Each game had a winner.

No need to add up the score.

The game was in overtime.

There was only one way it would end.

Sudden death.

62

CORA GOT BACK TO HER ROOM, to find the phone ringing.

"Oh, Cora, glad I caught you." It was Becky Baldwin.

"Me too. Listen, I'm sending you some people."

"Oh?"

"Freddy and the producer. For Dennis to take a look at."

"You told them that?"

"What, are you nuts? Quentin thinks he's IDing Dennis as the guy who's been hanging around the set. Freddy's there to help."

"Help?" Becky said, suspiciously. "What do you mean, help?"

"Oh, run errands and stuff."

"Damn it, did you tell this lunatic he could be my P.I.?"

"Not really."

"What did you tell him?"

"Oh . . ."

"Never mind. I'm calling because the D.A.'s got a witness."

"To the crime?"

"Not exactly. This is a truck driver. Drives an eighteen-wheeler on I-95."

Cora's voice hardened. "Oh, really?"

"The guy was on the road that night. He heard about the murder under the overpass. He came forward to report seeing a girl on the side of the highway near there around the time of the murder. The only thing is, he took one look at the victim and said it wasn't her. He was also under the impression that the girl he saw was wearing a nightgown."

"So it couldn't have been Jennifer."

"No, she was fully dressed on her way back from the bar."

"Just some young girl. Probably snuck out to meet her boyfriend."

"Yeah." Becky paused a moment, then went on. "When I say *girl,* this guy's a trucker. He would probably consider *me* a girl. Or any woman in her twenties."

"Men are pigs."

"Aren't they? Anyway, I keep thinking about that puzzle you came up with. The second one. The one Aaron saw on Jennifer's body. I'm wondering if maybe you weren't the one who took it off the body."

"I have no comment about any puzzle."

"Of course not. I'm just wondering if this trucker should take a look at some other people."

"Damn it, Becky! I brought you in on this! I set you up with Lance!"

"He's no longer my client. The new attorney his parents hired got him out, and they took him home."

"Is that my fault?"

"No. But I have *another* client to defend. I can't sit on any leads."

"No one's asking you to."

"Glad to hear it. So, you wanna have Sherry bring Freddy and the producer down to the station?"

Cora's rather curt ejaculation tended to convey the opinion that she did not consider Becky's suggestion to be a particularly good course of action. The slamming of the telephone receiver was mere punctuation.

Cora grabbed her drawstring purse, fished out her cigarettes, and lit one up right there in the room. If they kicked her out of the motel, that was just too bad. Cora inhaled deep drags of nicotine, and tried to calm down.

The phone rang. If it was Becky, she was going to get an earful.

Cora grabbed the receiver, growled, "Hello?"

There was a moment's pause, then an uncertain voice said, "Miss Felton?"

"Yes."

"Oh. I wasn't sure. You didn't sound like you. . . ."

"Who is this?"

"Oh, I'm sorry. This is Morton Giles."

"Who?"

"Morton Giles. I'm the assistant manager. Of Food 4 Less."

"Oh," Cora said, though she still had no idea who he was.

That must have occurred to Mr. Giles. After a moment he added, "In Stamford. Where you had the robbery. The stolen wallet."

"Oh, yes, of course." The details about Ginger's wallet had pinned down the incident, though Cora couldn't remember the man at all.

"I knew you'd remember," the assistant manager said. "We watched the surveillance video together. What an experience! Finding the perpetrator right on the tape."

Cora smiled in spite of herself at hearing a pudgy ten-year-old boy referred to as a perpetrator. "It certainly was. But why are you calling? And how did you know I was here?"

"How did I know? It's on TV. What a thing! That poor girl!"

"Yes, terrible." Cora hoped she didn't sound too brusque, but she wanted to get the guy off the phone.

He seemed to sense that. "I'm sorry. You asked why I was calling. You see, I know you're interested. Because you kept watching the video. Even after we found the wallet."

"Ah, yes," Cora said. That was because she'd spotted Freddy Fosterfield. She'd watched to see if he reappeared.

"On TV they were talking about the poor girl who got killed. That nice publicist. And then they mentioned the *other* girl who was killed. And it was *her*. The girl on the tape. They showed her picture, and it was *her*!"

So that was it. Cora was relieved it was so simple an explanation. "Yes, I know."

"Of course you do. But I didn't know. Boy, was that a shock! And then I remembered how interested you were in the video. So I went down to the store and I watched it again."

"Why in the world would you do that?"

"You were interested, and the girl who had her wallet stolen got killed. I wondered if there was any connection."

"Well, there isn't. The two things have nothing to do with each other."

"Are you sure?"

"Why do you say that?"

"I watched the whole tape. Not just the part we did, but the whole thing. And I saw something I don't understand."

"What's that?"

"I don't want to say on the phone. In case I'm wrong. But I saw something, and I think you should see it too."

"That's very nice, but I'm a little busy at the moment."

"I know. The store closes at ten. I'll hang around and wait. If you're not here by midnight, I'll assume you couldn't make it."

"I *can't* make it. What's this all about?"

"You have to see for yourself."

"No, no, no, you moron!"

"I beg your pardon?"

"You're doing just what every numbnuts does in the type of mystery book I want to throw across the room. You know something, but you won't tell me on the phone, so I show up to talk to you and find you dead."

"Stop. You're scaring me."

"I hope so. What is it you want me to see?"

"It's too hard to explain. If you can come tonight, fine. If you can't, I'll call you tomorrow."

"Goddamn it!" Cora shrieked. "Tell me now!"

The line went dead.

63

A SYRUPY VOICE SAID, "Information for what city, please?"

"Stamford."

"What number would you like?"

"Food 4 Less."

"Which one?"

"There's more than one?"

"There are three."

"The one at the mall."

"I have Food 4 Less at Arbor Mall, and a Food 4 Less in Lincoln Mall."

"Wonderful."

Cora called the Lincoln Mall store first. They had never heard of Morton Giles.

Arbor Mall had.

"Morty? He's not in right now."

"Well, when will he be back?"

"I have no idea."

"Isn't he the manager?"

"He's an assistant manager."

"So, wouldn't you know when he's there?"

"Hey, I'm an assistant manager. So's Carl. I could tell you my shift. I can't tell you theirs."

"You're sure Morty's not in the manager's office where the security-cam monitor is?"

"Lady, *I'm* in the manager's office. Trust me, it's not that big."

"Can you give me his home number?"

"No. You wanna give me your number, when I see him I'll pass it on."

"Damn it, this is an emergency."

"You got a food-shopping emergency? This I gotta hear."

Cora called information and got Morton Giles's home number. After four rings the answering machine picked up. *"Hi, I'm not in right now, but leave your name and number when you hear the beep."*

Beep.

"Damn it, this is Cora Felton. Call me back at— Oh, hell, I don't know where to call me back at. Call the number you called before. I *might* be here."

Cora slammed the phone down.

Then she grabbed her drawstring purse and slammed out the door.

64

SHERRY OPENED THE MOTEL ROOM DOOR to find Brenda standing there. "Sherry, we have to talk."

"Oh, for Christ's sake!"

"Don't oh-for-Christ's-sake me. We got problems. You wanna fix 'em, or you wanna grouse about whose fault it is?"

Sherry stepped aside and let her in.

Aaron Grant was sitting on the bed. "Hi, Brenda."

"Am I interrupting something?"

"I can't begin to tell you how you're not."

"Are you guys fighting too? This thing is tearing everyone apart." Brenda flopped down on the bed. "Sherry, why are we fighting?"

"I wasn't aware we were fighting, Bren."

"You know what I mean."

"I'm not sure I do. I have nothing to do with Dennis coming here. I have nothing to do with any of this, and it has nothing to do with me."

"Yeah, right," Aaron commented sarcastically.

Brenda looked at him. "What?"

"Oh, tell her, for Christ's sake," Aaron told Sherry.

"Tell me what?"

"Sherry had nothing to do with Dennis coming here. It's what she's done since he did."

"Aaron," Sherry warned.

"What did you do, Sherry?"

"She found some evidence that incriminated Dennis. So she hid it. That's what we're fighting about."

Brenda gaped at him. "Are you telling me Dennis did it?"

"Of course not, Bren," Sherry said. "It's absolutely ridiculous. But the police would have thought so."

"They think so now."

"Because they found the evidence."

"How did they find it?"

"It's a long story."

Sherry filled Brenda in.

"You did all that?"

"Yeah."

"To protect Dennis?"

"You think I should have let him hang? What if I'd done nothing? What would you think of me then?"

"I'd think you were over him."

"Bren, you're my best friend. Could I let that happen to your husband?"

"That's what you were thinking?"

"I wasn't thinking."

"I beg your pardon?"

"I was on autopilot. I'd just found a dead body."

"And your first reaction was to save Dennis? No wonder you guys have trouble."

"I really can't take everyone ganging up on me."

"Hey, I'm on your side," Aaron said.

"There shouldn't be sides," Sherry said. "We're all in this to-gether."

"Yeah, right," Brenda scoffed. "My husband's chasing around after you. You're acting like you're still married to him. But it shouldn't bother us."

"Wait a minute, Brenda," Aaron protested. "That's not what happened, and you know it. What Sherry did was perfectly natural. In her position you'd have done the same thing."

"*You* didn't," Sherry told him.

"What?"

"You found the body with the puzzle. You knew it implicated Dennis. You left it there and called the cops."

"I said it was natural for *you*. I've never been married to the guy."

Before Sherry could retort, Cora Felton pushed through the door, took in the scene at a glance. "Good, you're all together. Let me borrow your car."

"What?" Sherry said.

"Not you. You don't have a car. Aaron, give me your car. You guys can use Brenda's."

"Where are you going?" Sherry said.

"I'm going nuts, that's where I'm going. I gotta get out of here. Aaron, give me the keys."

"You just going to drive around?"

"You got a problem with that?"

"No, but I'm coming too. You're not driving around in the dark alone with a killer on the loose."

"I'll be safe enough in the car, Aaron. Can I have it? If not, I gotta ask Freddy Fosterfield. And I don't want to owe the son of a bitch."

Aaron fished his keys out of his pocket. "Okay, you can have it on one condition."

"What's that?"

Aaron fished in his pocket again. "Take my cell phone. Anybody even looks at you funny at a stoplight, you call and tell me."

"Oh, come on."

"Is it a deal?"

"I hate cell phones."

"You just don't know how to use them. It's easy. You press this button, it's on. Then you dial the number."

"What number?"

"The motel." On the bedside table was a notepad with the motel address and phone number. Aaron tore off the top sheet, handed it to her. "Call here, and ask for my room."

"Or Sherry?"

"No, Sherry's staying in your room, remember? At least as far as the motel knows."

"Where's Becky staying?"

"Becky's not staying anywhere."

"This is confusing."

"Stop it," Sherry said. "Take the phone. You call the motel, you ask for Aaron, end of story."

"Fine." Cora thrust the phone and the piece of paper into the depths of her drawstring purse and slammed out the door.

"She's not going to use it," Aaron said. "She just took it to shut us up."

"She has it for an emergency."

"If she can find it in that purse."

Cora pounded down the motel stairs, unlocked Aaron's car, and slung her drawstring purse onto the passenger seat. She climbed in, started the car, and switched on the light.

Aaron had a full tank of gas, God bless him. She'd fill it up again when she got back. But right now she was rushing out on a fool's errand. A ten-thousand-to-one shot. The least productive lead one could imagine. For the sole reason that if she didn't go and someone died, she'd feel guilty. Even though the real guilt would belong to the addle-headed moron who couldn't talk over the phone. Who had to have his ideas ridiculed in person. And, oh boy, was he going to get a show. Cora had a few pet phrases she'd been saving up for just such an occasion. She wondered if she'd have to edit them for television. But there would be no TV cameras if this venture was as unprofitable as she supposed. If it wasn't, Cora realized sourly, in all probability the damn fool would be dead and wouldn't know it.

Muttering to herself, Cora tore out of the parking lot.

As soon as she was gone, Freddy Fosterfield backed out of his parking space and tagged along behind.

65

HE MERGED ONTO INTERSTATE 95 just as an eighteen-wheeler came roaring by, kicking up dust from the road, blurring his vision, making it impossible to see. It didn't matter. He knew where she was, and he knew where she was going. He'd given her a good head start, not wanting to follow too close as she maneuvered through the series of turns leading to the highway. He could take his time, play with her like a cat plays with a mouse. No, like a mouse plays with a cat. Here, kitty, kitty, kitty. Come and get it. You set your traps, I'll set mine.

Who's fooling who? That was the question. That was the puzzle. That was the payoff.

How stupid she was. For a supposedly bright woman, how incredibly stupid. How easily duped. Here she was, in a car, all alone, dashing off in the middle of the night. And the people who were supposed to be guarding her—her niece, the lawyer, the young reporter—they'd all let her go. Of course, how could they know? How could they have any idea?

On the other hand, they should have. It wasn't as if they thought the moron in jail had done it. Only the police were that dumb. So they knew *he was out here somewhere. And they still let her go. As if she'd be safe in a car.*

There she was, up ahead. Racing to her doom. Pretty fast, actually. He checked the speedometer. Very fast. Very fast indeed.

But not quick enough. With her wits or with her car.

Grinning gleefully, he stomped on the gas, pulled into the left-hand lane, and whizzed on by.

66

It was a quarter to twelve when Cora pulled into the Food 4 Less parking lot. Had Morty given up and gone home? It would serve her right if he had. The parking lot was nearly empty. The store was dark. The security light by the front door was on. And was that a faint glow from inside? Another security light? Or could it be the light from the manager's station?

There were three cars parked near the Food 4 Less. Could one of them be his? Then whose were the other two? People from the area who occasionally left their cars overnight? Could there be two of them? If two, why not three? Why was she even here? Why had she come? Was this another wild-goose chase?

She hoped so.

Cora pulled into a diagonal parking spot in the row facing the Food 4 Less entrance. She rolled down the window and tossed her cigarette out. The wind whipped it across the pavement, sending up sparks. With grudging good citizenship Cora heaved herself from the car to put it out. Easier said than done. The glowing end skittered along the ground like a wounded firefly. Cora caught it up against the curb of the shopping-cart return area and ground it out with her heel.

A twig snapped.

A twig?

This was a parking lot, not a forest. There were no twigs.

So what was it?

Her imagination?

More than likely.

Cora realized her hand was in her purse, holding the butt of her gun. She wasn't conscious of having reached for her gun. Well, no reason to let go now. Cora started for the store, her left hand gripping the purse, her right hand gripping the gun.

Why was she so jumpy? The killer was a hundred miles away, bent on God knows what. She was just going to the mall. True, it was later than she would have liked. Much later. It was almost twelve. If Morty was still here, he'd be leaving soon. Maybe she should wait. Stay in the car, wait for him to come out.

Assuming he was here. Assuming one of those cars was his. Assuming he hadn't parked at the back of the store in some employee's space and gone in through some employees' entrance.

For God's sake, get it over with. You got a two-hour drive when you're done. You'll be shooting tomorrow, if those morons have their way.

Shooting.

Cora gripped the gun tighter, headed for the front door. Which was locked, of course, this time of night. No way it would be open. She'd bang on it a few times, get no answer, and go home. Feeling like a fool. Not that she didn't feel like one now, but more so.

At least nobody would be dead. That was the point of the trip. She wouldn't have to live with the knowledge that someone had died because she didn't listen. Talk about a guilt trip. A hundred miles each way.

Never mind, you're getting giddy. Get it over with and go home.

Cora walked resolutely up to the entrance, stepped on the mat.

The automatic doors slid open.

So he was here. Damn. That was annoying. Why wasn't he waiting out front?

Cora stepped inside. Expected some light to switch on. It didn't. Instead, the front doors slid closed behind her. The hollow thud reverberated through the caverns of the empty store.

Cora looked around in the dark. To her left was the row of cash registers silhouetted in shadows, fading away to the horizon of the far wall. Where the restrooms were. Where Cora had changed. And the wallet had been stolen. Not two weeks ago.

Ahead of her were the darkened grocery rows. To her right was the produce section.

Above and to the left, by the cash registers, was the manager's station. Light was spilling out of the booth and down the narrow stairs from the elevated platform. It seemed to come from a single bulb, most likely a desk lamp. Was the manager at his desk?

Cora started to call out, suddenly couldn't remember his name. What was it he'd said? Martin? Marvin? No, Morton. The other assistant manager had called him Morty. Should she call him Morty?

What, was she nuts?

"Morton!" Cora called.

There was no answer.

She tried again, louder, to no avail.

He was probably dead. It would serve him right. For being so stupid. For not telling her over the phone.

But telling her what? Some extraneous and totally unimportant bit of nonsense that had nothing to do with the price of eggs. Which she could check in aisle four. Good God, she really was losing it. Just because it's nearly midnight in a dark, deserted superstore.

Fairly dark. Could that light in the manager's office be the video monitor?

Cora headed for the light. She crept through the dark toward the elevated booth.

Someone was watching her. It was the creepiest sensation.

Someone was watching her in the dark. Not really, but that was the way it felt. Cora had never had this sensation before. Her flesh was tingling. Her hand stayed on the butt of the gun.

The office was behind a huge wall of beer cases. Poking up over the top of the cases was the glass partition of the manager's booth. Not glass. Plastic. Plexiglas. Or whatever. Was it bulletproof? And was the light reflected on it from within or without?

"Morton!" Cora yelled. If he was there, there was no way he couldn't hear.

She stepped around the corner of the wall of beer.

The light was coming from inside. Cora could see the top of the narrow stairs leading down from the platform. It was shining out. A dull, diffused light, flickering and changing intensity, like the light from a TV, still strong enough to light up the steps. At least the top. The bottom was obscured by an Entenmann's display. Every type of cake and doughnut piled high.

Cora stepped around it, a moth to the flame, drawn to the light. As she cleared the last pound cake, she could see the bottom of the steps.

The body of Morton Giles lay in a crumpled heap at the foot of the stairs. His head was twisted to the side, his face was pasty in the flickering light.

There was a crossword puzzle on his chest.

Cora involuntarily stepped back into the Entenmann's display. It toppled. Doughnuts flew. The wire racks and metal shelves clattered in the cavernous night. Her heel caught on the edge of the rack and she found herself going over backward. She flung out her hands to break her fall. The purse flew in the air, landed with a thud. Cora fell on her right arm, felt the pain jolt her shoulder as she rolled onto her back, crushing a coffee cake. She scrambled to her hands and knees, discovered her arm wouldn't support her weight. Was it broken or just badly sprained?

Cora struggled to sit up, then stopped in shock and horror. Blood drained out of her face.

Freddy Fosterfield stood in the flickering light.

He was holding a gun.

He looked horror-stricken, like some ghoul from hell. His eyes were wide, his mouth was open, his breath came in ragged rasps.

His gun was pointed straight at Cora.

"Don't move!" His voice was high-pitched, strained, hysterical. As if he'd failed the course in Cold-blooded Killer 101. Couldn't handle remorselessness, calm determination. Settled for running scared. "Don't move!" he repeated. "Stay right where you are!"

It was better the second time, but still shaky, and now he was coming at her, gun raised, finger on the trigger, hand trembling so much, he might pull it accidentally. Not meaning to kill her, just losing control.

"Freddy!"

"Shut up!"

Cora did. He was tightly wound, losing it. No way to reach him. She just had to pray he'd hold together long enough for his current rage to pass. Rebuking her seemed to strengthen his resolve. He came at her faster, reached her in two strides.

He stepped over her, hurried to the body of Morton Giles. He bent down, snatched the crossword puzzle from the assistant manager's chest. Held it up in the light.

"Jesus Christ!"

Cora gawked at him, ventured, "Freddy?"

He waved the gun, not at her, but dismissively. "Stay down! Stay right where you are. The killer's here." He held up the puzzle. "This proves it. This crossword puzzle was left for you. The question is, was it meant to be the last?"

"The killer," Cora said dully.

"Yes, the killer. Someone killed this poor man because of you. I don't know why. I just know you're not safe."

"Freddy, put down the gun."

"Like hell!"

"Put down the gun, Freddy."

"Why?"

"To prove you're not the killer."

"Don't be silly."

"Freddy. You picked up the crossword puzzle from the corpse. That is either very dumb, contaminating a crime scene, or very bright, accounting for any fingerprints you might have got on it when you left it there."

"I didn't leave it there."

"Then put down the gun."

Fosterfield was still kneeling by the body. He put the gun on the floor by his right side, the barrel pointed forward, the handle pointed away, so he could reach it in a second, a cowboy preparing for a quick draw.

"I didn't leave the puzzle there, Cora."

Morton Giles sat up, picked up the gun, held it to Freddy's head.

"No. I did."

67

FREDDY FOSTERFIELD NEARLY FAINTED FROM SHOCK.

Morton Giles smiled. "Game's over, Cora. Checkmate. I know, I know, that's not a crossword-puzzle term. What is it they say at the National Tournament? 'Done!' That works too. I'm done, and you were just beginning."

Cora pretended she didn't notice the gun aimed at Freddy Fosterfield's right frontal lobe. "I'm not even playing, Morton. I don't even know the game."

"Call me Morty."

Cora hesitated, tried not to look repulsed by the suggestion. "Okay, Morty. What exactly do you want?"

"I would think that was rather obvious."

"Then I guess I'm dumb."

"Oh, I don't think so. Or you wouldn't be here."

"You invited me here."

"True. But only after you figured everything out. And with so much interference. Talk about a handicap! Your niece, and her boyfriend, and her ex-husband, and his wife, and the lawyer, and the movie people, and those clueless cops. Hell, they even brought you a dog."

"Oh, God. I forgot to walk Buddy."

Sweat was pouring down Freddy Fosterfield's face. "Cora," he croaked.

"And then there's *this* guy. Talk about a red herring. I bet you suspected him, didn't you? Ridiculous. He couldn't have done it. He wouldn't have had the nerve."

"Why'd you do it, Morty?"

"I told you. It's a game. A puzzle game. Just for the two of us. At least it was supposed to be. People kept getting in the way."

"I don't understand."

"So I win. A Pyrrhic victory, perhaps, but a victory nonetheless. That and the consolation of you knowing it was all your fault."

"Why, Morty? What did I do?"

"What *didn't* you do? High and mighty Puzzle Lady. Too good to play with me. What do you think now?"

"I think you're very clever. I think—"

"Don't patronize me!" Morton pushed the gun to Freddy's temple. "You do and I'll pull the trigger."

Freddy whimpered.

"Sniveling fool! You really thought him capable of murder? Just one in a long line of snubs."

"Snubs? What snubs?"

"You never answered my letter."

"What letter?"

"My fan letter. I wrote it just for you. And not a word."

Cora stopped herself from saying, "Are you nuts?," realizing it could get Freddy killed. "You never sent me a fan letter."

"Yes I did. With the crossword puzzle in it."

"What?"

"Didn't she give it to you? She said she would. But I couldn't be sure, so I had to stick it to your door."

"So that was you?"

"Of course. Didn't you solve the puzzle?"

"Something about a little sign."

" *'I want to know you are mine. Can you give a little sign?'* But you didn't give one, did you?"

"You didn't sign your name. You didn't leave a return address."

"That would have spoiled the game, now, wouldn't it?"

"How was I supposed to answer you?"

"The same way I wrote you. In a puzzle. Every day I grabbed the paper, looking for your message. Which never came."

"I was supposed to put a crossword puzzle in the paper with a message just for you?"

"Couldn't you do that?"

"If I were omniscient. And knew that's what you wanted."

"Oh, I think you knew." Morton glanced at Freddy Fosterfield. "How you doin' down there? I want to thank you for bringing this gun. It's a beauty. Gives me a chance to have my say." He looked back at Cora. "I know what you're thinking. I'm like the villain in a James Bond movie, holding the hero at gunpoint while gloating about his plan. It's not quite the same thing. My goal was never world domination. Telling you my plan *was* my plan, if you know what I mean."

"So tell me."

"You came to my store. What a coincidence. *Not!* I'd lobbied for you. Talked up how much business it would bring in. Then the storm. What a disaster. Raining on my parade. Ruining my predictions. Making them fall way short. And then, just when the weather clears, just when things are picking up, that silly twit of a girl has to get her wallet stolen. Wrecking what was left of the day."

"Oh, my God!" The horrible realization swept over Cora. "That's why you killed Ginger? Over that?"

"I wouldn't say over that. But if someone had to go, why not her? She fit just fine. *'Just be glad it's not you.'* The perfect message. Except . . ." His face darkened. "Another meddlesome girl. Little Miss Fix-It. Steals the puzzle before it could be found. I was ready to give you an assist on that one. Of course, you didn't need it. You tracked her down, made her confess. You got the puzzle out of her."

"How did you know that?"

"She told me."

"When?"

"When do you think? She was surprised to see me. Surprised but not afraid. 'What are you doing here?' I don't think I ever answered that question to her satisfaction. Instead, I asked a few of my own. Until I found out everything I needed to know. Then I did everything I needed to do, and left the puzzle for you to find. I understand that puzzle made an even more circuitous route before it finally got to you."

"What about Dennis? What was that all about?"

"Oh." Morty chuckled. "That was fun. Sitting in a bar. Wearing a wig. Spinning tales. Looking for a scapegoat. And here he comes, large as life, your niece's ex. A lovesick moron gullible enough to swallow anything. A love poem for his lady. 'Claim you wrote it.' Sap enough to try? You bet he was. Fell for it hook, line, and sinker." He grimaced. "Sorry. I'm coming out with clichés. I never had anyone at gunpoint before. You don't really do your best work."

"You were telling me about Dennis."

"Yes, and wasn't that a beautiful ploy. He would give the puzzle to his ex-wife, claiming it was his own. You would solve it for her. Then the same puzzle would turn up on the body. It worked out better than I'd planned. He only shows the puzzle to your niece. She thinks it's his, and steals it off the dead girl. But not before her boyfriend sees it and tells the police. And the whole resultant comedy of errors. Leading to the young man's arrest."

"Which brings us here."

"Why here, you might ask. Why here in my store? With everything revolving around the film crew, why would I want to bring the police straight to me? Wouldn't that make me stick out like a sore thumb? Oh, another cliché. I really gotta watch myself."

"You were explaining why here," Cora prompted, patiently.

"Oh, yes. Well, you have to sell the premise. Buy the premise, buy the bit. Remember, that's what Johnny Carson used to say. Not that I'm old enough to have watched much Johnny Carson, but as a boy sometimes I'd stay up."

Cora wondered if she could risk another prompt. Luckily he didn't need it.

"The answer is at my fingertips. The answer lies with this gentleman here. Who ties the whole thing together. He shows up in the videotape of the girl. He shows up again and the girl dies. I uncovered the evidence. And called you to come see it.

"Which he must stop at any cost. He follows you here, as I knew he would. He's been following you around all the time, did you know that? He's been your shadow, from a distance, to be sure. I knew who he was. From your reaction to seeing him in the video. So while he's kept an eye on you, I've kept an eye on him. And he followed you here like I knew he would, only I drove fast like the wind, and got here first and set the stage."

"Uh-huh," Cora said. "And why did I come here, again?"

"To see the videotape."

"To see what on the videotape?"

"I didn't tell you what."

"No, but you'll have to tell people what you told me."

"I'll say it was him. I saw him on the videotape."

"But I'd already seen Freddy on the videotape."

"Yes, but they won't know that. And you, alas, will not be in any position to contradict me."

Cora fought back the icy chill. "You were going to show me him?"

"Yes."

"Which I hadn't seen before?"

"That's right."

"Then how did you know it was him?"

"Huh?"

"How did you recognize him on the videotape if you'd never seen him before?"

"They'll never raise the point. If they do, I'll think of something.

You pointed him out that morning in the store as someone annoying you. I was shocked to see him still hanging around late in the afternoon. Don't worry, it will fly. After all, he came here to kill you. To prevent you from seeing the tape."

"That's nice. You happen to know Dale Harper?"

"Who?"

"The Bakerhaven chief of police. I told the chief about seeing Freddy on the tape. He'll remember. He'll want answers. He won't stop till he gets 'em."

"He may have his suspicions, but he can't prove a thing."

"What if Dennis IDs you? You ever think of that? What if he gets a look at you in a wig?"

"Never gonna happen. Guy's so wrapped up in himself, he wouldn't know anyone else was in the bar. He couldn't describe me at all."

"He knew you wore a wig."

"Wanna bet he can't pick me out of a lineup of guys with wigs?"

"Doesn't matter if he can or not. If the police get to the point of asking him to try, you're in trouble."

"So we'll just have to see that they don't. To make sure, we have to carefully set the stage. Here's how it's gonna work. Freddy followed you here to stop you. He shot you with his gun. I assume this thing's loaded, Freddy, or you wouldn't be cowering so cravenly. So he shot you. I tried to stop him with a crowbar. See it lying there by the foot of the steps? I picked it up and bashed his head in. Alas, too late to save you from being shot."

"You just happened to have a crowbar?"

"I didn't just happen to have it, no. I borrowed it from one of the shelf stockers to break the lock on my woodshed door. Yes, I even broke a hasp on the door of the woodshed—always pay attention to detail. I brought the crowbar back, left it in the office before I went on vacation. None of the assistant managers knew to give it back, but you can bet they noticed it there. It's a bold move, admitting to killing this guy. But you wanna bet I get away with it?"

"I would, but as I understand it, I won't be in any position to collect."

"Well said. Not well reasoned—you're dead wrong—but well spoken. Gamely, and with spirit."

"The cops will never buy Freddy as a serial killer. You said so yourself. He's not the type."

"True, but who am I to fly in the face of overwhelming evidence?" Shifting the gun to his other hand, Morton pulled a handkerchief from his pocket and picked up the crossword puzzle that had been lying on his chest. He flipped it open, held it out to her.

"Here. Can you solve that in your head?"

"Not under the circumstances."

"If you say so. Some people function better under stress. Well, trust me, the theme entries gloat over your undoing. This will be in Freddy's jacket pocket. As you pointed out, his fingerprints are on it. His and his alone. He brought it here to leave on your dead body. Thanks to me he never got the chance."

"Because he shot me and you bashed in his head?"

"That's right."

"That's the story you intend to go with? That's how you'll explain it to the police?"

"Yes. What's wrong with that?"

Cora shook her head. "Nothing. It's a perfectly good explanation. It would probably work. I'm very glad you intend to use it."

Suspicion clouded Morton's eyes. "Why?"

"Because if that's your plan, you *can't* shoot Freddy." Cora jerked her gun from her purse, leveled it at Morton. "Not with his own gun. Not in the head at close range. You can't do it. So why don't you put the gun down."

Morton considered. "Okay, new scenario. Freddy shot you, I wrestled for the gun, and shot him. They can't tell the order of the bullets. No one will know I shot him first. I've got the gun to *his* head. Why don't you put *your* gun down?"

"Oh, I don't think so."

ACROSS

1 Family members
4 Rabbit's foot, e.g.
9 Borscht base
13 Popular "numero"
14 Perfect, as a rocket launch
15 Data, for short
16 Fictional first baseman
17 Start of a message
20 "It's a darned lie!"
22 Heavy weights
23 One or eleven in twenty-one
24 "That's all there ___ it!"
25 If not
26 Sound rebound
27 Part 2 of message
31 Dr. Seuss's Sam ___
32 Without warranty
33 Half or third of a dance
34 Exceptionally good
36 Remain in one place
40 Letter-shaped pipe bend
41 Ran away
42 "Be My Yoko ___" (Barenaked Ladies song)
43 Part 3 of message
48 Burden of proof
49 Well-ventilated
50 Pub servings
51 Place for phys ed class
52 Fluid-filled skin sac

53 Snickering laugh
55 End of message
58 "Much ___ About Nothing"
59 Swiss painter Paul
60 Bias
61 *Do the Right Thing* director
62 Orwell's alma mater
63 Schoolbooks
64 The Mormons, initially

DOWN

1 Gulf War victims
2 "... stuck a feather ___ and
   called it macaroni"
3 Midday
4 Crow cries
5 Jolly laugh
6 Alias letters
7 Infant's toys
8 "Gee whiz!"
9 Life stories
10 Grand finale
11 Obliterate
12 Comment after a witty retort

18 Short play
19 Advertising light
21 Lean-___ (shelters)
25 Abu Dhabi dignitary
26 Auction website
28 Ernest or Julio
29 In a predictable way
30 Elm tree's offering
35 See-through glass
36 Do in a dragon, say
37 Setting for *The Hustler*
38 Not necessary
39 Ballet slippers
41 Able to bear children
43 Hobgoblin
44 Free oxen, in a way
45 Ruckus
46 Most like Solomon
47 "Zip-a-Dee-Doo-___"
52 Ethan or Joel of *Fargo*
53 Give a clue
54 Tolkien tree creatures
56 Bill Clinton, astrologically
57 Car-wash option

Cora fired.

Gunpowder flashed from the barrel.

The explosion echoed through the empty store.

The gun kicked, but no more than it had when her least favorite husband, Melvin, had taken her to the shooting range.

The bullet ripped through Morton's right shoulder, knocking him backward. Freddy's gun jerked. Morton's finger squeezed the trigger.

The gun went off.

The bullet missed Freddy's head, hit him in the leg. He moaned and slumped over.

Morton's arm went limp. The gun clattered from his hand, skidded across the floor.

Cora crept close, gun raised. She stood over him.

Morton was on his back, writhing around. His wound did not appear life-threatening. It was, after all, one shot, in the shoulder.

Cora thought about Ginger and Jennifer, and what Morton had done to them, and what he had meant to do to her.

It would be so easy to pull the trigger one more time.

"Freddy!" Cora hissed.

Freddy Fosterfield had rolled away into a ball, and was clutching his wounded leg. He managed to raise his head. "Yes?"

"My purse is on the floor. Somewhere in it there's a cell phone. If you know how to use the darn thing, call the cops."

68

THE SUN WAS SHINING BRIGHTLY on the motel parking lot, which, Cora noted, was somewhat ironic since it was the twilight of the tour. The crew were hard at work, or as hard as their union rep would let them be, packing up the equipment van. The van *was* packed, of course, before they started, but apparently there was a difference between loading the equipment to use and stowing it when the shoot was wrapped.

Which it indeed was. Even if they'd had a publicist on board to put the best spin on everything, the tour was history.

"It's a shame," Quentin said. "If there were any way we could continue . . ."

"You would still have a job," Daphne reminded him. "Face it, it's over. Back to the drawing board. Come up with a new concept. Get yourself back in the game. Don't worry, you'll live."

"I'm glad you can be so cavalier about it."

Daphne shrugged. "Hey, my agent's already lined up two public-service spots and a beer ad. And I might get a *Law & Order: SVU*."

"No wonder you wouldn't fight to keep us going."

Daphne patted Quentin on the cheek. "Schnookums, she *shot* an assistant manager. When you're booking grocery stores, that's a tough sell."

"I quite understand," Cora said, contritely.

Buddy was tangling his leash in Cora's legs. She scooped up the toy poodle and cradled him in her arms, as if to present a more sympathetic picture.

"It's not like we don't have enough footage to make the ads," Daphne said. "It's up to Granville Grains if they wanna do it."

"I'll let you know," Quentin said.

"You mean they'll let *you* know. Take care, Cora. I gotta go pack. Quentin, give me a ride to the motel?"

Daphne and Quentin drove off to check out of their posher rooms.

Cora set Buddy down, walked him over to the grass. While the dog sniffed around, she watched the sun gleam off the Granville Grains tour bus. Her smiling picture graced the side. The face of a pistol-packing mama. She wondered how quickly the public would forget.

A door slammed. Cora looked around to see Dennis and Brenda coming out of one of the units. There were two cars parked out front. His and hers. Probably just as well, Cora figured. At least until they got some therapy.

Aaron and Sherry were in the parking lot. Dennis looked in their direction, but Brenda took him by the arm, led him to his car, stood there until he got in.

The cars pulled out, Dennis leading, Brenda following behind. Dennis slowed as they passed Sherry and Aaron, and Brenda honked the horn, either to hasten her husband or to bid them farewell.

Sherry watched them go.

Aaron watched her watch them. "Sherry?"

"What?"

"They're gone. Can we talk about this now?"

"Ask me some other time."

Aaron ignored her dismissive tone. He smiled. "That's the same as saying yes."

"No it's not."

"It is so. You're *asking* me to *ask* you."

"I'm asking you *not* to ask me *now*."

"Boy, talk about splitting hairs."

"Splitting hairs, hell. These are not ideal circumstances."

"Give me a break. I ask you to marry me and you won't do it because it would serve the useful purpose of not allowing me to testify against you and put you in jail. I can understand that. I certainly wouldn't want to deprive you of your right to go to prison for your convictions. No pun intended. And I can understand why you'd be very angry at me for suggesting such a thing. I'd like to point out, with the case solved, that is no longer an issue. My marrying you could accomplish no useful purpose whatsoever. There is, to all intents and purposes, no earthly reason why I should propose to you at all. Under such circumstances, I don't see why you can't take a proposal as being a voluntary act, perhaps whimsical, perhaps capricious, perhaps foolhardy, but in no way coerced by the long arm of the law or the pressures of society, merely an expression of simple desire."

"How can you term something simple when it's couched in so many words?"

"I don't know. I forget my premise. Perhaps I was calling myself simple."

"You're not that perceptive."

Cora, noting the tenor of the conversation and deciding an intervention might be in order, walked over. "How you kids doing?"

"Not at all well," Aaron said. "I'm proposing marriage, and Sherry's giving me a hard time."

Cora nodded. "A good tactic. I've played hard to get I don't know how often. The thing is, sweetie," she told Sherry, "once they *propose,* the tactic's *worked.* That's when you can ease up a little.

You don't get proposed to that often, so you don't understand some of the finer points."

"That's not funny."

"No, but it's certainly true." Cora smiled coyly. "I, for instance, received a marriage proposal just this morning."

Aaron's mouth fell open. "You're kidding!"

"Is that so hard to believe? Ah, the arrogance of youth. Yes, Freddy Fosterfield popped the question from his hospital bed."

"What did you say?"

"I told him I'd have to think about it."

"But you *hate* Freddy," Sherry protested.

"Yes, but if that were a deterrent, no one would get married. I hated all of my husbands at one time or another." Cora frowned. "Granted, usually not *before* the marriage."

"Aunt Cora. Can you be serious?"

"I *am* serious. I didn't say I'd *do* it, I said I'd think about it. It's only polite. It's impolite to turn down a marriage proposal from someone who got shot for you. No matter how obnoxious they are."

"Cora."

"Well, I do think *one* of us ought to get married, Sherry. You want me to leave it up to you?"

"Damn it, Cora. First Becky Baldwin, now you. Isn't it the groom who's supposed to propose marriage?"

"I *am* proposing marriage."

"You're not the groom yet."

"I'm the potential groom."

"Everyone's a potential groom." Cora lowered her voice. "So, did you do the puzzle? Not that I give a damn, but the cops want it."

"In my purse," Sherry said. "Stand in front of me and I'll slip it to you."

Sherry popped the snap on her simple leather bag and slid out a folded piece of paper. "Here you go. You can fax it to them, if they haven't solved it themselves. It's not that hard."

"Speak for yourself."

Cora unfolded the paper.

" *'What good fun this game has been. But now we are done. You lose, I win,'* " Cora read. "Cheery."

"The cops should like it," Aaron said.

"I'm sure they will. It's sort of the icing on the cake. The killer bragging of his accomplishments."

"But it was supposed to frame Freddy Fosterfield."

"It does both."

Sherry seemed unwilling to pick up on the conversation. Every time Cora and Aaron stopped speaking, there was an awkward silence.

Cora looked from one to the other. She smiled mischievously. "Well, don't let me interrupt."

Cora left the young couple to their own devices, and intercepted Becky Baldwin, who was bouncing a suitcase down the motel steps. "Sherry's going back with Aaron. Can I catch a ride with you?"

Becky raised her eyebrows. "Oh, are you talking to me again?"

"Well, the case is solved. You're not threatening me with any truck drivers."

"Is that my fault? If Sherry's going to go running around in her nightgown—"

"Hey, hey! What happened to innocent until proven guilty?"

"That only applies to clients. Not to people meddling with evidence."

"Fair enough. So who's your client now?"

"I have no client."

"Really? Last week you had three or four."

"Those were the days."

"You're not representing Morton Giles?"

"He hasn't asked me."

"That's a shame. You want me to put in a good word?"

"Would he listen?"

"The guy adores me."

"That was before you shot him."

"You think he holds a grudge?"

K	I	N		C	H	A	R	M		B	E	E	T
U	N	O		A	O	K	A	Y		I	N	F	O
W	H	O		W	H	A	T	G	O	O	D	F	U	N
A	I	N	T	S	O		T	O	N	S		A	C	E
I	S	T	O		E	L	S	E		E	C	H	O
T	H	I	S	G	A	M	E	H	A	S	B	E	E	N
I	A	M		A	S	I	S		C	H	A
S	T	E	L	L	A	R		S	T	A	Y	P	U	T
	E	L	L		F	L	E	D		O	N	O
B	U	T	N	O	W	W	E	A	R	E	D	O	N	E
O	N	U	S		A	I	R	Y		A	L	E	S
G	Y	M		C	Y	S	T		H	E	H	H	E	H
Y	O	U	L	O	S	E	I	W	I	N		A	D	O
	K	L	E	E		S	L	A	N	T		L	E	E
E	T	O	N		T	E	X	T	S		L	D	S

ACROSS

1 Family members
4 Rabbit's foot, e.g.
9 Borscht base
13 Popular "numero"
14 Perfect, as a rocket launch
15 Data, for short
16 Fictional first baseman
17 Start of a message
20 "It's a darned lie!"
22 Heavy weights
23 One or eleven in twenty-one
24 "That's all there ___ it!"
25 If not
26 Sound rebound

27 Part 2 of message
31 Dr. Seuss's Sam ___
32 Without warranty
33 Half or third of a dance
34 Exceptionally good
36 Remain in one place
40 Letter-shaped pipe bend
41 Ran away
42 "Be My Yoko ___" (Barenaked Ladies song)
43 Part 3 of message
48 Burden of proof
49 Well-ventilated
50 Pub servings
51 Place for phys ed class
52 Fluid-filled skin sac

53 Snickering laugh
55 End of message
58 "Much ___ About Nothing"
59 Swiss painter Paul
60 Bias
61 *Do the Right Thing* director
62 Orwell's alma mater
63 Schoolbooks
64 The Mormons, initially

DOWN

1 Gulf War victims
2 "... stuck a feather ___ and called it macaroni"
3 Midday
4 Crow cries
5 Jolly laugh
6 Alias letters
7 Infant's toys
8 "Gee whiz!"
9 Life stories
10 Grand finale
11 Obliterate
12 Comment after a witty retort

18 Short play
19 Advertising light
21 Lean-___ (shelters)
25 Abu Dhabi dignitary
26 Auction website
28 Ernest or Julio
29 In a predictable way
30 Elm tree's offering
35 See-through glass
36 Do in a dragon, say
37 Setting for *The Hustler*
38 Not necessary
39 Ballet slippers
41 Able to bear children
43 Hobgoblin
44 Free oxen, in a way
45 Ruckus
46 Most like Solomon
47 "Zip-a-Dee-Doo-___"
52 Ethan or Joel of *Fargo*
53 Give a clue
54 Tolkien tree creatures
56 Bill Clinton, astrologically
57 Car-wash option

"He might. Men are so unreasonable." Becky cocked her head at Buddy. "You bringing that dog with you?"

"I got a crate."

"I'm happy for you. But what does the dog ride in?"

"Ha, ha."

Cora went up to the room, packed up Buddy's kibble and bowls, and wrestled the bag and crate and suitcase down the stairs. Becky helped her load the suitcase in the trunk, and the dog crate in the backseat.

Becky started the car. "They charging you with anything?"

"I don't think so. You wanna represent me if they do?"

"I might. At least you had the good sense to shoot the guy in Stamford. It's not such a bad drive."

"You have a fine legal mind, you know."

Becky pulled out of the parking lot. "Say, what's that all about?"

Cora looked up from buckling her seat belt.

On the side of the parking lot, Aaron Grant and Sherry Carter were locked in an embrace, his arms around her, her head back, her chin tilted up, his lips on hers.

Cora smiled.

"I think they just settled an argument."

ABOUT THE AUTHOR

Nominated for the prestigious Edgar, Shamus, and Lefty Awards, PARNELL HALL is the author of six previous Puzzle Lady mysteries. He lives in New York City.